The
VATICAN
CONSPIRACY

The VATICAN CONSPIRACY

JOHN LEIGHTELL

THE VATICAN CONSPIRACY

iUniverse books may be ordered through booksellers or by contacting:

iUniverse
1663 Liberty Drive
Bloomington, IN 47403
www.iuniverse.com
1-800-Authors (1-800-288-4677)

ISBN: 978-1-4917-7970-5 (sc)
ISBN: 978-1-4917-7969-9 (e)

Library of Congress Control Number: 2015918626

Print information available on the last page.

iUniverse rev. date: 11/16/2015

Contents

To: Jackie, Judy, Suzy, Steve, and Chris.
For their encouragement, enthusiasm and patience.

List of Main Characters:

Cardinal Damien	American Cardinal, Vatican
Cardinal Karmazin	Ukrainian Cardinal, Vatican
Petra Salodin	Attaché: Russian Embassy, Rome
Willi Charpentier	Head of Interpol Office: Lyon, France
Waltmir (Walter) Russak	Russian Intelligence
Leonard Morse	Russian Intelligence
Alex Metachev	Drug Dealer: Toronto
Boris Radovic Sokalovsky	Russian born Assassin: Toronto
Father Bernado	Archdeacon: Castillo de Chipiona, Sanlucar de Barrameda
Antonio Messi	Computer Expert: Castillo de Chipiona, Sanlucar de Barrameda
Michael Kinghaven	Professor: Univ. of Stockholm
John Hampton	Physics Professor: Toronto,
Marius Sorensen *Dialogue* Member	Anthropology Professor: Copenhagen
Father Michael	Monk: Uncle of Jose Rodriguez, Toledo, *Dialogue* Member
Father Emile *Dialogue* Member	Priest and Physicist: Munich,
Jose Rodriguez	Detective: National Police Corps Madrid
Franz Millar	Detective: Bavarian State Police, Munich
Isobel Alverez	University Librarian: Toledo
Inspector Mason	Detective: Metropolitan Police, Toronto

PART ONE

Chapter 1

Sistine Chapel, Vatican City
Rome, Italy

The Cardinal electors were seated inside the Chapel at the start of the conclave to elect a new Pope. It was sixteen days since the previous Pope had died. His ring and Papal seal had been destroyed, and now the world waited for the College of Cardinals to elect a new Bishop of Rome.

They had all placed a hand on the Bible and repeated an oath to maintain the secrecy of the conclave and avoid all secular influences.

Once everyone else had been asked to leave, and the Master of Papal Liturgies had sealed the chapel, balloting was ready to commence.

Cardinal Karmazin, a Ukrainian, looked up at the ceiling frescos; Michelangelo's masterpiece, the story of creation, the fall from grace and, the adjacent panels foretelling the coming of the Messiah. The eternal message of God's saving grace.

Across the aisle Cardinal Damien, from the United States, was looking at Karmazin with an angry expression, although angry was perhaps too strong a word; Cardinals do not let their feelings show. But that was how he felt.

Within the Vatican a power struggle was taking place, between those who wanted to move the Church to a more liberal position, evaluating scholastic research and its impact on Church doctrine. The opposing Conservative group insisted that the Church should remain exactly as it was, a tradition and theology that had stood the test of time. The revelation of God's will, through Christ's teachings, crucifixion, and resurrection. It was not for men, scholastic or otherwise, to change.

The Liberals were led by Cardinal Damien. He believed that unless the Church modernized its beliefs it was doomed. Already it had lost members in large numbers in Western Europe and the United States; as much as fifteen percent, in some estimates. The reason was simple, in Damien's mind. The essential truths of the Catholic faith needed to be expressed in modern terms that spoke to the lives and hopes of contemporary people. To continue to base them on a Mediterranean society, as it existed two thousand years ago was to lose relevance. Christ's message was eternal, but its backdrop had to be germane to prevailing attitudes and problems. It was getting harder and harder to sell an ideology that was out of step with modern thinking.

Karmazin, the most outspoken of the conservatives, would have said that that was precisely the point. Modern-day cultures had no guidelines, no directions. Personal gratification was all that people cared about. Hedonism had become a way of life. The Church must stand firm against this decadence not change its views to be more acceptable. It wasn't a popularity contest. More than ever it must defend its values and refute the profligacy of today's societies.

The two men led the division within the conclave. No actual count was available, but the general consensus was that the conservatives held the majority. Damien believed this was a function of the Cardinals advancing years. Like arteries, opinions hardened with age.

In 1970, Pope Paul VI had limited the conclave to those cardinals under eighty. Even so the average age was still 71. The American suspected the conservatives would win the day and elect a hardline Pontiff.

Outside, the crowd watched the chimney on the roof of the Sistine Chapel. For three days, once in the morning and once in the afternoon, black smoke had emerged. Finally on the early evening of the fourth day the smoke was white. The crowd cheered and clapped. They had a new pope.

Inside Cardinal Karmazin was jubilant. The new Pope, who chose the regnal name, Aquinas, was known to be conservative. His views were more in line with the Ukrainian than the American. The only factor that gave Damien any hope was his age. The new Pope was 79 years old. Hopefully, it would be a short papacy.

Chapter 2

Piazza Trevi
Rome, Italy

Cardinal Vladislav Karmazin and Petra Salodin were seated at an outdoor table across from the Trevi fountain. They met each other occasionally at different locations, sometimes a restaurant, sometimes a gallery or a museum. In this way, they hoped that their meetings wouldn't be observed. There was nothing sinister in them, just a chance to exchange and discuss different points of view. But any meeting between a Russian Diplomat—Salodin was a cultural attaché at the embassy—and a Catholic Cardinal would cause a few eyebrows to be raised.

The origin of these meetings traced back to the Russian occupation of Ukraine. Karmazin strongly opposed the invasion of his homeland by the Soviets. They were ruthless and at times brutal, but not everything about the occupation was bad. They brought order to the country, enforced at the point of a bayonet when necessary, but you obeyed the rules, or you disappeared. It was a structure and a system that did not tolerate change. Karmazin admired that kind of discipline. Something sadly lacking today.

Before Karmazin became a Cardinal and was appointed to the Vatican, he was the Bishop of Lutsk, in Northern Ukraine. The church was frowned on by the Soviet overlords, but, in general, they left him alone.

He had an instinct for identifying who was important; who were just functionaries and who wielded real power. And he was good at it. He developed personal relationships that were to prove useful even after 1991 when most of them went back to Russia.

Karmazin's appointment to Rome was in part—though never stated—a recognition of these skills. But more an acknowledgment of his personal discipline and belief in the rule of law, both civil and religious. And the relationships he had fostered in Ukraine found one reincarnation in Rome. This time, it was the Russians who came calling.

Shortly after he had taken up residence in the Vatican, he was invited to a function at the Russian embassy. He was introduced to Petra Salodin, a cultural attache, which as everyone in diplomatic circles knew, was a cover for espionage.

They were important in another way. In any spat between two countries, when one of them had been caught spying or eavesdropping on the other, it was usually a cultural attaché who was expelled. Convenient. Like pawns in a chess game, they were disposable. When it was time to begin a new game, they could quietly be recalled.

It seemed they had a mutual acquaintance. One of the Cardinal's Russian 'friends' from Lutz was a cousin of the attaché. Whether it was a true relative or expediently arranged, he never knew for sure. In any event it didn't matter, he was quite happy to have a 'comrade' at the embassy. The flow of information is bi-directional; even if the message is suspect, and the messenger has an ulterior motive. The channel might be as valuable to the Vatican as it was to the Russians.

They sipped their coffee and watched the tourists gathered around the Trevi fountain. They could hear snatches of the guides' descriptions:

Built . . . 1762
Discovered . . . virgin . . . 19 B.C.
1960 . . . 'La Dolce Vita.'
Three . . . in the . . .
Next . . . Spanish . . .

They exchanged the latest 'gossip'—the name they used for passing on misinformation—wondering how much of it might be believed, then talked about the weather, sports, and other trivia. Karmazin picked up the newspaper that Salodin had brought with him and was lying on the table. While the attaché paid the bill, he scanned the headlines. More rumors, fewer facts, as always.

They agreed on the date and location of the next meeting, then stood up and left, Salodin heading for the Embassy and the Cardinal towards the Vatican.

Neither of them noticed the man drinking his coffee at a nearby table and occasionally looking towards them. Even if they had, they would have been unaware that he was a detective with the Carabinieri, responsible for investigations that were multi-national, and for liaison with Interpol.

Chapter 3

36 Gayton Road
Hampstead, London

Waltmir Antonovic Russak—Walter Russak was the name he used outside Russia—was back in his flat, on Gayton Road in Hampstead. It was the first time he had been back in almost a year. He was opening the windows and removing dust sheets from the furniture. Other than a cleaning service once a month, it had been undisturbed. It was good to be back. It was where he was born and grew up.

His father had been a diplomat attached to the Russian Embassy and Walter, and his younger brother Greg had been educated at a private boarding school near Oxford. As a result, Russak spoke fluent English and was comfortable with British customs and habits.

They had moved back to Russia when Walter was twelve, and he had been sent to a military academy to finish school before joining the army at the age of eighteen. He was tall, 6' 2", with sandy colored hair, a lean, sinewy frame and a black belt in Taekwondo. He was accepted into the elite Spetsnaz—the Soviet SAS. After two months of brutal training, he was posted, with his unit, to Afghanistan to infiltrate the Afghan resistance and eliminate the command core.

All they carried was a single NRS-2 knife, hence their nickname *Shivs.* It could, in emergency situations, be used as a gun, able to fire a single bullet, but they rarely needed it. A hand over the mouth, the *Shiv* between the third and fourth ribs and a quick thrust upward. It was all over in a few seconds.

After the withdrawal from Afghanistan in 1989, followed two years later by the break-up of the Soviet Union, Russak like many others faced a very uncertain future. But with his military training and experience, it didn't take long before he found a fit for his skills. He was hired by the Russian Police as an undercover agent. His first assignment was to an intelligence unit investigating Russian drug gangs operating out of London. This brought him into contact with the Soviet drug lords, and he was moved to the drug enforcement agency in Moscow. He followed the supply lines and found that the drugs originated in Eastern Russia. He joined the Primorsky Krai unit, based in Vladivostok, where his cover was a police detective, passing information to the networks. It took him four months to work his way up the chain of command gradually identifying the top people in each supply network.

The drugs came out of North Korea, across the border at Rajin-Sonberg and then by boat from Chongjin to Vladivostok. Once in Vlad the drugs were unpacked and hidden in several warehouses on the waterfront.

Russak made sure the wheels of the border patrols were well greased and looking in the wrong direction. He fed the traffickers warnings when police sweeps were planned. In return, regular payments were made to his Swiss bank account.

They came to rely on him and with everything in place, he was kicked out of the police; someone leaked the information that he was taking kickbacks from the dealers.

This was the dangerous part. His usefulness to the drug networks disappeared. And the protection that came with his police job evaporated. It was open season. He had to move first before they tried to take him out. In preparation, he had reassembled his *Shivs*, paying them out of the money he had received from the drug lords.

He arranged a meeting with one of his contacts to try and buy some time. "I think I need to renegotiate my position," he said, knowing the answer he would get.

"Why would we do that? We don't have any use for an ex-cop."

He needed a few more days until his *Shivs* were ready for the showdown, so he pressed his point. "After all the warnings I've given you and the officials I've bribed. The new dealers in Moscow I've given you. Don't you think that deserves a little loyalty?"

His contact wasn't buying it. "You must be out of your fucking mind. The only loyalty in this business is the needle sticking out of a junkie's arm."

Which is what Russak expected. He would need to keep his head down until everything was ready.

Fortunately, the delivery they were expecting was delayed by two days. He took it as an omen, and they used the time to finalize their plans. On the fourth day, he got the call he was waiting for.

The ship carrying the merchandise from Chongjin had just docked. They would start unloading the first thing in the morning.

He took along two of his *Shivs*, this time carrying semi-automatics. It was still early, the middle of the night for most people and for the most part, the streets were deserted. He was driving down Pogranichnaya Street on his way to the warehouse when he spotted them in his rear view mirror. He kept an eye on them taking some side street diversions then coming back to the main road. Wherever he went, they followed. It was a light gray Audi, a big one—an A8 by the look of it—the kind only drug dealers or bent officials could afford. It was keeping the same distance behind, about fifty yards; probably waiting until they reached the warehouse. He checked the mirror again; he thought there were four of them, but hard to be sure at that distance.

"What's wrong? Has the company arrived?" Androv, one of the *Shivs,* asked as he pushed a clip into his automatic. Sacha, the other one, followed suit.

"Yes. They're staying back, hoping we won't notice them. Doesn't say much for their smarts, since they're the only other car on the road. Let's try a little detour Hold on!" As he said this, he jammed the accelerator to the floor of the Mercedes. The tires screeched, and they shot down the road. A blue Lada came out of a side street, and Russak wrenched the steering wheel to the right to avoid it. The Merc hit the curb and mounted the sidewalk. It slewed sideways, and it took all his strength to avoid slamming into the buildings that lined the street. Fortunately, there were no pedestrians out this early, or he would have plowed them down. As it was, he bounced off two street lamps before he got the car back on the road. They were approaching the intersection with Svetlanskayat; Russak braked hard and swung the car to the right, narrowly avoiding a parked truck. The car fishtailed, but the Traction Control kicked in and kept it on the road.

He looked in the mirror and saw the Audi, tires protesting, fail to make the turn. It skidded past the intersection before coming to a stop fifteen yards further on. The driver threw the car into reverse, hit the accelerator hard and shot backward, blue smoke billowing.

It slid to a stop, and the driver gunned it down Svetlanskaya, but the Merc was nowhere to be seen. Russak had turned the car into a small alley and watched as the Audi shot by.

"Fuck!" the driver yelled as the traffic light ahead turned red. "Close your eyes and say a prayer. I'm going to run this light." Apparently God wasn't listening, and the driver's luck ran out. A tractor-trailer carrying a load of steel beams was crossing the intersection. The Audi didn't have a chance. It slammed into the side of the sixteen-wheeler, the hood jamming underneath the trailer. One of the heavy beams broke loose and went through the windshield of the A8, decapitating the driver. Whether the others survived, the collision was a moot point because the gas tank ruptured and the fiery explosion killed the remaining occupants as well as the driver of the truck.

Russak backed out of the alley and drove to the warehouse. He opened one of the main doors, put the Mercedes inside and closed the door. Two blocks away the sirens of police cars and ambulances shattered the quiet of the morning and drew a crowd of curious onlookers. "That was close," he said, "We need to get rid of the car." He walked around it, assessing the damage. "There are too many dents and scrapes and someone may have seen what happened. The police will be looking for it."

"I'll take care of it." Androv volunteered. "Once it's dark, I'll run it over to Gregor's. He'll break it up and dispose of the parts."

"Thanks. So far, so good. Now we move on to the next step. Are you all ready? If so let's do it tomorrow?"

Although Russak had outlined the plan, he had left the *Shivs* to work out the details. "Tell me how it's going to go down."

Androv, who had assumed the role of leader explained. "We take all three out at the same time. If we do it one by one when we hit the first one, the others will take precautions. I take out Karlov. I'll use the four *Shivs,* who've tracked him for the past two weeks. We know the best place to take him out. He always has two minders, but they won't see us. We'll take them out as well."

"Sounds like you've done your homework. What about the others," asked Russak?

He gave him the details of the other two drug barons and explained that everything was timed to go at eleven thirty the following day. He should expect a phone call mid-afternoon.

Russak didn't like senseless violence, at least that was what he told himself, but after the horrors of Afghanistan, he wasn't so sure anymore. Either way in this situation it didn't bother him. The drug dealers were destroying lives so they could line their own pockets. Communism was hard, but at least it kept order on the streets. These bastards were part of the rot that was ruining his country.

To implement his plan he had to take over the Eastern end of the supply route. And he had to make it clear that he would not tolerate any opposition. Send a message to anyone who might want to get in his way.

The next day his *Shivs* went to work. It didn't take long. He received a call at 3:30 p.m. that everything was finished, and the bodies were in a meat freezer at the warehouse.

Two days later the bodies of the three men were found hanging from an unloading crane in the docks. Each was attached to the boom with a meat hook that had been inserted into an eye socket.

The police in Vlad knew who the men were, known criminals and drug dealers. They looked the other way. Even left the bodies hanging for a few hours. As far as they were concerned, justice had been served. They also had instructions from the top brass, to turn a blind eye.

News travels fast, and it wasn't long before he was attracting attention from Moscow. He now had control of one of their main sources. He offered them a better deal; improved delivery and better prices. He knew he was playing with fire. One wrong move and he was a dead man; Russian roulette with a loaded gun. But that was the only way he could get close to the power players.

It took six months hard work and a lot of risks, but once he had the deals with the Moscow bosses, and everything was running smoothly, he got out. He documented everything and told everyone that he was moving to London to extend the networks into the UK and Europe. He sent a copy of his report to the police chiefs in each federal district of Russia. And attached a memo that he would let them know when it was time to go *fishing*.

Russak spent the first few weeks back in London planning how he would settle a personal matter. Then he enjoyed life in the capital, eating in his favorite restaurants, looking up some old girlfriends and taking in a few football matches. He dropped by his local pub, where the regulars greeted him like a long-lost brother and quizzed him on where he had been. "I had to go back to Russia quickly to sort out some property issues," he lied. "When the Soviets came to power they appropriated our family estate in the Urals, as well as our home in Moscow. I've been meeting with lawyers trying to get it back. The government gave me two days to present my case. No time for any farewells." It was a flimsy excuse for his long absence, but it fit the bill. This was his local watering hole, not MI5.

"And it took so long?" someone asked.

"Oh yes. Bureaucracies are the same everywhere. They only have two speeds, stop and reverse."

That brought a few laughs and then one of the regulars, asked, "And did you, get it back?"

"Not yet but it looks possible. The last letter my lawyer received said that my claim was being processed. The house in Moscow will be dealt with one month from now, but the country estate won't be done for another year. At least it's progress. I have to go back next month when the committee will deal with it."

"Sounds like you're going to be a man of means. You could buy us all a round to celebrate." Russak laughed and brought out his wallet.

Chapter 4

The paper in front of Cardinal Damien contained a list of names; the Cardinals who agreed with the need to modernize the church, and underneath, those who were sitting on the Vatican fence. Since the conclave and the inauguration of Pope Aquinas, he had spent a lot of time on the phone with the latter group.

He had persuaded three of them—from Helsinki, Berlin, and Naples—to make the jump but he knew that it still wasn't enough. He needed to become pro-active rather than re-active. He also knew that before deciding on a new direction it was important to take a careful look at where he had come from.

* * *

Pennsylvania, U.S.A,

William B. Damien was the second son of a wealthy American Industrialist. It was always assumed, by his family that Billy B, as he was known, would follow the family tradition and attend Princeton, before joining the family business. Damien 'men' had done this for as long as anyone cared to remember. And no-one had any reason to doubt that he would follow in the family footsteps.

During the summer, following high school graduation, before he went to Princeton, he went on a three-week visit to a small village in Northern Nigeria. It was organized by the Church through its Mission Service. What he saw there appalled him. He had never seen hunger and poverty on that scale. The hopelessness was beyond words. And the tribal and religious conflicts made it worse, often erupting into bloody massacres.

15

He could not ignore the starvation and the fear that were constants of their daily existence? And he saw his life of privilege as part of the problem.

For the first time, he understood the epiphany that had happened on the Road to Damascus. And like Saul it changed his life forever.

When he returned home, he canceled his enrollment at Princeton and informed his family that he was entering the priesthood, and once he had taken his vows he was going back to Northern Nigeria as a missionary.

His mother was appalled, but not his father, who knew that for life to be meaningful it must be lived with a passion. And Billy B. had found his.

True to his conscience, a few weeks after he was ordained he moved to Nigeria, where he established a small mission. It consisted of a church, a one-room school, and a small hospital. It was funded by family money. Although he had taken a vow of poverty, his family hadn't. And Father Damien was no fool. He named it Damascus.

For ten years he headed the mission; the school grew to ten classrooms and over two hundred students. The hospital added two patient wards and an operating theater. The church remained as it was, only room inside for twenty worshippers. The rear wall was removed, so that it provided outdoor space for any overflow. It was his opinion that schools and hospitals served a much more important and necessary role in this part of the world. The size of the congregation grew and multiplied year after year.

He would happily have spent his life there, it was where he belonged, doing what he knew was the work God intended him to do. He guided the mission through famines, a pestilence that destroyed the crops they had planted, and a fire that destroyed much of the hospital. Ethnic wars threatened the lives of everyone who worked in the mission and resulted in a massacre that killed two female doctors and fifteen female students. He ignored the requests from the Church and pleas from his family to return to America.

In the end, however, he was forced to go home by a much smaller enemy, the mosquito. He survived a number of malarial attacks but the final one almost killed him, and he knew he had to leave.

He spent six months recuperating at his home in Pennsylvania; it was time he spent deciding what he wanted to do next. Not surprisingly it involved the commitment of the Church to the service of those in need, not just in the missions, but to the millions who lived on the fringes of society in his own country.

Salvation is fine for the next world, but this one is much more in need of food and shelter.

Once his health had returned, he was appointed curate in the Greensburg Diocese. It was hoped that the duties of his office might muffle his 'crusade'. It didn't.

But Vatican politics change and a new Pope, Elias, was elected, whose views were similar to Father Damien's. He issued a Papal Edict that could have been written by Damien himself. It emphasized the importance of service to the poor and downtrodden. To emphasize his intentions, he announced several new Cardinals, including Father Damien, who was appointed to the Congregation of the Faith in the Vatican.

When in Rome, he did exactly what he had always done. He spoke his mind. He argued that the Curia was old and outdated, even though he was now part of it. In private he described it as a bunch of old women more concerned with the furnishings of their apartments than with furnishing support for the millions in need around the world.

The biggest obstacle to the fulfillment of the Church's role in society was the Curia. Layer after layer of bureaucracy had buried the very truth it had been created to deliver. It had become a self-serving institution.

It marked the beginning of his attempt to bring the College of Cardinals into the modern world. He knew it was an uphill battle. But he also knew that unless it changed the Church would continue to lose relevance until finally it would be moved from the center of life to its margin.

The Church had to address the changes that had, and were, taking place in society. Much of what had emerged in the last two centuries had a direct bearing on religion. There were groups both inside and outside the Church reviewing the findings. Their work should be encouraged and their recommendations studied.

With encouragement from Pope Elias, Damien made progress and assembled a group of like-minded Cardinals to begin the work. They had hardly begun when Pope Elias suffered a fatal heart attack and died, to be replaced by the hardliner, Pope Aquinas.

* * *

Vatican City, Italy

Now he had to make his decision. If he went ahead with his plan, he would put himself in direct opposition to the Pope; the man to whom he he had pledged allegiance. It was not something to be taken lightly. It needed careful thought and meditation.

For a few days, he hid away in his apartment on *Via Crescenzio*. He played Devil's advocate: was it arrogance, was he overstating his own importance, was he substituting his will for God's will?

After three days, he was still sure. It was why he had become a priest. The path was the same; it had never varied. He knew the road he had to take, even though it meant deliberately opposing the Pope; God's emissary on earth.

He returned to his office in the Vatican and began to put his plan into action.

* * *

Papal Apartment, Vatican City

Pope Aquinas was reading the report about Cardinal Damien. Some of it was factual, some of it rumor, but both pointed to the Cardinal's, and his supporter's, opposition to his instructions. A direct threat to his Papacy. He could not let it go unchallenged. He needed someone he could trust, who could neutralize the threat; and he knew exactly who that was.

He would also review Cardinal Dominic's request to use one of the Vatican owned estates in Northern Italy. It was a reasonable request from a loyal friend. The summers in Naples could be quite brutal.

Chapter 5

Office of the Pope
Vatican City, Italy

The secretary showed him into the inner office. "Your Holiness, may I present Cardinal Karmazin of Lutsk."

Pope Aquinas dismissed his secretary and stood up to greet him, "Welcome Cardinal. It is good to see you. I had hoped this meeting could have been arranged earlier, but since the inauguration, there were so many things to take care of. I wanted to thank you personally for the support you offered me before and during the conclave. Without your help, I'm not sure *we* would have been successful."

"Holy Father, you are too kind. I'm sure my help was only marginal, even without it I'm sure you would have prevailed."

The Pope waved the Cardinal to a seat before stating the purpose of the meeting. "I have spent some time over the past few week deciding why I have been called to this Holy Office. I believe it is God's will that the message of the Scriptures and the Church Father's edicts be re-established. These modernists would have us *cut the cloth to suit the coat*. The cloth was cut two thousand years ago by the Master Tailor. It is not for us to alter it."

"Exactly Your Holiness. Your election is a sign that God is instituting a return to our fundamental beliefs."

"I believe that to be true, which is why I have called you here this morning. I want to ask you to join my circle of advisors and also to ask you to undertake a special assignment."

Cardinal Karmazin tried to hide his delight. It was what he had hoped for but in the devious planning that takes place within the Vatican, nothing is ever certain. He concealed his pleasure and simply said, "It will be my pleasure and my duty to serve you in any way I can."

The Pope ran a finger down his temple, a habit he had when he was choosing his words. *"We* know that there are some Cardinals who oppose us. Even now they are planning to gather information that they think they can use to attack us. I think you know who I am talking about."

"I know the Cardinals you are referring to, but I don't know about their plan."

The Pope did not tell him about Cardinal Dominic's report. Karmazin didn't need to know. He continued, "I want you to stop them. They must not be allowed to succeed. Their work must be destroyed."

"It is a task I will enjoy. I will stop these heretics. You can rely on it." Karmazin replied.

They talked for another thirty minutes and agreed that the Cardinal would provide occasional reports, but not too frequently; they didn't want to raise any suspicions.

Back in his apartment Cardinal Karmazin poured himself a generous glass of Vodka and sipped it slowly. A chance to prove himself and bring those dissenters to heel. Something close to his heart.

Chapter 6

Castillo de Chipiona,
Sanlucar, Spain

Father Bernado had just arrived at the Castillo, near Sanlucar, a short drive from Seville. He was taking a tour of the buildings that were to be his new home.

The Castillo dated back to the fifteenth century and was constructed by the Bonacci family, who had made their fortune plundering silver and gold from the Spanish conquests in Central and South America. It had two storeys; dining room, drawing room, and library on the ground floor and bedrooms above. Also, on the ground floor was a completely circular room with a table and chairs for thirteen people. It was called the Room of the Apostles.

The Castillo even had a basement, or Sotano, unusual in this part of Andalusia, where the ground was hard. It contained rooms for the servants, as well as a complete kitchen and dining area.

In the sixteenth century, the Inquisition used the Castillo as its base in the region and the Sotano to house those accused of heresy. The entrance was at the end of the dining room, concealed behind a false wall and with a solid copper door at the top of the stairs that led down to it.

Over the centuries, more buildings were added, staff quarters, a separate dining room, even a small hospital, eventually growing to a self-sufficient compound. A defensive wall was erected around the compound in the eighteenth century.

In 1830, the last of the Bonacci family, who never married, and had no heirs, left everything to the Spanish church.

Up until 1950 it was used by the Church for different purposes; conferences, retreats, even a monastery. But for the last thirty-five years it had remained unused and had fallen into a state of disrepair.

The Church was planning to demolish it. It was saved by a little-known group called the *Christian Heritage Society* who offered to restore it if they could use it as their official headquarters. In 1985, they were granted a one hundred year lease with the stipulation that they would carry out all the required repairs and renovations.

The *Society* was founded in the eighteenth century, by a religious faction who believed that all heresies should be stamped out and those promoting them, executed. The *Society's* belief in the power of the Church was absolute, and their commitment to it was unconditional. And in accordance with Christ's commission of to his disciples, only men were admitted.

The initiation rules ensured that they had a well-funded treasury—each member had to attach an irreversible codicil to their will, leaving half of their estate to the *Society.*

As secular law gradually reigned in religious powers, the *Society* was forced to operate in secret. In some ways, this strengthened their position. If the authorities were unaware of them, they could not restrict their activities.

Father Bernado had been appointed the Archdeacon of the *Society* in March, and six months later he had been summoned to Rome for a meeting with Cardinal Vladislav Karmazin.

He was met at the airport by a black limousine with Vatican plates and driven to the Cardinal's office. He was shown into an antechamber where he was told that the Cardinal would be with him shortly. Ten minutes later he appeared and led him into his study. He was tall and thin with a receding hairline. He looked to be in his late sixties, young for a Cardinal.

"Thank you for coming, Archdeacon. I trust you had a pleasant journey. Can I get you something to drink, tea, coffee, water?"

"No, I'm fine thank you."

"I have another meeting to go to, so let me get straight to the point. There are rumors beginning to circulate about a group who, I think, call themselves the *Dialogues*. From what little we know they claim that the gospels are simply a written record of oral traditions; stories of Christ passed on by word of mouth. If their views are made public, they could undermine the faith of millions of Catholics around the world. They are also heretical and a challenge to the veracity of Church doctrine".

The Cardinal coughed and took a sip of water. "The rumors were so infrequent at first that we felt they were best left alone. Recently; however, they have become more common, and now something must be done before they are sufficiently ubiquitous that they attract the attention of the media. Also, they have extended their work to include cosmology. They want to remove God from the universe altogether. They have also been critical of our stand on gender issues. Already there is chattering on the Internet, and we need to take action immediately. This is what I would like to discuss with you." He paused waiting for a reply.

The Archdeacon realizing he was expected to say something, nodded and said, "I have heard something about this, but not in any detail."

The Cardinal ran a hand through his thinning hair before continuing, choosing his words carefully. "We think that any involvement by Rome would draw attention to the issue; quite the opposite of what we want. We need an organization within the Church, loosely connected, not well known and separate from the Holy See. The *Society* fits the profile perfectly; it is off the radar and ideally purposed to investigate. This is a challenge to our Christian Heritage, exactly what the *Society* was formed to preserve."

He then said, forcefully, "We need to find out who these people are? Do they have academic or theological credibility? Where are they located, and how they are organized? And how we can stop them and destroy their research!" He paused, then emphasized, "This task is of primary importance. We want you to develop a plan of action. You will be provided with some initial funding, through a grant to the *Society* but beyond that there is to be no link between us. And, of course, everything about this mission is confidential. Absolutely confidential. Only disclose the information to those who are involved and even then tell them only as much as is necessary. Are there any questions?"

"Several Excellency," he replied, noticing that the Cardinal had used the word *We* twice, indicating that this came from the highest authority. "However I will wait until I have had time to consider the matter in more detail and will present them with my plan. When do you need it?"

"One month from today."

"That isn't a lot of time."

"I understand, but it is urgent. Deputize your other responsibilities and give it your undivided attention. The Cardinal looked at his watch. "Now I'm afraid I must attend another meeting."

He touched a button at the side of his chair, and his secretary appeared. "Father please call for a car for the Archdeacon to take him to the airport. Thank you for coming, Archdeacon." He made the sign of the cross. "God go with you."

Father Bernado flew back on a late flight to Seville and was back at the Castillo just after midnight. Next day, he called his personal secretary and told him to free up his calendar for the next five weeks. His assistant would take charge in his absence.

Chapter 7

University of Stockholm
Stockholm, Sweden

Michael Kinghaven had been Registrar at the University for six years. Tall and thin, with the light hair and blue eyes of his Nordic ancestors, he had never married, although he had had lots of chances. He preferred the freedom of being able to do what he wanted when he wanted.

After teaching undergraduates in philosophy and religion for twenty years, he was jaded and needed a change. Opportunities in the private sector were very limited for burned out professors, and he didn't want to give up the security that tenure brought with it. The registrar's position was a plum. It only required him to teach one course per semester, and the duties were fairly light leaving him the time to research his abiding interest; the interaction and interplay between science and theology. He had published two important papers on the topic and was regarded as an expert in the field.

So it was not entirely surprising when he received a letter asking him to coordinate a project involving those topics. He would have filed it with the rest of the junk mail, except it was addressed to him personally and included a significant financial commitment. He read it again.

> *Professor Kinghaven;*
>
> *I am addressing this letter to you because of your reputation and interest in both science and theology. I have been a member of the Church all my life, and I believe in its mission to be the voice of God in the world. But now I am afraid that that voice is losing its*

relevance; it is failing to adapt to the changes that are taking place.

I do not like these changes, but that too is irrelevant. They are happening, and they will leave behind all those, individuals and organizations that do not deal with them. The Church is one of those. If it does not meet them, head on, it will find itself marginalized and in the process forever lose its authority.

There is already a group of researchers studying these issues. And their findings need to be considered by the Church. Unfortunately, they lack focus and discipline. Their meetings are infrequent and irregular. The time devoted to research is haphazard and only done after their 'other' work is complete. They are called the 'Dialogues', and they have been in existence for several years.

What I would like you to do is to bring some organization and focus to their work, including deadlines by which their reports are expected. To this end, I have created an account at the EGF Investment Bank in Stockholm naming you as the trustee and signatory. If you undertake this commitment, I will transfer 500,000 euros into it and instruct the bank to provide you with whatever assistance you need.

You should use the money to create a structure within which the 'Dialogues' can operate and within that structure identify the specific disciplines involved. Identify points of conflict that challenge orthodox beliefs and those that do not. For the former recommend how the Church can adapt them to its teachings and for the latter provide arguments and explanations that will stand the test of academic and theological scrutiny.

If you are prepared to undertake this commission, please place an advertisement in Thursday's Atfonbladet newspaper, in the Home Services section and include the phrase; 'Good foundations provided.' Once I see that message, I will arrange the transfer of the money.

In His name, I thank you.
Bethlehem

Kinghaven did not recognize the *nom de guerre,* but he had heard it referenced once before. He knew what he was referring to. A group calling themselves the *Dialogues* had been reviewing modern research into areas they considered impacted on Christian teaching. They had been in existence for a few years, but their progress was slow and lackadaisical. They had no specific targets or timetable. There were concentrating on three main topics:

- Science and cosmology; in particular, the latest theories of the universe's origin
- Christian Origins; especially the Q document that predated the gospels and may have been used as a source document.
- Gender issues, especially the role of women in the church, the admission of gays and lesbians into the ministry, and married men and women into the priesthood.

He knew a few of the members personally, but he wondered how they would view someone from outside telling them how to organize their work and meet deadlines. It would be, to say the least, contentious. He would have to frame it very diplomatically. The money would certainly help.

Tomorrow was Thursday. He phoned the Atfonbladet newspaper, asked for Classified and placed the ad. Two days later he went to the bank to sign the papers for the account. There was a letter waiting for him with further instructions, including how to contact *Bethlehem*, with the caveat that it is used only in emergency situations. It also specified what to do once the reports were complete.

Chapter 8

Museum of Contemporary Art
Rome, Italy

Despite their different backgrounds, Petra Salodin and Cardinal Karmazin had developed a respect, if not a liking, for each other. They were of similar ages and had both grown up under the Soviet system, which had instilled in them a sense of order and the need for control. Both despised the lack of discipline in modern society. Everyone had rights, but not responsibilities. There was a lack of discipline and very little order.

Karmazin had begun to look forward to their meetings. This was mainly due to Salodin's easy manner and social conversation. He had the practiced skills of a polished diplomat and effortlessly got past the Cardinal's stiff personality. He seemed to take a genuine interest in him.

The information they exchanged was accepted without question, even though it contained little of substance. A reflex conditioning to the old Soviet mantra, 'you can never have too much information', even if much of it seems to have no value. You never knew when it might be useful.

Their meetings had been going on for six months when the Cardinal received a request from the Archdeacon. He had set up a reporting structure that included twelve Regents, together with the priests and bishops who fed them relevant information. But Bernado realized that he needed someone to act on that information; identifying what was useful and what wasn't, and more importantly using the information to chase down the heretics and mete out justice. *Swift and Certain.*

At his next meeting with Salodin, he mentioned the request. Prompted skilfully by the attache, the Cardinal mentioned, without being too specific, what they were doing at the Castillo. He was careful to downplay his role and how it related to the power struggle taking place at the Vatican.

"Yes, I'm certain I can help. Investigate, Interrogate, Eliminate," he said, "the rules of the game."

"What game?" asked the Cardinal, a little confused?

"The game of espionage, of course. It's played by all the best countries. And I can certainly help you find someone. It's my stock in trade. I will need to check my files. I'm certain I can find a suitable candidate.

Back in his office Salodin looked at the files on his computer. He kept a list of Russians and their 'stock in trade'. They were on the list because the FSB—successor to the KGB—had something on them that could be used when needed to bring them to heel.

It wasn't as easy as he had indicated to the Cardinal, there was no index. He had to look at each file individually. Fortunately, there was a summary at the beginning of each file that saved him from having to read every page.

After four hours, he had narrowed it down to four people. He compared them by looking at the 'leverage' they had on them; which reduced it to two, both wanted on murder warrants. He looked at the details in the files. If the dates were correct, one of them was in his midsixties. Probably too old for what was needed. Which left him with one file as the best candidate. His name was Boris Radovic.

* * *

Lesozavodsk, Primorsky Krai

Borislav Radovic Sokalovsky was born in the slums of Lesozavodsk in Primorsky Krai, 250 miles north of Vladivostok, in a four-room hovel that was shared with two other families. He never knew who his father was; he suspected his mother didn't either. When he was eight months old, his mother left him with a neighbor while she went shopping. She never came back. He grew up in a string of foster homes and institutionalized care.

By the age of sixteen, he was 6' 4", 250 pounds and didn't take no for an answer. Most of the girls, attracted by his size and his looks—dark hair, aquiline nose, square chin—would have said yes, anyway. His most distinctive feature were his eyes, dark brown, almost black, hypnotic; they drew them to him like moths to a flame.

There was one girl he wanted. Dominika Karlov was fifteen but looked eighteen. She was beautiful, and she knew it. He had been trying to bed her for six months but every time he approached her she told him to fuck off. One night, just after dark, he was walking home when he spotted her on the other side of the street. He crossed over, walked towards her, "Hello Dominika. What are you doing not heading home yet, I hope."

He could tell she had been drinking, especially when she said, "It depends on what you had in mind," instead of the usual 'fuck off.'

She moved closer to him and placed her hand on his chest and moved it from one side to the other. "I heard you had a great body; now I believe it." She undid the buttons on his shirt and slid her hand underneath and slowly moved it down to his waist, then began sliding it lower and at the same time she pulled him towards her.

He put his arm around her and up inside her blouse. She looked him in the eyes, smiled and kneed him in the balls. He yelled in pain. "Now, fuck off."

The next day they found her half naked and bleeding. She had been raped. By then he was halfway to Vladivostok, where he disappeared into the waterfront.

He soon adapted to the rough and ready life. His size and strength gained him respect. Even amongst the stevedores and wharf rats there were very few that could take him on. And the two that did wished they hadn't.

Work was plentiful, and the pubs were as lively as the girls who worked the waterfront; they were young, soft and cheap. Five nights a month he catered to his landlady, while her husband was out drinking, in exchange for free room and board.

After he had been in Vlad for a year and a half one of the girls, Alexandra, approached him. "I have a question for you about your eyes," she said. "Is it alright if I ask?"

"You mean the color of them? Brown almost black." He had been asked about them before.

"Yes, but what I was going to say is that there is a woman who has eyes the same color. And I wondered if you knew her."

Boris was suddenly very attentive. "Where did you see her?"

"She works one of the streets on the other side of the harbor. On Okeansky Prospekt," the girl replied, becoming a little frightened as she sensed his anger.

"Can you take me there?"

"Now?"

"Yes, now," she didn't have any choice. She was half dragged by Boris, who was in a frantic haste to get there. When they reached the street, it was murky and hard to see.

"Where is she?" he asked, looking up and down but not seeing anyone. Gradually as his eyes got used to the dark, he saw several women on the street corners.

"She's down there," Alexandra said, pointing to a woman halfway down the street, talking to a sailor.

Boris ran down and pushed the sailor out of the way, knocking him to the ground. Then he looked hard at the woman. Alexandra had been right; she did have the same colored eyes, and the shape of her nose and jaw were almost identical to his. Boris had wondered so many times what she would look like if he ever found her. But not like this!

He knew she must be in her early thirties, but the woman he was staring at looked in her fifties. Her skin was gray and lined, even under all the makeup that layered her face. Her eyes were devoid of expression, and she reeked of alcohol. Her leather skirt was short, not hiding very much, and her top was cut low, revealing all of her cleavage and most of her breasts. This was his mother. The woman who had given him life. He felt shame, mixed with sadness. And anger. So much anger!

The sailor was so drunk he was having trouble regaining his balance. When he finally did he said, "Out of my way you bastard. I was here first. She's my fuck." Then he took a swing at Boris, who ducked, and the punch went harmlessly over his head. The momentum caused the sailor to lose his balance again but when he regained it, he was holding a knife and aiming it at Boris' throat, who instinctively raised his hand to block it.

Boris didn't know what happened next. It was a blur, all over in less than twenty seconds. When he looked down, there was blood everywhere. All over his clothes, on Alexander, on the pavement, and on the knife that was now lying in the road, close to the sailor who was clutching his throat, trying to stop the bleeding.

Radovic recovered quickly and got control of himself. His mother was screaming, and Alexander was being sick on the sidewalk.

He ran back to his room at the boarding house, found some tape and bound his hand to stop the bleeding, where the drunk had cut it. He threw his few possessions into a holdall, then moved the wardrobe and pried up two of the floorboards. Underneath was a solid looking black box and inside it was his new passport and fifty thousand dollars; most of it money he had been paid by the Mafia for two contract killings. He put the money into a hidden compartment at the bottom of his bag and the passport into a black leather wallet. There was a tramp steamer leaving that night, and he worked his passage to Hong Kong.

The waterfront there was not very different to Vlad, and he quickly found his feet. Ships carrying cargo between the two ports also brought along the latest rumors, not always accurate but usually more interesting, which is how he heard that the sailor had died. His name was Gregor Antonovic. There was a warrant out for Radovic on a charge of murder.

After a few months, he met a woman named Lily Wong, who was small and diminutive with an outgoing personality. He found himself drawn to her. He couldn't explain it. Perhaps it was her size; he felt he needed to protect her. And her cheerful attitude was in contrast to his taciturn nature. In Lily, he found the affection he had never had growing up, and in him Lily found the security and protection she had never known.

Three months later Radovic moved in with Lily and a few months later, she told him she was pregnant. Six months later their daughter, Lilette, was born. He had never seen anything so small and beautiful, and he had helped create this tiny miracle. She was part of him, and he was part of her. Somewhere in his dark psyche there was still a spark of humanity.

If it hadn't been for the transfer of Hong Kong back to the Chinese, he might have stayed and settled down with Lily. But the authorities were checking everyone's papers and he knew if they caught up with him they'd ship him back to Russia. He gave her half of the money he had accumulated and told her he would send for them both when he found somewhere safe.

On the run again he ended in Vancouver, courtesy of a freighter headed first to Shanghai and then to Vancouver. From there he traveled east, finding work as he went—usually illegal and always profitable. When he reached Toronto, he stayed, and after a few months he started working for a Russian drug dealer, Alex Metachev. Alex was well into his seventies and losing control. Much of his network had been taken over by the opposition. He recognized Boris' potential and gradually turned the business over to him.

Boris' first job was turning the tables and taking back what was formerly Alex's. At the same time, he decided to take the rest and destroy the competition at the same time. He followed the advice he'd been given by a mobster in Hong Kong. *If you want to get rid of someone, don't go after them, go after someone he cares about.*

He kidnapped the daughter of the biggest drug dealer in the city and gave him forty-eight hours to close down his network and suppliers. Radovic knew he wouldn't, and he was ready. Two days later the dead body of his daughter was dumped on his front lawn. She had been raped, and her left breast had been hacked off. The following night two of Radovic's heavies had set fire to his house after first pouring gasoline everywhere. There were no survivors, only the charred remains of the family and their bodyguards. He used equally vicious methods to remove the rest of the opposition.

Two years later, with the competition destroyed and everything under control, he was a powerful man. The profits were rolling in, and his bank account had grown to several million. He decided to change his image. From gangster to businessman. *Slowly, one item at a time.* Three piece suits, an upscale apartment, chauffeured Mercedes.

He was still as brutal as ever, but he was smart. He kept his hands clean and fingernails manicured. He had a team of trained baboons to take care of the nasty bits.

He indulged his passion for gambling and found his way into some high-stakes games where the ante started at ten big ones. And he was good at it, thanks to the games with the Roughnecks on the waterfront in Vlad. The main requirement was a *poker* face and that he had in *spades*.

The players included some of Toronto's business elite; part of the 'establishment'. They weren't that much different to him, still vicious and ferocious underneath, but covered with a veneer of respectability. But they were 'old-money', something that Radovic didn't understand. It all came from the 'Robber Barons', at one time or another. Not that he cared. He was happy to take their money wherever it came from. He even met a few of their wives who were fed up with husbands who spent more time at the office than with them. They liked the look of the 'new kid on the block'. They were ready for a little adventure, and they liked it a little rough. And he was only too happy to oblige. He soon earned the nickname 'Rasputin'.

He continued to send money to Lily. He thought about them occasionally. But that had been in another lifetime.

When Alex Metachev died, he was contacted by Alex's lawyers, Peter Todd and his partner Michael Sweeny. He was immediately on his guard—in Boris' experience lawyers were all bloodsuckers. They each owned twenty-five percent of the business, but Alex had left the rest to Radovic, including a mansion in Forest Hill, the chauffeured Mercedes, and his silver Lexus.

* * *

Russian Embassy, Rome

Salodin phoned Cardinal Karmazin and arranged to meet the following Thursday in the rooftop restaurant at the Museum of Contemporary Art.

At the meeting, after they had finished eating, Salodin told him that he had found a suitable 'interrogator.' He opened his diary and flipped through it until he found what he was looking for. He wrote a phone number on a blank page, tore it out and handed it to Karmazin.

The Cardinal looked at it, then glanced at Salodin with a confused look on his face, and said, "There's no name?"

"Exactly. If you used his name he would immediately be suspicious," said the attaché.

"What do I call him? And how do I explain how I got his phone number?"

Salodin took back the sheet of paper and added another name. "Tell him you got the phone number from him."

The Cardinal looked at the name, "Alex Metachev, who's he?"

"It doesn't matter, just make up some story that he did some work for you in Canada, a few years ago. He died a few months ago, so he can't check with him."

"How do you know this 'interrogator' and how do I know he's the best?

"He's Russian! Most of the top ones are. We seem to produce more than our fair share. He now lives in Canada. When you phone him don't tell him I gave you his name, he won't trust anyone connected to the Russian government. He is extremely cautious; part of his 'stock in trade'."

The Cardinal looked uncertain. Was Salodin setting him up? Was this 'interrogator' some kind of spy? "How do you know all this about him?" he asked.

Salodin recognized the Cardinal's suspicions. One of the essential skills of an accomplished diplomat is to know when to give the facts and when to bend them. *Use the truth to shade the lie!*

In this case his doubts were unfounded, so he told him the truth. He described how the man had fled Russia and ended up in Toronto. From nothing, he had worked his way to the top of the drug networks. In the process, he had removed most of the opposition. And he'd shown he could think as well as act. "He will find your heretics and dispose of them effectively and efficiently. The difficulty will be in getting him to work for you. In his rise to the top, he has amassed a small fortune."

He waited for a response but none was forthcoming, so he continued. "I know about him because we keep very careful records. Not much happens that we don't know about. And because he is still wanted in Russia we retain a measure of control. We can always bring him back to face the charges against him. Or we may find a use for his services.

For now we simply watch and wait. Like everything in life, timing is everything.

Now you know the score, you also have that edge. Although I don't advise you to use it. Remember he is an executioner, not always careful about who he executes. Exactly what you need."

When the Cardinal got back to his office, he contacted the Archdeacon and arranged a meeting. He preferred doing things face to face, away from prying ears and electronic equipment. At the meeting, he passed on the information, about the Russian 'investigator', but not the part about the outstanding warrant in Russia.

Chapter 9

University of Stockholm
Stockholm, Sweden

Kinghaven had taken some time deciding how to approach the project. He would try and persuade the existing members to focus on just one of the three topics. They could select their preferred group, and he would balance the expertise by inviting other specialists to join.

It took a lot of phone calls to explain why he was involved. Fortunately, his reputation opened the door; they knew that Kinghaven would add to the group's prestige. And once he mentioned the incentive that they would be paid fifteen thousand euros their interest turned into serious consideration and, in most cases, acceptance.

Of the names on his list, most were men, with a few women. All but two were from university faculties. The exceptions were both priests; Father Emile had a doctorate in physics and Father Michael was a retired Abbot, who had spent a lifetime studying early Christian writings. Kinghaven would act as coordinator for the project.

He arranged an initial meeting and then went in search of a computer system. For safety and control, it was essential that there was only one data repository. He had seen what happened when there was more than one copy. Before long they got out of sync and contained different information and no-one knew which one was correct. For this reason, there had to be strict control on the stored data. One copy only with online access for everyone. And no printed copies either. For safety and security.

To set it up and provide a security system, he turned to Larisa Glushenko, one of his graduate students. She was from Donetsk in Eastern Ukraine with a strong computer systems background and always short of money.

After he outlined the requirements and the compensation she jumped at the chance. She estimated that she would be able to complete it in four weeks.

His problem now was to find a computer system on which to install it. He remembered that a colleague in Copenhagen had told him that they had a new Mainframe that doubled their total computing power. It was a donation from NordVest, the wind turbine manufacturer. There was a joint project between NordVest and the university that used the computer but it only required twenty percent of its capacity. They were trying to decide how to make use of the other eighty.

He looked up his friend's number and called him and told him that he was setting up a project and was in need of computer resources to store the data. He also mentioned that there were funds available to pay for it. Two days later he got a return call that indeed they could always accommodate a paying customer, so the following week Larisa Glushenko arrived in Copenhagen and began work on the data system. It took three weeks to design and install it and a further week to test it. Then it was good to go.

Chapter 10

Office of the Archdeacon
Castillo de Chipiona
Sanlucar, Spain

Father Bernado looked around his study. The desk he sat at dated back to the sixteenth century; the wood-paneled walls were original, all perfectly restored by expert craftsmen hired by the *Society*. It had been expensive but to get the best you had to pay for the best. It had been well worth it. He stood up and went over to the bookshelves which lined one whole wall from floor to ceiling. The books stacked on them all related to the *Society*'s interests; religion, church history and the Inquisition. Some were original and irreplaceable, records of interrogations and confessions, which had taken place here at the Castillo.

He was excited by the commission he had been given by the Cardinal—the responsibility to uncover and destroy those who were working to undermine the Church. And it had come from the very top. This was exactly why the *Society* had been formed; to stamp out the heretics. This was a chance to prove they were worthy of that trust.

It must have been like this at the time of the Inquisition, he thought. The Holy Church was strong and enforced strict adherence to its rules. Those heretics, who strayed from the one true faith or opposed it, were quickly dealt with. They were given a chance to recant and renounce their sins or face a fiery death at the stake. Here in the Sotano they had been interrogated and made to pay for their sins.

The Archdeacon turned his attention to the task at hand. Working sixteen hours a day he had a draft finished in three weeks and he completed the final rewrite five days later. He decided that the name *Disciples of the Word* would make their mission clear, and twelve members would give it an appropriate significance. The members, called Regents, would each handle one geographic region within the

Holy See. They would meet as a group monthly in the 'Room of the Apostles'. There would be a ring for each of them, bearing the seal of the Inquisition.

He spent three days deciding which twelve should be chosen. The *Society* had its detractors, even within the church, who felt they were nothing more than a group of fanatics. But there were many more who understood the need for an organization that would stand firm and uphold the law as it had been created and handed down by the Church Fathers.

There were three members who were automatically included. They could trace their ancestry back to the original Inquisition. This gave them, and the *Society,* a credibility and a legitimacy as the modern day successor of 'Tomas de Torquemada'.

The other nine were more difficult. They had to be dedicated, relentless and uncompromising. But all the members were. Then the Archdeacon remembered something the Cardinal had mentioned; that the *Dialogue* groups were located through Europe and North America. So he chose the other nine from those who had contacts or networks that stretched into those regions.

He reviewed the twelve names. They were all men of character who would give their lives if asked, to defend the Holy Church against those who opposed it.

Next he developed a reporting structure that would ensure that all information, no matter how tenuous, would be channeled through the appropriate Regent and back to himself. He also guessed that, much as he disliked them, computers would be involved. Everything now was stored on them, and if you wanted to steal or destroy the information, you needed someone who could crack them, if that was the word? He would need to find someone in the *Society* to set this up.

Once he had finished, he sent the plan under diplomatic seal to Rome and received approval four days later, with a stipulation that he provide the Cardinal with a monthly report. Karmazin authorized funds to be transferred to a new account with the Archdeacon as the signatory.

It had taken Bernado a further two weeks to phone, discuss and inform the chosen twelve and set today, February 28, for their first meeting. They were now assembled, waiting for him to enter.

On his desk was a leather-bound book, the size of a Bible, inscribed on the cover in gold letters:

Disciples
of
The Word

He picked it up and walked from his office to the 'Room of the Apostles'. As he entered through his door, they all stood and waited for him to speak. He looked around the room. Each of them wore a black cassock with 33 buttons and a matching zucchetto on their heads. The trim and the buttons were in the color of the region which they were to represent. His own cassock was in purple with white trim and a purple biretta.

He could sense their eagerness. They began by reciting the Apostle's Creed and when they had finished and were all seated, he began. "Let me remind you of our purpose here. We have been chosen to defend the Holy Church and its teachings. It is a calling of the highest order. We are to root out and destroy all those who would do it harm. Remember God's word as it is written in the Psalms, '*for, behold, those who are far from You will perish; You have destroyed all those who are unfaithful to You.*'"

He paused to let the words of the *Inquisition* sink in. Then he continued, "There is an organization called the *Dialogues* who are trying to destroy the Church by spreading heretical lies about our faith. We have been asked by the Holy See to root them out and destroy them and their work. This is our responsibility and our undertaking. We are to use all means necessary."

In front of each one of them was a book that looked identical to his. He explained that inside they would find a map of their region, as well as a list of contacts; priests and bishops who felt as they did and would assist them in every way possible.

"These contacts have been chosen," he explained, "because they are sympathetic to our cause. After this meeting, please familiarize yourself in every way with your region. Arrange to contact those priests who will help you and set up whatever reporting network you deem best. Also, be sure they understand the need for absolute secrecy. Each month we will meet here where you will present your report. If you discover anything that is linked to the *Dialogues,* however tenuous, inform me immediately." He scanned the room, before continuing. "You are essential to our plan. You are the eyes and ears of our organization. Once you identify a member of these *Dialogues,* we will bring them back here to the Sotano. People who are skilled in getting people to talk are being hired. They will extract the information we need to lead us to the other members. We are also hiring computer experts, called hackers, who will be able to destroy the information they have compiled."

He could read in their facial expressions and body language their complete and absolute commitment to this cause. He was certain that together they would root out and destroy the *Dialogues* and all those guilty of sedition.

This is the will of the Lord.

"Finally please open the box in front of you." He waited until they had taken the rings from the box. He explained the crest and why it had been chosen. "Before you put the ring on, look on the inside, and you will see printed your name and region. Now please place them on the ring finger of your right hand. They will identify you as a Regent."

Then he closed the meeting.

The next day the Archdeacon met with the security chief who showed him the newly installed security system. It used a key and code method. When a key was inserted into a lock and turned, a numeric keypad was revealed, with the numbers 1 through 9. Each key would fit any lock, but the code entered was unique and had to match the key. All keys and codes would open common entry portals, but only executive codes would open doors to restricted areas; the Archdeacon's office, the security office, and the door to the Sotano. Each key was attached to a small white plastic square. On one side were the symbols CΦC and on the reverse a graphic that when translated identified the code.

Chapter 11

99 Via Crescenzio
Rome

Bethlehem had requested an initial report from Michael Kinghaven once the *Dialogue* groups were in place. After that, communications were to be kept to a minimum. He was to leave them, as agreed, at the EGF bank in Stockholm.

The bank had been instructed that when they received any correspondence for *Bethlehem* they were to phone him immediately.

Two days ago the bank had called and told him that there was a letter for *Bethlehem*. He had instructed them to send it by secure courier to the apartment on Via Crescenzio.

The following morning it arrived and it was with his morning mail in his study. He read it as he drank his coffee. It informed him that the *Dialogue* groups were in place and a timetable had been agreed on. He would receive a letter when the reports were ready. For security reasons, he would be given a special password that would allow him to read the reports. No paper copies could be printed.

Chapter 12

University of Stockholm
Stockholm, Sweden

One of the *Dialogues* had withdrawn; an anthropology professor from Milan. He refused to accept the new structure especially Kinghaven taking over. And placing time frames on the research was completely contrary to the accepted practice. Pure research could not be put on the clock.

Although Kinghaven tried to persuade the professor to stay, he didn't try too hard. It was better to cut him adrift now, rather than run the chance of his bitterness surfacing later and polluting the rest of the project.

Also, he knew where he might find a suitable replacement. He picked up his phone and dialed the number.

Marius Sorensen picked up the phone on the second ring. "Hello, Sorensen," he answered.

"Hello Marius, it's Michael Kinghaven."

"Michael, what can I do for you?"

"Well, first a thank you again for helping set up the database."

"I hardly set it up, Michael. All I did was ask the computer people."

"Nevertheless without you, we might never have known about it. Now I have another favor to ask. I mentioned the *Dialogues* before but I wonder if you might be interested in joining the group? We are holding our initial meeting, here in Stockholm, next month.

"But you said that the work involved science and theology. I'm an anthropologist. What could I contribute?" Sorensen queried.

"Because anthropology is important in interpreting religious beliefs. It is impossible to understand the history of a people or a region without considering the social patterns and practices. Anthropology and religion are intertwined."

Marius conceded the point and after some further discussion he agreed to attend, more as a favor to his friend than out of genuine interest. He wrote the date into his diary, followed by a note. 'Not certain about this, not exactly my forte.'

Two weeks later, towards the end of August, still doubtful about joining, he arrived for the meeting and was introduced to the other members of the group. Most of them were university professors; there were two clerics, who were also academics in their own right.

Kinghaven explained. "Our numbers are small because we want to keep the purpose tightly focused and to contain the information."

"Why?" asked Marius. "Usually it's the opposite. Researchers like to get their ideas published."

"In general I would agree with you but, in this case, it is not original research. We will be looking at existing findings to evaluate their relevance to the Church. There will be three groups, one for each topic: cosmology, gender issues, and the origins of the gospels. Our intent is not to damage the Church but to emphasize current opinions and attitudes. Our intent is not to publish; rather it is to get the Church to look at our findings."

The meetings went better than expected. They agreed on the topics, set up schedules and arranged the groups. They discussed how the members of each group would be assigned. There was a variety of opinions but a suggestion, from John Hampton, a professor of physics from Toronto, won the day. He pointed out that the focus of each thread was, first of all, to summarize the current academic findings, and secondly to evaluate it in relation to Church doctrine. The first requirement would require an expert in that field and the second would be best served by someone with a background in theology. The balance of each group would be best served by a mix of expertise to provide a balanced approach.

Using that as a template, the groups were organized surprisingly quickly and without too much ego stroking. Each member would be allocated to two groups. Each would have at least one specialist, one theologian and the rest from the other disciplines.

How long each group would take was difficult to predict, and each was left to set their own schedule. What was important was that the work be completed within eight months.

Despite his initial skepticism, Marius felt a growing interest. Up to now he had always avoided religion and the Church. It stirred memories that were best left alone. It had destroyed his childhood and even as an adult he had never been able to either forget or forgive.

* * *

Copenhagen, Denmark

Growing up as a young boy in Copenhagen under the Nazi occupation he had seen his father, who was a member of the resistance, arrested and executed along with four other resistance fighters. The Nazis had even forced his family, himself, his mother, and his sister to watch.

As he grew older, Marius blamed not only the occupying forces but also the agreement between the Church and the Nazi party. The *Reichskonkordat* was a treaty signed by the German Vice Chancellor, Franz von Papen and the Vatican Secretary of State, Eugenio Pacelli who later became Pope Pius XII. It stated that the Holy See would not oppose the political and social aims of the Third Reich. In return, the rights of the Roman Catholic Church in Germany would be protected. Many people believed it gave the Nazi's a moral legitimacy, a *carte blanche* to carry out their atrocities. Marius and his family, who to that point had been Catholic, renounced the Church.

After the war, he had learned that his father and his four comrades had been denounced by a Danish priest who colluded with the Nazis. He said that the *Reichskonkordat* required him to do so.

The priest died in mysterious circumstances shortly after the German surrender. The circumstances of his death were never investigated. What was never made public, probably because all those who knew about it were dead, was that the Priest's sister lived in Frankfurt and was married to a Jew.

Marius, throughout his career, had always tried to make sure that the events from the past did not affect his academic judgment in any way. But he knew that the influences of childhood were not so easily discarded.

Perhaps it was time to move on or at least try, and this seemed the ideal opportunity to do so. It would allow him to apply his academic training and at the same time challenge the Church because, no matter what Kinghaven said, it would be viewed as an attack on its authority. He had to be sure not to let his personal history prejudice his judgment but within that confine he felt he might be able to make a useful contribution.

Nevertheless, he asked for some time to make his decision. It took him two weeks to be certain but once he was, he phoned the secretary and told him he would be happy to contribute whatever he could.

Chapter 13

36 Gayton Road
Hampstead, London

He called the electronics expert—he knew everything there was to know about phone networks—and explained what he needed and how it had to work. He was assured that it could be done. It was going to be expensive, but he agreed to it.

The next day the two virtual phone numbers were set up in Moscow ready to be switched for the real ones. Two phone receptionists were hired, one for each number, and briefed on how to answer and how to transfer the calls.

Next he called his operators and briefed them on the details, times, and dates.

Chapter 14

Interpol, Quai Charles de Gaulle
Lyon, France

Inspector Willi Charpentier had been seconded to Lyon, from his native Holland some ten years ago. His father was French Canadian and his mother, Dutch. They had met during the Canadian liberation of Holland at the end of the war. After Germany had surrendered, the Canadian Forces returned home. After he had been demobbed, his father returned to Holland and two months later married his mother. Willi was the third of their children born much later than his siblings. Not exactly an accident, more an afterthought, and certainly a surprise. He grew up speaking two languages, French at home, his mother had been educated in France, and Dutch outside. After school, he joined the national police and was soon moved to the international section.

His ability was noticed by his superiors and he advanced rapidly eventually being seconded to Interpol. After the secondment had ended, he accepted an offer to work for them permanently. For the last two had been in charge of the Interpol Integrated Inquiries, known to everyone as 3-I, based in Lyon. His agency used specialized software to look for reports, filed with Interpol, that had a common link. It might be a common suspect moving across international borders, the same organization operating in several regions, large amounts of money disappearing in one country and reappearing in another, or a myriad of other factors.

When he found the links, he contacted the appropriate authorities in each country and asked if they wanted Charpentier to assign one of his agents to look into it. The answer was nearly always 'Yes'. Police forces everywhere were understaffed and could rarely afford to put a detective on it full time. And Interpol investigators could operate easily across borders.

He didn't fit the profile of a senior police official. When he joined the Dutch police, he was small, young, had a full head of unruly hair, and passion for chocolate. Unfortunately, he didn't have the active lifestyle that could burn off the extra calories. Now, ten years later, he was short, bald, overweight, and still with a passion for chocolate. He had grown a beard to offset his expanding waistline. What hadn't changed was his ever cheerful personality and his enthusiasm for his job.

He was looking at three reports, cross-referenced by the computer software. The first was a description, from the police in Rome, of regular meetings between an Attache from the Russian embassy and a Catholic Cardinal, from the Ukraine, but based in Rome. The second was a request from Germany for information about a Catholic Priest named Father Bernado now living in Spain. They were evasive about the reason, but Charpentier deduced it had something to do with income tax on undisclosed income. What tied them together was a third file that tracked a priest from Sanlucar travelling to Rome to visit a Cardinal in the Vatican. The Cardinal was from the Ukraine and the Priest's name was Father Bernado.

Charpentier read the reports again. What was the connection between a Ukrainian Cardinal, an attache from the Russian embassy and a Roman Catholic Priest? It might not be anything criminal, but it certainly needed checking out. He checked who had filed the reports and contacted them. They all gave him the go ahead.

He checked his computer for the list of operators but of those who were available, none were suitable. But he knew who would be ideal for this assignment. A Russian operator by the name of Morse, if that was still the name he worked under. They had worked together several years ago and had developed a mutual trust and respect. But trying to find him now would be difficult. He would have to look up his contacts in the former Soviet Union and see if they could locate him.

Chapter 15

Detective Inspector Mason, head of the Toronto Drug Squad, took the call. He listened attentively as the caller explained what he wanted, making notes on a pad on his desk, including the number on the call display *7 495 695 3786.*

He knew that the country code was Russia but not the rest of it. When the caller had finished talking, Mason replied, "I'm not sure I can do that. What you're asking is for us to get involved in something that really belongs to you. Where are you calling from? It looks like somewhere in Russia." He listened for a moment, "Moscow? Well I appreciate the heads up, and the name you mentioned is known to us but he has never been charged and I can't act without hard evidence. I'd be putting my job on the line. I can try and kick it up upstairs to see if they'll okay it. You'd better give me the number of your chief. He'll only talk captain to captain. His name is Captain Michael Donaldson."

The caller gave him the information, and they talked for a few more minutes before hanging up. The first thing he did was check the number, just to be sure that they were who they said they were. He called the police switchboard and asked them to check the two numbers. They called back a few minutes later and confirmed both were listed as Moscow police numbers.

Mason sat for several minutes deep in thought. What he had said to the caller was true. He couldn't get involved in a case that was out of his jurisdiction. In this case it was tempting; the person he had named, Boris Radovic, was someone they were sure was behind a number of drug-related murders in the city. A 'person of interest' was the official phrase—in plain English the bastard was guilty, they just couldn't make it stand up in court. And he was elusive; they still didn't have a handle on where he lived or where he operated out of.

If this sting by the Ruskies worked, it would rid them of the problem permanently. In fact, he might be able to use it to solve another problem. They suspected that one of their own—Dave Woodman—a drug squad detective, had been bribed and was feeding information to the drug rings. Not a lot, just enough for the dealers to disappear before the cops arrived. It could be a coincidence except Mason didn't believe in coincidences. Maybe he this could use this to flush out the mole. The chief had been under a lot of fire from the board to seal the leak. This just might get them off his back. He picked up his phone and punched in the extension. "Yes, Mason, what's up?"

He gave the chief the information and the phone number. "This could be a real chance to get them both, but it might mean a few rules being bent; justifying the end if you know what I mean."

"Thanks, I do know what you mean but let me sit on it for a few hours. I've got a meeting in ten minutes; I'll get back to you."

Later that afternoon the Chief dialed the number Mason had given him. It was answered by a receptionist speaking Russian. He asked if she spoke English. "Yes," she said with an accent, but perfectly understandable, "how can I help you?"

"I'd like to speak to the Police Chief?"

There was a click and a few minutes later, a man's voice, speaking English with hardly any accent. "Hello, is this Captain Donaldson?"

"Yes. How did you know?" the Chief asked, just a little suspicious.

"The receptionist said you didn't speak Russian, only English and my Detective Inspector told me to expect a call. He said he had spoken with a Detective Mason this morning."

Satisfied it was genuine, he confirmed the information that Mason had given him. They talked for another twenty minutes, going over the details before Donaldson agreed to call tomorrow, with a decision. He hung up and headed downstairs.

There was a knock on Mason's office door and the chief walked in. "I just called the Moscow number and they confirmed what you told me. I'm going out on a limb on this one. I'm sick of wearing the board around my neck so let's set it up. Two birds with one stone; that's too good an opportunity to miss. I'll call Moscow in the morning and give them the go ahead."

Mason was listening carefully. His chief, 'Slippy Mickey', as he was known—but never to his face—had advanced his career by taking the credit when things went smoothly. And laying the blame on someone else when things went wrong. Mason knew he would have to watch him carefully on this one.

It was risky, and illegal, to allow a foreign agent to operate in Canada; career suicide if the press got hold of it. Together they concocted a cover story—and Mason made sure that it was both of them—that the agent was just 'passing through'. As a courtesy, they had agreed to meet him to share information about a possible Russian dealer operating in Toronto.

If it went wrong, they would find their collective arses warming the sidewalk. If it worked, it would put a big hole in the drug network and give them the hard evidence to bust Dave Woodman.

The following day Mason met with his team of narcotic detectives. He told them they had received a tip-off that a major dealer, by the name of Walter Russak, was moving into Toronto, along with his enforcers. The existing snowmen wouldn't be exactly thrilled. "If what we heard is true we can expect bodies, from both sides, on the streets."

"So why would we worry," said one of the detectives, "let the bastards kill each other; save us the trouble."

"Wouldn't that be frickin nice but you know we can't. We have to protect the public from all this crap even if they don't know what's happening and those who do don't even give a shit."

There were several comments and questions. Mason let it continue for a while before bringing it back. "Okay, thanks for the input. Here is what we know at this point. The head of the organization is arriving next Sunday on a flight from London. I've got a meeting with the chief this afternoon. Once we've worked out how we're going to deal with it, I'll call you in individually to let you know your role. And remember this is information that we need to sit on. I don't want to read about it in tomorrow's Toronto Sun."

The following day, after his meeting with the Chief, he planned the details. They would have a detective at the airport, to tail Russak once he arrived and call the coordinating officer, who would be in contact with the rest of the team. There would be other detectives stationed at the Sutton Place hotel where the arriving Russian had booked a room. One of them would be dressed as the doorman, waiting at the main entrance.

He called the detectives into his office one at a time to explain their roles being careful to only give them their assignment without disclosing who else was involved. He assigned Woodman to the airport, "Here's your role Dave. You'll be our point man at Pearson. This is a contact in customs," he said, handing him a piece of paper with a name and phone number on it. "Talk to him and tell him to give you the nod once he arrives. Any questions?"

"Do I stay with him once he leaves the airport?"

"Absolutely. Stick to him like glue and if anything changes, like he doesn't head for the Sutton Place, call Mike, he's on the desk."

"Sounds good. What are the airport details?"

"It's all on the sheet I gave you, Dave. Let's get the bastard."

After the meeting, Woodman drove over to the Sutton Place Hotel and went to reception. He showed his police badge and asked what room had been assigned to Walter Russak, arriving the following Sunday. The clerk went over to a computer terminal, typed in the name and waited a few seconds for the information to appear. He wrote the details down "He's booked into a suite on the third floor," he said giving the sheet of paper to the Detective.

Radovic was watching the evening news when the phone rang. He picked it up, "Yes," he grunted. It was Woodman. After listening for a few moments, he told him to hold on. He got up turned the television off and grabbed a pen and a notepad. "Okay give me the details."

"Have you ever heard of Walter Russak?"

Sounds familiar." He sat thinking for a second, "Yes he's the Russian from Vlad, got himself kicked out of the police force for selling out to the other side. I thought his name was Waltmir, not Walter."

"We were told Walter and according to the info I was given he's some kind of drug czar who runs the Eastern supply chain into Moscow.

He's coming to town," he said writing the name Waltmir, alongside Walter on a pad of paper.

"Really, well I think I'll arrange a warm reception, personally, one Russian to another and then ship his parts back to Moscow, one piece at a time. When is he arriving and where is he staying?"

Woodman gave Radovic the details and told him he'd call him from the airport once Russak's plane touched down.

Next day, Radovic paid a visit to the hotel taking a side door that led down into the garage and took the service elevator to the third floor. He was careful to keep his face shielded from the close circuit cameras. He found Suite 305 and rapped on the door. If anyone answered, he was prepared with a story that there had been a complaint of loud noises and he was checking to see if they had been disturbed. No one answered. After checking that the hallway was empty, he took a black plastic box from his pocket, about the size of a pack of cigarettes. It had a black tab on top. He placed it underneath the door lock and pushed the tab into the slot on the bottom. There was a click, the light changed from red to green and he opened the door closing it gently behind him.

There was a small hallway with a door to the bathroom off to the left and just beyond that it opened up into a large room. It had a desk at one end, a king bed at the other, and a chair and small table in front of a TV in the center. There was a window overlooking the front of the hotel.

He studied the layout and decided that the bed was ideally placed, not visible from the door but giving him a clear shot at anyone entering the room. He went over the hit in his mind, mapping it out. Satisfied, he opened the room door an inch and listened for anyone in the hall. There was no sound and he left quietly.

Chapter 16

University of Stockholm
Stockholm, Sweden

The *Dialogues'* group dealing with Gender Issues, had completed their initial report and posted it to the database. They had sent Kinghaven, and the other members, an email informing them that they should read it and post their comments.

Kinghaven logged on and went to the reports section, found it and read it.

The findings and recommendations were much as expected; the Church needed to accept the modern understanding of gender. Much had changed since the time of Christ, not least the role of women. And the committee could find no reason why their role within the Church should not change as well.

They had looked at Church doctrine on the subject; *'Only a baptized man validly receives sacred ordination.'* It precluded women becoming priests. What made it even more intractable was that it was considered part of the Divine Law, which comes directly from scripture and revelation and, therefore, cannot be changed by man.

The committee disagreed. The New Testament is man-made; an anthology of books, written in the first and second centuries, and compiled into the twenty-seven books of the New Testament over the next four hundred years. These decisions about what to include and what to exclude in the canon were made by religious leaders who were all men—then, as now, no women were involved. Decisions made in that context had no relevance for today.

The report went on to apply the same argument to the priesthood.

After his resurrection, Christ told his disciples to travel to *all nations* and teach them to *obey everything I have taught you.* This was the Great

Commission that could only be carried out by single men. But it too has little, or no, relevance for today.

The committee, therefore, recommended that priests, women or men, should be allowed to marry. It did not preclude single priests of either sex, But hopefully, it would move towards a priesthood and a Church that would end the inequality towards women and begin to mitigate the shame of paedophilia.

The report went on:

We accept that the Church has constantly reviewed its position on these issues, including commissions and Papal interventions, seeking God's will. But they have still come to the same conclusion. Until this changes, they will continue to be out of step with modern society and run the risk of becoming irrelevant and impotent.

At the end of the report, there was an added note:

It is hard to accept that God's revelations ceased two thousand years ago. To do so precludes the insights and breakthroughs that have occurred in every field of human endeavor, since then. If we are *created in the image of God*, it is surely in our intelligence, understanding, and creativity that the parallel is most evident. Within the Catholic Church, this classification already exists. It is called Natural law; the use of reason to analyze human nature, both social and personal.

This is the same *rationality* that has propelled humankind to question the unknown and look for answers. This timeline has marked humanity's evolution through the ages. Art and music have enriched and ennobled our culture. Medicine has brought an end to diseases that once killed large swaths of the world's population. Psychology and psychiatry have furthered the understanding of the mind and the complexity of human nature. And science has produced a topography of the universe that maps its journey from the beginning to the present day.

This search for meaning is both personal and universal; to understand ourselves and the world in which we live. This too is part of God's revelation.

Kinghaven sat back in his chair, remembering how he had felt when he was a young man, some twenty years ago. He had believed then in the Church. Fully and completely. He had felt its power, and he thought he could base his life on its message:

Crucifixion. Resurrection. Absolution.

Except it was not enough. There was a world out there that he wanted to change. Today not tomorrow. The teaching of the Church was bookended in events that took place two thousand years ago and a future that might never come. He couldn't wait that long. So he had exchanged a theology rooted in the distant past and the unforeseeable future, for a political ideology focused on the here and now.

He added his comments to the report, pointing out a few minor points, but essentially agreeing with its recommendations. Once the others had posted their comments, he would finalize it, then send *Bethlehem* a password that would allow him access to the report.

Chapter 17

Pearson International Airport
Toronto, Canada

Woodman was waiting in the arrivals hall at the airport watching the screen. The Air Canada flight from London had just changed from 1:45 p.m.to 2:15. He picked up his phone and dialed a number.

Sitting in his car across from the hotel, Radovic picked up his phone and looked at the display; Woodman's number. "Yes, what's happening?"

"The flight is thirty minutes behind, so sit tight and I'll call you when he's cleared customs." Woodman then called Mike at the coordinating desk with the same information.

When Russak finally appeared it was 3:15. Woodman was busy calling Radovic and didn't notice a man in a Maple Leaf Hoodie hand Russak a black bag, the size of a carry-on.

Radovic closed his phone and pulled on his gloves. He locked his car and went into the hotel through the side entrance. His revolver was in his shoulder holster and the silencer in his pocket. He went in as before, through the garage, taking the service elevator and avoiding the cameras. He walked quickly along the corridor and let himself into room 305.

The hotel clerk, at the front desk, was watching the CCTV cameras and noticed the man in a Fedora walking across the garage, and a few minutes later he was visible on the camera in the elevator.

Russak was riding in the back of the airport limousine, on his way to the Sutton Place hotel. He was feeling tense; a nerve in his cheek twitched. His phone rang, and he looked towards the driver to see if he was listening. He didn't appear to be, and the sound of traffic on the

65

highway would make it almost impossible to hear what was being said. Nevertheless, he cupped his hand over the phone.

He looked at the number. It was Androv. "Everyone in position?" he asked him, watching the CN tower and the downtown high rises come into view.

"Yes, I'm in the coffee shop watching the main entrance."

"Good. Do we have the side entrance covered?" He listened to the reply, then said, "Hopefully you won't see him. I should be able to take him out, but in case anything goes wrong, it's down to you two."

Radovic scanned the room. Everything was the same. He moved a chair over to the side of the bed. He took off his top coat but kept on his gloves, screwed the silencer onto his gun, and placed it on the bed. Then he waited, wishing he could turn on the TV, but the sound would give him away. There was a newspaper on the bed, but he wasn't a big reader. Occasionally he would look at the rack on the Sunshine Girl but that was about as far as it went. After going over how he would do this, he let his mind wander.

For the last few weeks, he'd been screwing Olivia, who he had met in Petrograd's, a bar on Queen Street. But last week he had met Nadia a Russian with great looks and even bigger tits. Olivia must have heard about it. They had just had a great fuck when she yelled at him. "You're seeing someone else, aren't you?"

"So, what's it to you!"

"You don't even deny it. You motherfucker."

That got his attention. He walked over to the bed; she was still in it, and with his right hand he grabbed her hair and lifted her up, so the top half of her naked body was exposed. "Don't you fucking swear at me, you bitch! I'll see who I like when I like. Got it." Then he hit her hard across the face.

Her head slammed back from the blow and then she collapsed back onto the bed crying in pain. "The next time you talk to me like that I'll take my knife and cut your face so that no one will ever want to look at you again."

To emphasize his point he pulled her head up and scratched his fingernail over her face in four different places. "Maybe I should do the first one now," he said taking the knife from the special pocket sewn into the inside jacket of his coat." She screamed and tried to cover her face, "No please don't. I won't ever say anything again. I promise. Please."

"Good now you can prove it," he said as he climbed back into bed. Violence always gave him an appetite. He found the two went well together.

The doorman opened the door and Russak stepped out. "Welcome to the Sutton Place, sir," he said and then added, almost in a whisper, "your visitor has arrived."

When Russak got to the door of Suite 305, he didn't immediately open it. He put the bag down and from one of the side pockets, took out an industrial strength smoke mask and placed it over his nose and mouth and pulled the strap tight behind his head. From another pocket, he withdrew a small canister about the size and shape of a hand grenade. He opened the door of the room, pulled the pin and rolled it into the room with sufficient force that it rolled all the way across and stopped at the far side, below the window.

Radovic's pleasant thoughts had been interrupted by the sound of the door opening. Immediately he was fully alert. He took the gun from the bed and waited for Russak to come into view. But he didn't. Instead, he saw the grenade rolling across the room. "You bastard," he yelled as he flung himself under the bed and waited for the explosion. There wasn't one, but he smelled the tear gas. His eyes were stinging and he could feel it burning the back of his throat. He pulled himself out from under the bed and stayed low hoping there would still be fresh air closest to the ground.

Russak was now in the room, with the door closed behind him. He held his *shiv* in the firing position, with a cartridge in the chamber. The smoke was too thick to see anything, but he could hear Radovic moving around and he knew at some point he would have to make a run for it. He heard a creaking sound, like a hinge that needed oil and saw the smoke beginning to disappear. It was being sucked out of the room.

Russak, both hands on his *shiv*, edged into the room. The window was open and there was no sign of Radovic. He looked out and realized what had happened. They were directly above the hotel entrance, which was covered by an overhanging portico. Radovic had dropped down from the window onto it and from there down onto the ground. He could just see him racing down the street in the direction of the parking lot.

The smoke had activated the detectors and all the alarms were ringing. There was general chaos as guests headed for the stairs. The police detectives posted on the ground floor wouldn't know what had happened. Russak just sat on the bed still wearing his smoke mask, soaking wet from the sprinkler system above his head.

Radovic reached his car and jumped in. He felt like putting the gas pedal all the way to the floor, but he knew that would be the worst thing he could do so he forced himself to drive at the speed limit. But he was furious. He had been set up and it had to be that bastard, Woodman. He would fucking make him pay. If he hadn't made it out of the window, he'd be a dead duck. He'd underestimated Russak, maybe it was time to lay low until he had figured out what was happening and just who he was dealing with.

A white Buick, Androv driving and Sacha in the passenger seat, stayed close behind. Sacha had a notebook in his hand and wrote down the license number of the Mercedes. They followed it north on Bay St., onto Davenport, and right onto Avenue Road. He had to run a red light at Dupont to keep him in view, but he lost him just north of St. Claire Avenue. Traffic was restricted to one lane for road repairs, and the Mercedes got through just before the northbound traffic was stopped to let the southbound cars proceed.

The Buick was trapped between the car in front and the car behind. He didn't have any room to manoeuvre. Even if he had, his only way to get past the road works was on the sidewalk and that was full of pedestrians.

He watched the Mercedes take the next left and as soon as traffic flow was reversed he took the same turn but there was no sign of it. He drove around the area, noticing the large mansions and Sacha made a sketch map of the streets: Heath Street, Forest Hill Road, Davenport, Warren.

Russak had booked into the Hilton, under a false name. With all the confusion of fire trucks and police cars, sirens wailing, no one had noticed him leaving the Sutton Place, through a rear entrance.

He had just made it into his room when his phone rang. It was Sacha. "Shit!" Russak said in frustration, then forcing himself to stay calm, he asked, "What happened?" He wrote the street names in his casebook before hanging up.

Then he sat down in an armchair and reflected on the *sting*. Everything had gone wrong. Radovic had got out of the window and escaped. His operators who had been in position for exactly that eventuality had lost him. And it wouldn't be long before the Toronto police checked the Moscow numbers and found out they were bogus.

He was further behind than when he started. Radovic or his goons would be looking for him. Not to mention the Toronto Police Force. It was time to disappear before they got him in the cross-hairs.

And pulled the trigger.

Chapter 18

Cherry Beach, Lake Ontario
Toronto, Canada

Two kids saw it first. They were swimming in the Lake. It looked like someone's coat floating on the water. They swam towards it. The girl got there first and then she screamed and half swam, half ran, as fast as she could, back to the beach. She told her mother who immediately called 911. The police arrived followed by the paramedics. They dragged the body from the water, loaded it into the ambulance and drove it to the city morgue on Grosvenor Street.

The Coroner's report, two days later, showed the body was a male, aged 45, killed by two bullets to the chest. It was identified as that of Dave Woodman.

The Chief was in Mason's office and angry. "What the fuck went wrong? This was supposed to get rid of that asshole Radovic. This detective, Rissole, or whatever his name is"

Mason interrupted him, "You mean Russak, I think." Then immediately regretted it.

"Don't fucking interrupt me," the chief yelled, his face red and the veins in his temple pulsing, "I'll tell you when you can speak. Got it."

Mason had never seen him this angry and he knew who was going to take the blame. He just nodded.

"Where was I? I know," he said picking up where he had left off before Mason had interrupted him. "Russak was supposed to flush Radovic out and then ship him back to Russia. Either that or put a bullet in him? And what happens; he doesn't do either. Instead, Radovic is alive and well, and it looks like I'll be taking a long vacation, courtesy of the police board. I got a call this morning, they want to see me tomorrow. So what went wrong?" When Mason didn't respond, he added, "Now you talk!"

"I don't know yet. We're trying to put the pieces together, but at least we got Woodman."

"Don't tell me we put those bullets in him. Christ this is going from bad to a fucking disaster. I'll be lucky to get out of this with my pension. And if I go down, you'll be right behind."

"No, we didn't pop him, it must have been Radovic, or more likely one of his goons," Mason said, thinking that Slippy Mickey was doing it again. Although this time, he was *sharing* the blame. At least so far.

"I'm sure Radovic has disappeared but what about the other motherfucker?"

"Right now, we can't find either of them. They've both gone to ground."

What Mason didn't tell the Chief was that after the fiasco, he had checked the Moscow phone number that Russak had called from, as well as the one he had given to the Chief. They were both numbers for Moscow police, but neither of them had received any calls from Toronto in the last several days.

Chapter 19

Hilton Hotel, Richmond Street
Toronto, Canada

He was in his room trying to figure out what to do next. Androv had given him the street names in the area where they had lost him. He had the license number of the car, but he doubted if it was registered to his home. Probably some phony address. Anyway, he could hardly call the police and ask them to check. Maybe they would have to do a search of the streets, hoping that the Mercedes was parked in a driveway visible from the street. In that area not very likely.

Androv phoned and asked, "Any progress?" Russak looked at the paper where he had made his notes. It was mostly scribbles, rectangles and circles that he drew subconsciously when he couldn't solve a problem. "No, not much. Have you had any ideas?"

"Not so much an idea, just something I noticed, that might help. You know the frame that holds the license plate, it usually has the dealer's name on it. I'm pretty sure that it said 'Mercedes-Benz Middletown' or something like that. According to Sacha, who knows every car ever made, it's a two-year-old, E250. Couldn't we check with the dealer to see who it was sold to?"

"Good thinking," Russak replied as the glimmer of an idea began to form. "They wouldn't release that information to anyone but if it was a query from an official, say a police detective, then they would have to. We could say it had been seen near the scene of a crime and we need to ask the driver a few questions."

Androv pointed out the obvious, "I don't think the Toronto Police are likely to cooperate. We're hardly flavor of the month."

"I know," he answered, running his idea through his head, thinking how it would work. "Suppose we tell the dealer we are detectives with the police."

"And why would they believe us?"

"Because we show them our police badge."

"You're getting weird," Androv said. "Have you been into the vodka? How do we get a badge?"

"We buy one!"

"Where?"

"Have you heard of eBay? You can buy practically anything. So you check out the dealership location and I'll see what I can find on eBay."

It didn't take him long to find what he needed. It was even better than a Toronto badge. It was a wallet and badge for the RCMP, Canada's national police force. It was out of date, discontinued several years ago, but it would be enough for what he had in mind. Rather than put in a bid. He bought it and arranged for overnight delivery.

They found the location of the dealer, Mercedes-Benz Midtown on Eglinton Avenue and drove there in a rented black Dodge Charger, one of the models used as unmarked police cars. The combination of the car and the RCMP badge convinced the salesman that they were who they said they were; police detectives.

It didn't take long, thanks to a customer database, to find out that the car had been sold, just over two years ago, to an 'Alex Metachev, 101 Forest Hill Road.'

Although the name didn't mean anything, the address was close to where they had lost the Mercedes. "We need to set up surveillance on the house to see if the Mercedes turns up. I'll get two of the Shivs to alternate, twelve-hour shifts, and keep an eye on the place."

For the first two days, the only car they saw coming and going was a silver Lexus. The driver had the size and bulk of Radovic, but since no-one had seen him close up—they had only seen him running from the Sutton Place hotel—they could not be certain. On the second day, the Lexus left just after dark but never returned, but the next day they hit pay dirt.

The Mercedes—same license plate; same dealer name—appeared from a garage behind the house, driven by a chauffeur, with the big man in the back.

They stayed close behind, this time risking recognition rather than losing it in traffic. The journey was quite short, eventually arriving at an apartment complex on Eglinton West. The Mercedes went to the back of the building and reappeared ten minutes later, with only the chauffeur. The big man was not in the car.

They phoned the Hilton and told him where they were. He told them to stay there and keep the place under surveillance.

Back in his hotel room he decided that the time was right. He sent the message to each federal police district in Russia. It was terse and to the point.

Subject: Fishing:

You can reel them in whenever you want.

Chapter 20

Triumph Apartments, Eglinton Ave.
Toronto, Canada

Radovic was drinking his morning cup of coffee and thanking his lucky stars—whatever they were— that he had got out alive. It had been a close call and without that canopy he wouldn't have made it. At least he had got that bastard, Woodman. He wouldn't be double-crossing anyone again. *Ever.*

He had moved back to his apartment on Eglinton. He had tried living in the Forest Hill mansion, but he couldn't get used to it. It was so large he often got lost in the place. It also came with a cook, a housekeeper and the chauffeur. He always had one of them interrupting him. The cook wanting to know what he would like for dinner, the chauffeur asking whether he would need the car, and the housekeeper needing to know when she could clean the bedrooms. It was driving him crazy. He started driving himself in the Lexus and left the Mercedes and the chauffeur at the house. He would only use them for business purposes.

He tuned the television to RBC, a Toronto channel that carried news of interest to expat Ruskies.

The first item made him sit up. The police and security organizations had made a huge drug bust in nearly all the major cities across Russia. This wasn't an ordinary raid, where a large haul of drugs was intercepted, although that had happened as well. What made this different was that it reached right to the top and right across the country. The authorities had nailed the top men who ran the networks. Something this huge must have been planned for years and needed someone on the inside. With the networks down there would be chaos on the streets; without their meds, the junkies would go crazy. His own supplies came mainly out of Central and South America, but he wondered if any of his suppliers would try and divert some of it to Russia. He made a mental note to have a word.

The second item brought him to his feet. Peter Todd, the lawyer who had handled Alex's will was being led away in handcuffs from his Bay Street office. He was charged with stock manipulation; defrauding his clients of over one hundred million dollars. So much for white collar business ethics.

But why, Radovic thought, was this on the Russian news channel? He didn't have long to wait the answer. The reporter explained that the police suspected that Todd was fronting for Russian mobsters operating a drug network in Toronto.

Radovic knew it wouldn't be long before the police started looking into his affairs and uncovered the link between Peter Todd and Boris Radovic.

The schmuck would almost certainly sing to reduce his sentence. Their kind always did. And he was pretty certain that his name was probably already on some police file linked to the Russian mob.

After the fiasco with Russak, and now this, it might be time to get rid of the drug business, altogether. Pass it on to one of his assistants. They were running it day to day anyway. Split the profits. He would be out of sight and free to move on. To what he hadn't decided. But it made sense. A good time to disappear.

And reinvent himself!

Chapter 21

6100 Decarie Blvd.
Montreal, Canada

His thoughts were interrupted by the phone ringing. He picked it up, "Elite Property Brokers, Can I help you?"

"I'm calling to see if the property is still for sale," the voice on the other end asked.

"You mean the one by the lake. I'm not sure, I'll check. Give me your number and I'll get back to you."

Fifteen minutes later the Property Broker called back. "I take it you're looking for a change in your personal affairs. Is that right?"

"Yes. How do I go about it?"

"Get a pen and paper and write down what I tell you, but first the price. It's going to cost you forty big ones twenty now and twenty when it's finished."

"Forty thousand, that's fucking gouging."

"Well that's the price and you wouldn't be calling me if you had any choice."

He knew he was right. "Alright," he said, "give me the details."

The man gave him an address in Montreal and a date and time as well as a list of documents and instructions. "Bring all the items and half the money, cash only, as a down payment."

He had accounts at four different banks—for exactly this situation—and over the next few days he withdrew the money in different amounts. The following Friday he packed all the documents and the twenty thousand in his briefcase and put his favorite weapon, just in case, in the glove compartment of his car. Then he headed for Montreal. Once on Highway 401, the traffic thinned and he set the cruise to 110. He let his thoughts wander. He'd got out of the drug business, but he wondered if he'd made a mistake. Been too hasty. He hadn't realized how much he enjoyed it and how much of his time it occupied. He took up golf and played poker three times a week. The upper-class bimbos filled part of his time, but he needed something else. Like contract killing; he enjoyed that.

Not from a hundred feet away; from a window or building where the target couldn't see you. That was a coward's way. He did it 'face to face'. He liked to see the expression in their eyes when they realized that this was the end. The power of life and death as he squeezed the trigger. It gave him a 'high' like nothing else.

Traffic was light and he made good time and at Kingston he pulled into a rest area to get gas and some food.

A blue Camaro pulled into the other side of the parking area.

When he pulled back onto Highway 401, the Camaro followed him at a safe distance. All the way to a small hotel on Rue Metcalfe, in downtown Montreal.

The next day Radovic drove along Sherbrooke and north on Decarie. It took him two attempts to locate 6100, the address he had been given. The first time he was on the wrong side of the street so he crossed over on Van Horne and found it half a block further south. He parked and got out of his car and thought he must be at the wrong address. Directly across was a police station. He went into the lobby of 6100 and checked the Business Directory; 'Elite Property Brokers, suite 301'. This was it.

He took the stairs rather than the elevator. When he could, he always avoided small enclosed spaces that had only one way out. He found Suite 301, rapped on the door and opened it. He was expecting some kind of security, but he was greeted by a man, standing by the window, impeccably groomed in a grey suit, white shirt, and a blue striped tie. His hair was close-cropped and brown. He was olive skinned, with an oval shaped face. Radovic estimated that he was about sixty, slim and looked every inch the successful businessman. As they shook hands, Radovic noticed the index finger on his right hand was missing.

"The result of being careless with a knife," the man said, reading his visitor's thoughts, "Their knife. My finger!"

He recognized the voice from the phone call earlier in the week. "Careless but I'm sure you didn't make the same mistake again."

"No, I didn't. And the man who did it isn't making any mistakes at all. *Ever.*"

"I expected more security. Anyone can just walk in here. And there's a police station across the road."

"Oh there is security, take a look," he said as he turned the computer monitor towards him. On the screen was a shot of the parking lot and his car. "We tracked you from the moment you arrived. The door frame on the ground floor is actually a scanner. Anything metal you were carrying, such as a gun or a knife would have shown up and we would have been ready. It's as well that you left your gun in the glove compartment."

The visitor looked at him in surprise, "You can actually see inside a car? From inside the building?"

"That's what they tell me. Gamma rays or something like that. And directly across the hall there's a room with two heavily armed security guards on duty at all times. They monitor the system 24/7. And the police station is the perfect smoke screen, no one with criminal intentions would locate straight across the road. I even know some of the police by name. I see them at the local coffee shop. And what is there to find? My filing cabinets contain legitimate properties and you can see from the diplomas, that I'm a legitimate property broker." He pointed at several framed certificates hanging on the walls.

Radovic looked at them, one citing his real estate license, one his broker's, and one acknowledging that he had been president of the Montreal Real Estate Board from 1989 to 1992.

"I'm impressed. Are they real?"

"Absolutely. I still sell several properties each year."

They talked for a few minutes about baseball and hockey and then got down to business. "Let's see what you brought me."

He placed the briefcase on the table, opened it and turned it so it was facing the broker. It contained the money and a legal sized envelope He removed the envelope and emptied it on the desk, sorted the documents and carefully studied each one. "Everything looks in order. I'll need to make a copy of them."

He picked up the intercom and punched in two numbers. When it was answered, he said, "Mary can you come in for a moment." When she did, he placed the documents back in the envelope and the envelope back in the briefcase. He handed it to her and told her to make a copy of all the documents in the envelope, and to put the money in the safe.

When the secretary had left, he detailed the procedure. "When you leave here I'll be in touch with a plastic surgeon we use. Nothing major, just a subtle change. His fee is covered by your deposit. They'll phone you with an appointment date and time. It's a small clinic in Westmount. You'll need to stay overnight. Since you're currently clean shaven, I recommend you grow a mustache. In two weeks' time, you come back here with the balance of the money. And we'll provide you with a complete set of documents in your new name and new address. Make sure you bring the old documents so we can destroy them. And that's it. Any questions?"

"Not that I can think of. Everything seems straight forward."

As he left, he didn't notice the Camaro across the road, on a side street. The driver called in and gave the address. He was told to stay with him.

The plastic surgery was done a few days later.

Two weeks later he went back to the broker's office and stood in front of his desk. "What do you think?"

"My God. Your own mother wouldn't recognize you. You've taken my advice and grown a mustache and you've even shaved your head. A nice touch."

He gave him the balance of the money. The broker produced a camera and took a series of head shots, for his new passport, driver's license, and health card. "When they arrive you can assume your new identity and say goodbye to the old one. We'll register the demise as death by misadventure. One last thing, you need to get rid of your car. It's still registered in your old name. We have a dealer who works with us. Leave it with us; he'll give you a good price. We'll forward the money to you. When your new documents arrive, you can buy a new one in your new name and new driver's license."

"You think of everything. Your prices are high but worth it."

"We aim to please. Now when you leave here go out the rear door of the building. There's a car there waiting to take you to the airport."

"Why the back way?"

"My security people have reported that the car parked across the road is the same one that was there when you were here two weeks ago. Maybe it's nothing but it's best to be safe."

When he got back to Toronto, he went straight to his new apartment, Suite 504, in the Edwardian, 755 Lawrence East, that backed onto Edwards Gardens. While he waited for his new identity to take shape, he picked out a new car, a dark green BMW 550. He would complete the purchase once he had his new documents.

They arrived the following week via UPS. A day later his passport arrived. They were perfect. Expensive but worth every last cent. It gave him a sense of freedom. No police record, no suspicious past. Every ending is a new beginning.

Until you're fucking dead.

Chapter 22

Office of the Archdeacon
Castillo de Chipiona
Sanlucar, Spain

The Archdeacon picked up the phone and dialed the Canadian number that the Cardinal had given him.

It was answered on the third ring, in English, spoken with a strong accent. "Yes, how can I help you?"

"Hello. My name is Father Bernado. I was told that you might be interested in carrying out some investigations we need doing."

"It depends on who gave you my number and on the work and the fee. Give me your number and I'll call you back."

"Why?" the Archdeacon asked.

"Because in my business there is no room for error and I like to know who is at the other end of the line. My call display didn't show your number, just *unknown.*"

Karmazin had told him he would be cautious; he had been right. "Very well. It doesn't look like I have much of a choice." The Archdeacon gave him his private number at the Castillo.

Immediately the call ended, he pressed his speed dial and asked for a trace of the Archdeacon's number. A few minutes later the phone rang and the nerd—an expensive nerd—told him that the phone was a safe line and located in Spain near Seville.

So that explained his accent. He took his cell phone, left the office and headed outside. Although it was prepaid and not traceable to him, he always worked by the maxim that *walls have ears,* and there was a modicum of safety outside. He dialed the number he had been given and the voice with the slight accent answered.

"Okay, Father Bernado; so far everything checks out, so tell me who recommended me and gave you my number?"

"I was given it by Alex Metachev."

"He's dead?"

"Yes, I had heard. So sad. Such a nice man. He helped me on a number of occasions. Does that mean you are no longer available?"

He was going to say that he had never heard Alex described as a *nice man* but decided it really wasn't relevant. "Not necessarily. I did the kind of work I think you have in mind for Alex. Tell me what it is you need."

"We need someone to take over the enforcement side of our business. I can't discuss the details over the phone, even if it is a secure line. But let me give you the essentials. The assignment is ongoing and may last up to a year, but probably no more than eight months. The Remuneration is negotiable but is in the seven figure range. And there would be an expense account to cover personnel, travel and equipment purchases."

So far he was interested, especially by the mention of seven figures. And it was perfect timing. *The enforcement side.* A lot of possibilities. He was excited, but he kept his voice flat, "Very well Father I am interested enough to suggest we discuss the opportunity in more detail. We should meet. Can you come to Toronto?"

"That would be difficult. I have an organization to run and it is difficult for me to be away for more than a day or two. Couldn't we meet somewhere in Europe?"

"I'm busy too. I'll call you back tomorrow when I've looked at my schedule," which was an invention since he kept his schedule in his head, and he knew he was available. The only thing on his agenda was his current bimbo, Ida Goodwin, and that could be postponed.

"I'll await your call. And I look forward to meeting you."

He decided London would be suitable. Big enough for him to fade into the background if it became necessary. Easy to get to and they spoke English, even if it was with a strange accent. The next day he called the Archdeacon, "We'll meet in London on Tuesday next week."

"Just a minute," the Archdeacon interrupted him, "Let me check my schedule."

"Perhaps you don't understand. When I take an assignment, I have to control what I do and when. If that's not possible, our conversation is over."

"Sorry, that date and location will be fine," said the Archdeacon, controlling his temper, realizing that if he wanted someone to take this on he had to go along with them. The problem of controlling him would come later. "Where and at what time do we meet?"

"You'll find that out just before the meeting. Let me know where you are staying and under what name and you'll get a call from me one hour before the meeting."

The Archdeacon disliked this man, already; he disliked anyone who told him what to do. It wasn't personal it was just part of what he believed.

Few people understand the true nature of power. It does not come from brute strength. When the strength fades, as it always does, the power disappears with it.

Real strength comes from within; it is based on an understanding of human nature; on the fears and prejudices that people try to hide. Power, real power, comes from harnessing those fears, turning them inside out until they become desires, then amplifying them until they become a nation's voice. A glorious crescendo that give the people a vision and a purpose.

Just as it happened in Berlin as our country rose to its glorious destiny; the conqueror of Europe. The dream of world domination. And my family had been part of it; my father as an army surgeon, myself a proud member of the Hitler Youth.

If you truly want to understand power, study Hitler, and Goebbels. The great orator and the great persuader. They understood so well. First the Vision—the third Reich. Der Ubermensch—then the purpose; identify and destroy the enemy, first the soul, then the mind, and finally the body.

But at the end of the war his whole world had collapsed, his hopes destroyed, his heroes gone, his country destroyed and beaten. The enemy was pouring into Berlin and the Hitler youth had been called on to protect the fatherland. To stand. To fight. To die.

He had been given a Luger and told to shoot the enemy, soldiers. But he had failed. A moment of doubt, indecision, inaction. What good would his dying do? The war was over. He was only a boy. Wasn't it better to live? To fight another day! He had run, in fear, to the first organization that offered him shelter, the Catholic Church.

He detested weakness. He hated cowards and the shame was still with him. To remind himself he kept his gun in the safe next to his desk. Ready and loaded. He would not fail again.

Chapter 23

Boulevard Lasalle
Montreal, Canada

They had lost him in Montreal, at the address on Decarie. A few inquiries revealed it was called Elite Property Brokers.

An Avis location in Toronto reported they were missing a car. They had expected it to be returned three days ago, but there was no sign of it and the phone number on the contract wasn't answering. They reported it to head office in Etobicoke.

Two kids playing ball on a deserted lot in a park by the river found it. A late model Camaro with a body inside it, not moving. They ran home and told their parents who called the police. When they arrived, they found the driver slumped over the wheel with a bullet hole in the back of his head. From the smell they guessed he had been dead for quite a while. The coroner later confirmed it had been three days.

There was no id on the body; whoever killed him had taken everything that would identify him. Even the glove compartment had been emptied. The only lead was an Avis sticker on the inside door panel. It took three more days for all the pieces to come together.

Chapter 24

Hotel Continental
Oslo, Norway

Morse was sitting across from Charpentier in a suite on the top floor of the hotel, overlooking the harbor in Oslo. It had taken him three weeks to run him to ground.

Charpentier explained the assignment. He described the meetings between the Russian attaché and the Cardinal and now the Priest from Sanlucar. He needed Morse to set up surveillance, find out what was going on and then to decide on a course of action.

Morse was interested. It was the kind of work he enjoyed. But there was a problem. He had some unfinished business to take care of.

"How soon do you need me to start?" he asked.

Charpentier thought about it. The attaché and the Cardinal only met once a month and the meetings with the Priest were spasmodic. "It doesn't have to be right away, but within the next few weeks."

Morse took his time answering. A practice designed to unnerve the other person; learned under the Soviet system and difficult to change. At length he said, "I think we have a deal Charpentier. Let's say three weeks from today."

They reached across the table and shook hands; then spent the next four hours working out the details.

Morse looked out of the window overlooking the harbor, watching the tugboats maneuvering a large Cruise Ship into its berth. To the right he could just see the Royal Palace and the National Theatre where many of Ibsen's plays were first performed. His family originated not far from here, in Lillehammer, the site of the 1994 Winter Olympics.

He looked at the time. Still three hours of daylight but a storm was moving in. His Saab had all wheel drive and the main highway was well plowed. He should be able to make it.

He was right. He made it in two and a half hours, just before the snow began to fly. He would have liked to have stayed there longer but he needed to get moving again, before the trail went cold.

He made flight arrangements; still no direct flights. He had a choice; he could fly SAS, via Copenhagen, or Icelandic via Reykjavik. The length of the flights was the same, eight hours. He decided on Icelandic; Keflavik was always less crowded than Kastrup.

Three days later he headed to Gardermoen, to catch his flight. He already had a reservation at the Hilton.

Chapter 25

Pearson Airport
Toronto, Canada

He flew from Toronto to London, first class as he was now used to doing. A man his size needed the extra room. As soon as he was seated he was provided with a newspaper and a drink; vodka, which he drank, Russian style, in one gulp. Before he could ask there was another one in front of him. He liked the service. And the stewardess who delivered it. She looked interested and interesting. As he sipped his vodka, he wondered what she was wearing underneath her uniform. Not now, he had business to take care of. Maybe on the return flight.

Once the flight was in the air the man in the seat next to him, smartly dressed in a navy blue suit turned to him and said, "Hello. My name is Paul Sadlon." and he held out his hand.

He shook it but didn't tell him his name.

"What takes you to London?" the man asked.

"I'm meeting a client to arrange a contract."

"What kind of business are you in?"

Radovic looked at him and didn't answer. But the expression on his face and the darkness of his eyes got the message across. There were no more questions.

The Archdeacon was staying at the Waldorf Hilton and his friend had suggested that *what's good for the Goose is good for the Gander*; another one of those strange English sayings! No wonder they conquered the world, no-one could bloody understand them.

He had decided to stay at the more modest—if such exists in London—Excelsior Inn at Kings Cross in part because of its proximity to the tube and rail stations. In case he had to make a quick exit.

He had told the hotel that he wanted a standard room and a small meeting room, visible from the lobby. They had arranged the Trafalgar room for his meeting. It was on the ground floor and visible from the main foyer. His room was on the second floor almost directly above it.

Once he had settled in he did a careful check of the hotel. He began outside his room, noting the closest entrances and exits, service access and entrances to the underground garage. He then repeated the process for the meeting room.

The next morning, after his workout, he ordered breakfast from room service and while he waited he dressed. He decided to wear his shoulder holster—just in case—and a loose fitting sports jacket to conceal the slight bulge. At 9 a.m., he picked up the phone and dialed the Waldorf and was connected to the Archdeacon's room.

"Good morning," the Archdeacon answered, "I trust you had a safe journey."

"I did. And I'm ready for our meeting. I've arranged to meet in the Trafalgar room at 10 a.m. The room will be open. Coffee has been ordered and I'll arrive slightly later." He gave him the name and address of the hotel and then added "I'll see you shortly Bernado." He deliberately avoided either Father or Archdeacon, which would have established an authority between them, that he was determined to avoid.

He went over to the desk in his room, opened his briefcase and withdrew a buff-colored envelope. He shook out the contents and picked up two photographs of Bernado. They were part of the requirements that he had insisted on before agreeing to the meeting. He had refused Bernado's request for the same. He looked at them again; unnecessary since he had already committed them to memory. He put them in the top pocket of his jacket and went down to the lobby.

He bought a newspaper, went to the meeting room and opened the door, making sure to leave it slightly ajar. Then he found a seat in the lobby from which it was visible; just to be sure that Bernado had not ordered an advance party. At ten minutes to the hour, he saw a taxi pull in and a short, stocky man get out. This was him; exactly as he appeared in one of the photographs. He hardly needed them, since he was wearing clerical garb; a purple cassock and a matching beanie. He looked to be in his sixties with grey hair protruding from under his hat.

He put down the paper and took out his cell phone. He punched in a number at random and got a recording telling him that the number didn't exist. Precisely what he wanted. Hiding behind a newspaper can be a giveaway; being on the phone is much more natural. It also gives you an unobstructed view.

Bernado went to reception and was given directions to the meeting room. A few minutes later the waiter delivered the coffee. After five more minutes, he was satisfied that no one else was watching. He made his way to the Trafalgar room.

The meeting went smoothly. The Archdeacon was impressed by his appearance and size; not someone you'd want to meet in a dark alley. And his resume, delivered verbally—nothing in writing—was perfect.

They discussed what was needed. It was exactly the kind of work he enjoyed. He answered Bernado's questions with directness. Bernado liked the clarity of his answers. His *modus operandi* was refreshingly straightforward; identify the target, isolate, abduct and get the information you need; then remove and dispose. It didn't take long for the Archdeacon to make up his mind. He was exactly what he needed. The only problem would be who gave the orders. But that could be decided later.

They discussed the terms of the contract. It was his turn to be impressed; by the amounts of both the initial retainer and the monthly amounts. Far more than he would have asked for. The requirements were to track down a group called the *Dialogues* and to investigate and eliminate as necessary. Also whatever information they had compiled would need to be destroyed.

They discussed the extra staff that would be needed at the Castillo. They would need computer personnel, as well as a super nerd, who could hack his way into the *Dialogue's* computers. And it went without saying that they would all need to be on the wrong side of the law.

They shook hands to indicate their agreement. As they did so, the Archdeacon noticed the scar on the palm of his right hand. He told him he would be ready to start in one week and gave him his name. *Andre Balinska*

Balinska set up his own operation, to keep an eye on Bernado's people. Just in case! He kept it to a minimum, much easier to control and much more efficient. He hired five operators, three in Europe, and one each in Toronto and Montreal.

Back at the Castillo, the Archdeacon set things in motion. He asked Leo Ronaldo, one of the members of the Society, who was in the computer business to set up a system at the Castillo. Also to find him an expert who could 'hack' his way into any computer and was not handicapped by any moral or legal scruples. Leo pointed out that you never used 'hacker' and 'scruples' in the same sentence. It took him a few days to put together the network team and a few more to find the ideal hacker, Antonio Messi, who lived in nearby Seville. They were all hired and moved into the Castillo.

Father Bernado went to a small cabinet in the corner of the lounge next to his study and took out a bottle of Lagavulin and poured himself a generous amount. He took a hand-rolled Cuban cigar from the humidor and sat down at his desk. He lit the cigar and took a sip of his scotch. He was satisfied. The work was about to begin.

Balinska waited until the Archdeacon had sent him the names of the people he had hired. He then had a company that specialized in investigating people, check out the main ones; the Archdeacon, the man in charge of security, and Antonio Messi. He told them it was a rush job. So long as he had the results within a week he would pay double their normal fee.

The report was delivered five days later. The head of security was formerly with the Spanish branch of Brinks' security. The Archdeacon had been born Karl Vessel in Germany in 1930 and had been a member of the Hitler youth and a fervent Nazi. There was a note about him avoiding paying taxes on the estate that had passed to him from his parents. Not exactly 'devastating' but not something the upstanding Archdeacon would like advertised.

The security guard was clean, but Antonio Messi was interesting. Very Interesting. He had been a top student at the University of Tavosa in Central Romania, specializing in Information Technology, when he suddenly quit in his final year.

There was nothing on file to explain why, but the investigator had dug a little deeper and found the reason. Messi had hacked his way into the University's record system and would alter a student's marks for one hundred euros a pop.

When he was caught in his fourth year, he gave the university an ultimatum, either buy him out or he would go public. In the end, they had no choice. If it got out, no-one would trust the academic credentials of any of their graduates. They agreed to pay Messi a fixed sum each year to keep quiet.

The kid has balls, thought Balinska.

After he had left the University, he ran several successful scams until a credit card hack went wrong and put him on the police radar. He had left Bucharest in a hurry and didn't stop running until he reached Seville; waiting for things to quiet down.

Chapter 26

Castillo de Chipiona
Sanlucar, Spain

Balinska made his first visit to the Castillo, a week after he had been hired by the *Society*. The security chief and the Archdeacon took him on a tour of the compound. He would have preferred a guard on each of the gates, but once he saw the control room, with its bank of monitors, he withdrew his objection.

"And who would want to break in here?" the Archdeacon said, "We are a peaceful Christian society. If we put guards on the gates, it would look as if we had something to hide."

Balinska didn't bother replying; agreeing with the Archdeacon would suggest he was right and the lines of demarcation, who was going to run this operation, had not yet been defined. But when he saw how the Castillo had been built; with three foot thick walls and beams carved out of thick natural timbers, he realized that the place was almost impregnable. And the Sotano, with a copper door concealed behind a false wall, showed that whoever had designed the Castillo had been a genius, a man ahead of his time.

He found out later that the rooms had been used by the Inquisition. They still contained some of the instruments of torture; the Rack, the Judas chair, the Boot, and the 'tortura del aqua'. He became quiet, lost in his own thoughts.

He had been born in the wrong century. What must it have been like; to tighten the rack, to hear their bones crack, to hear their screams, and to watch them burn at the stake?

Most of them were crumbling relics, more than 400 years old, but the water torture had recently been renovated. Balinska went over to and ran his fingers along the metal table, where the prisoner would be held immobile by the series of straps. It was pivoted in the centre so it could tilted until the prisoner's head was directly below the spigot that protruded from the wall. There was a retractor to keep the mouth open and a hood with a slit for the water to run through. With the head in position, the tap could be set to a constant drip that gave the prisoner the sensation of drowning. With a hood over his head, left alone and in the dark, even the most hardened individuals would soon be pleading for mercy.

"Has it been tested?" Balinska asked.

"No, but now you're here I'll have my security guards pick up a derelict from the streets of Seville. Someone who won't be missed. Then you can put it to the test; see if it's to your liking. Perhaps after dinner?"

* * *

Castillo de Chipiona

The three of them, Balinska, Messi and the Archdeacon had spent the first week studying the organization and the reporting structure. Balinska's initial comment was critical and intended to undermine the Archdeacon. "It shows how information passes from the priests to each Regent and from there to us, but it doesn't specify *exactly* how the priests are intended to find the information in the first place. We need a plan that shows how they can find the names and locations of these *Dialogues*; who they are and where they are."

The Archdeacon, who saw what Balinska was trying to do, responded somewhat angrily, "And how *exactly* would you suggest we do it?"

"Isn't that what Messi is here for?" He turned to him and growled, "This is where you come in. Get onto your computer and start doing a sweep, or whatever you call it and find them. That's what you were brought in to do. Do it now."

Messi was used to running things his own way and he wasn't about to have some oaf high on testosterone, give him instructions. He looked directly at Balinska, "You have no idea what I do or how I do it. You have neither the acuity nor the inclination to understand. What I do, requires both aptitude and acumen. Neither of which you possess. So remember that. I don't take orders. Not from you! Not from anyone! I decide what I do and when I do it. If you don't like that just say so and I'll be out of here and you can try and find someone else. Capiche."

Balinska was furious—partly because he only understood every other word, which was Messi's intention and also because he was sure it was insulting. He was having a difficult time resisting the urge to smash Messi's face into the wall. But he remembered the advice that Alex once gave him. *If you lose your temper, you lose control, and then you lose everything!* So he choked it back and said. "Very well, let me rephrase. How do you propose we find them?"

The Archdeacon had been watching the two of them carefully. Despite his dislike of Balinska the Archdeacon knew he was more than just a cold-blooded assassin. That's the reason he had been hired but, in this case, he had got more than he had expected. He was pleased to see Messi wasn't going to be cowed. He was no pushover. He could hold his own with Balinska and, in fact, he had the advantage of a formal education. And according to his academic record, assuming he hadn't altered it, his knowledge of IT was outstanding.

But the Archdeacon was concerned that animosity between the two of them could affect the operation. He needed them to get along. He moved to diffuse the situation, "I think we need to calm down. We have to work together or we'll get nowhere. Let's break for an hour and then come back and see if we can move forward." To his relief they both agreed, assuming that Balinska's grunt meant 'yes'.

When they regrouped an hour later, Balinska had obviously thought about the situation. What he had thought before about him, *this kid has balls,* had been re-affirmed. He could—would have to—work with that.

The Archdeacon sensed a calmer atmosphere and asked them what could be done. There was a pause before Messi said, "I'll take a look at the chatter although with no idea of the location it will be difficult."

The Archdeacon broke in, "Sorry to interrupt." With a slight emphasis on *Sorry,* "but when I met with the Cardinal he said something about that; let me think . . . Yes, he said that there is already chattering on the Internet, about the *Dialogues*."

"The word is chatter and it's a way of tracking information that is flashing back and forth on the internet. I'll see what I can find out, but it could take a while."

Balinska stared at him, still not fully appeased, "I have to go back to Canada for a few days . . . " he paused thinking how to phrase the next part, as a request or as an order. *This kid has balls,* so he concluded, "Can you have the report on my desk when I get back?"

Messi returned the stare, "I'll see what I can do."

The Archdeacon breathed an inward sigh of relief. It looked like his 'interrogator' and his 'hacker' might be able to work together.

"While you're away I'll contact the Regents to get started by asking the Priests to report anything that looks at all suspicious. And I'll send a note to the Cardinal." The Archdeacon added.

Balinska flew back from Seville to Montreal to meet with his operator, Pierre Molatov and update him on what he had learned at the Castillo and what to expect.

He had intended to spend a day in Toronto, doing the same thing with his operator there, Yuri Beratovsky before heading back to Sanlucar. He ran out of time and flew and flew back to Toronto the afternoon before his flights to Spain. He booked into the airport Hilton and had Beratovsky meet him there. He gave him the same information he had given Molatov and went over what he expected while he was in Europe. He gave him his contact information at the Castillo.

Chapter 27

Hilton Hotel, Richmond Street
Toronto, Canada

He needed to pick up the trail and he guessed that there had been an identity switch.

He knew he would need help on this. He had to get into official records to see if he could figure out what had happened. He used his contacts in Russian Intelligence. He was redirected several times but finally he got to the right person, Colonel Mikhail

Beratov. Once his encrypted security code had cleared he was told to expect the information within twenty-four hours.

Knowing how slowly Russian bureaucracy worked, he didn't hold his breath. But he was wrong. It arrived the next day.

> *Arrangements made Ottawa; access to records. Contact*
> *Henri Borassa Passport Department.*
> *Toronto contact: Peter Gillard, Registrar General.*
> *They have been contacted and will provide you with all*
> *assistance.*
>
> *mb*

He was going to have to move quickly to finish on time. The following day he flew to Ottawa, took a cab to the Passport Office and asked for Henri Bourassa. When he appeared—a dapper little man wearing a charcoal suit and a red bow-tie—he took him to the Information Access section. He showed him how to access passport applications that had been processed in the last three months.

He spent the first hour making mistakes but once he got the hang of it, he found it easy to use. He was looking only for eastern European names, figuring that it would be necessary, to explain his accent. Even so by the time he had finished three hours later, he still had over 100 names. He checked his watch. It was 2:30. He thanked Henri for his assistance and grabbed a taxi back to the airport. Traffic was light and he made the four o'clock to Toronto.

In Toronto, he spent two days matching the list of names against birth and death records. By the end of the second day, he was seeing black spots in front of his eyes. Was this going to be like finding the proverbial needle in a haystack?

He took a break and came back two hours later feeling better, at least the spots had disappeared. An hour later, he got a match, between a birth record, a death record, and a passport record. The death record indicated the boy died when he was two years old. The name was Andre Balinska. And the information he had from the passport office, included a photocopy of the application, with a photo and an address to which it was to be sent: *Suite 504, 755 Lawrence Ave. East. Express Delivery. Urgent!*

Now he had everything he needed, he could finish it! He contacted one of his operators, gave him the address, sent a copy of the photo and told him to monitor his comings and goings. What he needed was a fixed window of a least an hour when Balinska was always out. That would give him time to break into the apartment and wait for him to return. He had him in his sights again.

But there was a problem. For three days, his operator reported, there was no sign of Balinska, coming or going! Not again, he thought. Has he escaped a second time? He went over the events, piece by piece, but couldn't explain what had happened. Until he took another look at the passport application. Why did it specify, *Express Delivery? Urgent!* He answered his own question. *Because he needed to get somewhere in a hurry!*

He needed to get a look at airline flight lists and reservations for the past few weeks. Fortunately he knew someone who worked for the airlines. It was just a matter of offering the proper incentive. She checked the name against airline passenger lists going back three weeks and forward two. When the report came back, it showed Andre Balinska had been on a flight from Toronto to London, returning three days later. It was followed a week later by a flight from Toronto to Madrid and on to Seville. He was scheduled to return after ten days to Toronto, but he flew instead to Montreal. He was booked on flights from Toronto to Seville next week.

So that is why he never appeared at the apartment on Lawrence Avenue. He had gone instead to Montreal. Why? He had no idea. And to try and track him down in Montreal would take too long.

He reasoned he must have planned on coming back to Toronto, but something changed and he went to Montreal instead. He might fly to Seville from there.

Just to be safe, in case he did return, he told his agent, to keep an eye on the apartment and to contact him if Balinska appeared. And to be safe he booked himself on flights from Toronto to London and then on to Seville two days later. It would put him in Seville eight hours before Balinska. Providing nothing changed.

Chapter 28

Heath Row Airport,
London, England

The flight from LHR to Madrid was smooth. He even enjoyed the coffee if not the cardboard wrapped 'breakfast sandwich'. The Iberian flight was the opposite. The small plane bounced up and down in every air pocket it encountered. It landed at San Pablo Airport at 10:15 a.m. local time. It had been cool and raining when he left London and he was overdressed. As he walked across the tarmac to the terminal he removed his topcoat; it was short sleeve weather in Seville.

He had cleared customs in Madrid and for a change his suitcase was already on the carousel. He grabbed it, walked outside and hailed a taxi and fifteen minutes later he was at the Airport Marriott. Once in his room he had a shower and then slept for a few hours; he had been up at 4 a.m. to make his flight from Heath Row. He would have liked to have slept longer, but he had a lot to do before Balinska arrived late afternoon.

After lunch, he took a cab to the Avis car rental, to pick up the car he had booked online. He told them that he had a friend arriving tomorrow and he wanted to be sure that he had reserved a car. He gave them the name, Balinska.

"Yes, sir we have his reservation. He's asked for a luxury car."

"That sounds like him. Only the best is good enough for him."

"Exactly. In fact we're giving him the Mercedes over there," said the rental agent, pointing to a maroon CLK that was being cleaned. "I'll be off duty when he arrives, but I could get one of the other agents to tell him you are here."

"Thank you but that's not necessary. I'll see him at the hotel."

He walked over to get his car and as he was passing the Mercedes, he made a mental note of the license plate. He found his mid-size, a silver Peugeot, and drove back to the hotel, and went over his plans.

At 4:30 p.m. he was sitting in his rental on a quiet section of the airport ring road with the glasses trained on the Avis Car Rental. He looked at Balinska's photo which was clipped to the rear view mirror. At this distance, even with the binoculars, it might be difficult to identify him. At least he knew the car he was renting, and he could follow that.

He watched the arrival and departure of every passenger who got on or off the Avis shuttle. After an hour, he was having trouble keeping his eyes focused but he knew that there were two shuttle buses and that each made two trips to each terminal, every hour. He knew their license; their make, one of them had a tire that needed inflating and the other had a tail light that had blown and they carried an average of 8 passengers. If pressed he was sure he could also pick out the drivers in a lineup.

Finally at 6:15 his man got off the shuttle and walked into the building. It was more the way he walked—identical to the way he ran, with his shoulders thrown forward—than his photo, which identified him.

He started his car and drove closer to the Avis exit gate. He saw Balinska get into the Mercedes, exit the airport and follow the signs to AutoRoute E5 heading south.

Once on the AutoRoute he was able to keep several cars between his Peugeot and the Merc. After about forty minutes, the CLK slowed down and took exit 44. Most of the cars stayed on the highway and now there were only two cars between them.

The access road led to a roundabout and the second exit took them onto the A-471 towards Sanlucar de Barrameda. He slowed slightly until there were several cars between them. They reached the outskirts of the town and the volume of traffic increased. He had to make sure he didn't lose him as cars weaved in and out. The A-471 changed into a two-lane secondary road, heading south and eventually became the A-480.

The fields all around were full of vines, heavy with grapes, obviously wine making country and judging by the size of the grape bunches. The harvest must be soon.

They travelled a further six miles and he caught the smell of the ocean. Suddenly the Mercedes slowed and turned right onto a narrow road. He slowed and followed; now there was no one between them but Balinska rarely looked in the rear view mirror unaware that he was being followed. Maybe he felt safe in Spain; his enemies an ocean away.

The road was no longer paved, just gravel, and the tires crunched over it causing him to slow to minimize the sound. There was a right-hand turn and when he came around it, the CLK had disappeared. He quickly stopped the car, opened the window and listened. Despite the trees which were thick on either side, he could just hear the sound of a car off to his right. He got out and walked back along the road trying to see where the car had gone.

At first he missed it, just a small clearing about fifteen feet wide, partially covered by the overhang of the trees. It was only when he went towards the back that he saw a gap on the right and a dirt road. The road led to a wrought iron fence and gate, set with the vertical spires two inches apart to a height of about six feet. He crouched down studying the gate looking for a security system. It didn't take him long to find it. Mounted on a tree to the right were a light and a camera. He guessed they were both motion activated.

He was hardly dressed for it, but he had no choice so he crawled through the dense brush to his left until he was certain he was out of range of the camera. Then he turned and on all fours elbowed his way to the edge of the tree line where he encountered the fence. The shrub had been cut on his side, providing a six-foot clearance that ran as far as he could see. The other side was manicured lawn. The fence ran to the North and West as far as he could see. The gate was on the East side close to where the two sides met. There was a motor that he assumed would open it once it was activated. There were two metal signs, one on either side, the first warned that the fence was electrified and the second advised that this was private property.

The road ran on for about one hundred feet then curved to the left and disappeared behind the trees. He would need to get over the fence to get a closer look and see where it led. There was a tall tree to his left that had a thick branch that overhung the fence that should be sufficient. He thought about what equipment he would need, how to get it and where. As he was about to go back to his car, he heard a low growling sound coming from inside the fence and a Doberman came towards him with its fangs bared. It was soon joined by three others of similar disposition. He would have to plan his closer look very carefully

Chapter 29

Security Control Room
Castillo de Chipiona
Sanlucar, Spain

The security guard in the Control room was watching every movement on one of the monitors. There were ten in total, one for each camera. The cameras were positioned at each corner of the wall that enclosed the compound, on either side of the main gate, as well as the perimeter gate and access road. There were two more on the ocean side. Their size and position made them difficult to see.

The guard had called Balinska as soon as he arrived to report a strange car on the access road; the driver had parked it and walked back to the clearing. After that, he disappeared out of view of the security camera. "What the hell is he doing," said Balinska, then answered his own question. "He apparently thinks this place needs further investigation. Do you think he's law enforcement?"

"Well," the guard replied, "he suddenly appeared . . . at," he paused to check a computer log, "19:40 almost immediately after you arrived at 19:38. So it's reasonable to assume that he was following you."

"All the way from the airport?" Balinska asked.

"I don't know, but I could check it out. I've got the license number," the guard said a little nervously. He had heard about Balinska's reaction to problems and he didn't want to become one of them.

"Do it. I feel like going out there and asking him what the hell he thinks he's doing but let's get all the facts first." As he said this, the door opened and the Archdeacon walked in.

"Hello, Balinska I heard you had arrived. Do you mind me being in here? I wanted to see who was outside."

"No. Help yourself, Archdeacon. I'm going to my office to see what came in while I was away. I'll see you tomorrow at 11 a.m."

"Right," said the Archdeacon."

He went over to the cabinet where the keys and cards were kept. "Any news on the missing card?" he asked the security guard.

"No Archdeacon, not yet, but we haven't finished searching all the buildings and the cars."

"No record of who had it last? I thought every card had to be logged in and out."

"That's the procedure but the guard on duty that night was new and forgot to write it in the book. He said he didn't remember who it was issued to. He's no longer with us, of course."

Actually the guard did remember. It was, Balinska, but he was too afraid to say so. He preferred losing his job, rather than an arm or a leg.

Once in his office Balinska looked through the documents and mail on his desk. Most of them could wait, but there was one, presumably from Messi, with 'Internet Chatter' typed on the envelope. He opened it and read the report.

> *I ran a program, called an Internet bot that looks at the chatter traveling across the internet and searched for 'Dialogues' I got few hits but nothing definite; mainly background, like white noise. My guess is that the locations are Northern Europe, possibly Scandinavia, but we need corroborating information to be sure.*
>
> *Messi*

"Shit," Balinska exclaimed, "Is this all he can come up with. There's nothing there that helps; *Northern Europe*, leaves it pretty wide open."

He pressed a button on his intercom and Messi answered. "I need to see you in my office."

"Right now, I'm busy. I'll be there in thirty minutes." He hung up before Balinska could say anything.

When Messi appeared, it was obvious that there was more than just blood circulating in his veins. He had been smoking something. Balinska pushed the report across the desk to him. "Is that all you can come up with in a week? What am I supposed to do with it? There's no names, no location—Northern Europe doesn't count, we need specific places where these people are —so what else have you got?"

"I need some more information to be able to pin them down. What is the network of priests doing? How many of them are there? And they haven't turned up a single clue. But you think I should be able to come up with answers. As I said before, you don't understand what you're talking about."

Balinska kept his anger in check because he knew Messi was right at least as far as the Archdeacon's network of priests were concerned. Not a bloody thing. But he still needed to have some control over Messi so he decided to use the *edge*. "Point taken, but I don't think you've been entirely honest so far. You never mentioned the credit card scam that blew up in your face in Bucharest."

If he expected Messi to have a guilty look, he was wrong. He just looked at Balinska and said, "You know about that do you. But I don't think you mentioned the rape of that fifteen-year-old or the sailor's throat you slashed in Vladivostok. You're not the only one who did their homework."

Balinska just looked at him; *this kid really did have balls.* He was going to have to watch him very carefully.

In the meeting and for the next two weeks they got nothing; not even a sniff. Just a big fat nada. Like hitting the wall. They couldn't even get started. Then they caught a lucky break.

The Archdeacon came down to his office, after breakfast. His mail was on his desk as usual. He went through it, dispatching some to garbage, others to a pile to be dealt with later until he came to one from a Regent in Germany. He opened it immediately.

The letter explained that he had been contacted by a Bishop in Munich, who was sympathetic to their cause. The Bishop had received a letter from a curate in the diocese, complaining about the appointment of a Father Emile, an outsider, as Parish Priest. According to the curate's letter Emile spends more time studying scientific topics than he does on parish business. He is extremely secretive about it and keeps his notes on the office computer, protected by a password that only he knows.

The letter added that Father Ulrich, the curate, had expected to get the appointment and was angry that he had been passed over. It is possible that it is simply 'sour grapes'. Nevertheless, given your instruction to report anything that might hint of the *Dialogues*, I thought I should inform you.

Attached was the letter from the curate. The Archdeacon read it. Maybe it was sour grapes but it needed to be followed up. He called Balinska and gave him the letter. "What do you think?"

Balinska read it, before saying, 'It's the first lead we've had. It may be nothing, but I think we need to check it out. I'll take Messi with me since there's a computer involved. The Archdeacon had his secretary make travel arrangements for both of them to go to Munich, the following day.

PART TWO

Chapter 30

The distinctive ring of the phone disturbed Jose's concentration. It was his private line and that meant it could only be one of the few people who knew his personal number. He recognized the number in the display window. It was his uncle in Toledo.

Jose Rodriguez was tall and slim with an entirely ordinary face set off by dark green eyes. A two-inch scar on his right cheek added a slightly mysterious look to his appearance. A rumor had started that it was a knife scar from a police raid gone wrong. He didn't bother correcting the story. It was a lot more intriguing than the truth; he had fallen off his bike when he was a teenager and gashed his cheek on a jagged piece of metal lying hidden in the grass verge.

He was seated in his office at the headquarters of the National Police Corps in Madrid, thinking that he hadn't seen his uncle, Father Michael, for almost six months. It had been a party to mark his retirement from the monastery of Espiritu Santo, just outside the town of Santa Isabel a few miles from Saragossa. His uncle had devoted his life to the monastery and to the study of ancient tracts about the origins of Christianity.

The monastery was more than just a devotional sect, it was an active self-sufficient community. Founded in the tenth century on two hundred acres of farmland. It grew its own food and kept both a dairy and beef herd; the pedigree cattle fetching premium prices at local and regional cattle auctions. More famous than that and infinitely more profitable was the Merlot wine, which they had been producing for over 200 years, made from the grapes grown in its own vineyards and fermented in its winery. The wine had won many international awards and was now shipped to over 30 countries.

But what set the monastery apart was the repository of books and medieval documents, some of them over a thousand years old. Many of them had been copied by hand to ensure that their legacy was not lost; others had been translated from original Semitic languages into Latin and Greek. It was this scholasticism that eventually became Father Michael's life work and interest. He worked as a translator, librarian and registrar amassing a voluminous knowledge of the subject and becoming one of the world leading experts on the first few centuries of the Church's existence. At the age of 55, he had been asked to become the Abbot. He was reluctant to accept the position because it would take him away from his beloved library. In the end, he had been persuaded to take the post and had served as head of the monastery for five years, before retiring to Toledo to resume his scholastic passion. The library at the university there had an excellent collection of books and reference documents that he was eager to consult.

Jose's own father, Mario was Michael's younger brother. Officially a lawyer with the Madrid police, he was, in fact, an officer with the Spanish Intelligence Service, based at the central headquarters in Madrid.

Mario's marriage to Clarisa Beneton, a former fashion model had been a mistake from the start. She had never settled to a life of domesticity. He had hoped that motherhood would mature her and indeed pregnancy seemed to give her a different focus and she looked forward eagerly to the birth. However, after only a few months she reverted to her old ways, her only interests were getting back her figure and restoring her career as a model at Madrid's leading fashion houses. She hired a nurse and left Jose in her care, sometimes not seeing her son for days on end. Also, there were growing reports of her sexual peccadilloes. In the end Mario gave up; the public embarrassments and humiliations were too much.

He waited until she returned home late one evening and then confronted her. "Clarisa, we've been married for five years and, to be honest, it's a disaster. I've waited for you to grow up, hoping you would learn to be a wife and especially a mother, but you haven't. You are not interested in our son or me. The only important things in your life are your shopping expeditions and your growing reputation for sexual dalliances."

"How dare you," she responded jumping from her chair, her face red and angry.

"Sit down Clarisa and try being honest for a change. If I wanted to, I could get several reports of your sordid little affairs and you know what, I no longer care. That's not what this is about. This is an ultimatum. You can do one of two things. You can start acting like a mother which means being home with our son, helping him grow, watching over him and loving him so that he knows who his mother is. You can also start to be a wife; put an end to all your sordid affairs, accompany me in public and show me some affection as your husband."

She was about to interrupt, but Mario stopped her. "Let me finish Clarisa. The second option is your freedom. You will accept a no contest divorce and give me sole custody of Jose. In return you will get to keep the apartment, it will be signed over to you, and you will be provided with an annual allowance that will be adequate to your lifestyle." He watched her face and he could see from her expression that she was considering it.

Nevertheless, she responded as if the offer was an affront. "How can you even suggest such a thing; you can't put a price on my love for my son and my marriage."

"What love," Mario exploded. "You're never here. Jose probably thinks his nurse is his mother and we haven't had sex for the past three months. Anyway, you can't make a decision straight away, take some time to decide what you want to do. I'll put all the details in writing and send it to your lawyer."

Four days later, after a meeting with her lawyer, Clarisa followed her heart and took the money.

Three years after the divorce Mario was asked to go undercover to penetrate the Basque network in Catalonia. This would involve being away for several months, even years. He knew he would regret it if he turned it down, but his son, who was now ten, had to come first. The plan had always been for him to attend boarding school, away from the crowded, dangerous streets of Madrid. As he had so often in the past when dealing with family matters, he turned to his older brother,

Michael. He phoned him and gave him the gist of the problem and arranged to drive down to see him.

The following Tuesday he drove the 200 miles to the monastery. It was a clear day and he brought out his favorite toy, his 1961 Jaguar XKE, one of the first off the production line. He had flown to England to get it. It was reserved for special occasions and he decided this was one of them—he hadn't visited his brother in over two years. Once on the AutoRoute, with the top down, he opened her up. Even with the constraint of right-hand drive, he still made in under two and a half hours; well over the speed limit, but that was one of the few perks that came with the job. When he arrived, his brother was waiting for him. "Michael, so good to see you," he said as he climbed out of the car.

"Hello, Mario. Good to see you. I see you still haven't got over your childhood obsession with fast, expensive cars."

"Thank you, Michael," he said, ignoring the sarcasm. "Glad you like her, she is a beauty isn't she? And since Clarissa is now gone, it is my only passion, except of course for my son. It helps keep me young, speaking of which you look the picture of health; the country life agrees with you."

"It's not just the country life," said Michael, "it also has a lot to do with an inner life of quietness and contemplation. You should come and try it, we run weekend courses. It could rejuvenate you."

"I don't think so, you know my responsibilities lie elsewhere." Michael was one of the few people, outside the intelligence service, who knew Mario's real occupation. "And that's why I've come down to seek your help and advice."

Michael took Mario's overnight bag and led him to one of the small guest rooms, little more than a single bed and a chest of drawers; with a shared bathroom down the hallway. "Get yourself settled and then join me in my office in the library."

Looking around Mario said, "Well that should take me all of five minutes. Does the monastery run to a cup of coffee or is that excluded from the monastic life?"

"I'll see what I can do, but only because you're my little brother."

Ten minutes later they were seated in Father Michael's office. Mario opened the conversation by outlining the problem. "I have a dilemma on my hands, Michael. It is no longer possible for Jose to live and go to school in Madrid. We had always planned to send him to boarding school when he was old enough and now that time has come."

"So what is the problem? Send him to boarding school and see him on weekends and school holidays."

"That's not the issue. The problem is mine, either I turn down this assignment and remain in Madrid or find someone who will accept the responsibility of being a second father to Jose."

"And who," Michael interjected, "do you have in mind, little brother?"

Mario looked up and saw the smile on his brother's face. "Well, what are big brothers for?"

"But first," Michael responded, "I want you to search your heart to be absolutely sure this is what you want. You are making someone else responsible for the life of your son. Are you sure that down the road, you won't regret it? Have you talked to Jose about it? He was abandoned by his mother and now he's going to be left by his father. Have you any idea what that kind of rejection can do to a child?" He said this softly; the years of monastic life had instilled in him a quietness, but there was a look in his eyes that left no doubt about the import of the question.

Mario understood the seriousness of it and the piercing look in his brother's eyes. He had seen that look so many times before; since childhood and he knew the weight of its meaning. It was reserved for those critical moments in life when a decision had to be made that was of crucial importance. He took his time answering, although he had gone over the question in his mind every day since he had been asked if he would accept the assignment in Catalonia.

"No, I don't know. And yes I'm frightened of what it will do to Jose, and me, both now and in the future. What I do know is this. My work is very important to me. No please let me finish," he said as he saw Michael about to speak, "I know what you are going to say. Is my work more important than my son? Of course not but it's not a black and white situation, there are many shades of grey. But I believe my country needs me. It is possible to continue in my work and have you act as a surrogate father for Jose. God knows, you know a lot more about human nature than I ever will and you can provide a much more stable upbringing than I ever could. Jose has spent the last two summers here at the monastery with you and loved every minute of it."

"Alright," said Michael, "it's far too complicated to make a snap decision. Let's think about it for a few weeks then meet again and decide on a course of action. Are you still around for a few weeks? Do you know when your assignment, if you accept it, will begin?"

"I told my unit that I would not be available for at least two months. I knew that I needed at least that much time to decide what to do. Let's meet two weeks from today and try to come up with a course of action."

"Very well, little brother but search your soul and pray to God that you make the right decision."

It took two more meetings and several conversations with Jose, who said he understood, but may just have been putting on the brave face that he knew was expected of him.

They planned for Jose to spend the summer with Michael at the monastery and Mario came down every weekend until his posting began. Together they identified suitable schools; coeducational to offset life at the monastery; close enough to Santa Isabel so that Papa Michael, as Jose called him, was close by, and with an established academic record. Of the three schools that met these requirements, they selected San Cristóbal de la Escuel.

During the last week of August, both Mario and Michael drove Jose to the school on the outskirts of the small town of Vuela. They were met by the house master, Señor Roberto, and to their great relief he and Jose seemed to form an immediate friendship.

"Tell you what, why don't you two old folks find your way to the cafeteria and see if you can scrounge a cup of coffee. Jose and I will go and explore the rest of the school."

It was over an hour later and Mario was getting concerned when they returned. Jose was excited and proceeded to tell his father and Papa Michael about the school; the classrooms, gymnasium, the dormitories and the sports fields. Señor Roberto guided Jose over to a group of students, boys and girls, of the same age and introduced him.

Once he was absorbed the housemaster returned to Mario and Michael and said, "So far so good. I have all the information you sent me and I'll keep a very close eye on him and let Father Michael know immediately of any problems. He looks like he's pretty resilient and there's so much to interest him that he may not be too upset. It's quite normal for students who are away from home for the first time to be homesick. My wife, who's the matron, and I are used to it, we know the signs to watch for; we'll keep a close eye on him".

He turned to Father Michael, "And before I forget Father, I did hear a rumor that you occasionally have a spare bottle of Merlot in search of a palette. Just a thought," he said with a smile.

Mario and Michael took their leave of Jose, who had already made several friends, including a couple of girls, so their goodbyes were not as painful as they had feared. "And I'll come and see how you're doing next weekend," called Papa Michael as they climbed into the car.

Jose brought his thoughts back to the phone. He reached over and picked it up. "Rodriguez," he answered.

"Is that you Señor Jose," a woman's voice asked.

He recognized the voice of Señora Romano, his uncle's housekeeper. "Yes Señora," he answered, detecting the alarm in her voice. "Is anything wrong?"

"Yes and I'm frightened. Papa Michael didn't come home yesterday and while I was out shopping someone broke into the house and went into his study. They ransacked the place; documents were scattered everywhere. They took his computer and some of his files."

"Did he tell you that he was going away?"

"No, Señor. He went to the University on Monday morning, as he usually does. I expected him home for dinner but he didn't arrive and I haven't seen him since."

"Has there been any contact? Did he phone or send any message?"

"No, nothing at all."

"Don't worry Señora I'm going to come down," he reassured her. He looked at his watch. It was 6 p.m. "It's too late now, but I'll leave early in the morning. I should be there by nine o clock. Don't touch or move anything."

Chapter 31

Bergandel Meetings
Sollentuna, Sweden

The Cosmology group had decided that the focus of their meeting was on those aspects of cosmology that had a bearing on Christian Doctrine. They met at the Bergandel Conference Center, north of Stockholm. There were five of them, but the sixth member, Father Emile had not turned up. They were relying heavily on his involvement. He was well known and respected for his knowledge of Quantum Theory as well as being a practicing priest, with real world experience, putting theory into practice. *Boots on the ground, so to speak.*

They assumed he was just delayed, but Michael Kinghaven called at lunch time. He had spoken to the housekeeper and she could only tell him that he was missing. The other two priests couldn't help, one was sick and the other was away for a few days.

They considered postponing the meeting, but it would be hard to get everyone together again, so they decided to continue. Their discussions lasted two days and Father Emile never appeared. In his absence, John Hansen agreed to write the report.

Rather than going back to Toronto, he decided to stay behind at the Conference Centre and write it there. It would still be fresh in his mind and there would be no interruptions.

They had recorded their discussions on a disk; Hansen turned it on and listened, then began to summarize it.

> *The Greek philosophers believed the heavens could be*
> *explained using only reason—the logos—and without*
> *a 'demiurge' i.e. a God or 'prime mover'.*

Fifteen hundred years later the great astronomers, Brahe, Kepler, Copernicus and Galileo pointed their telescopes at the moon and the stars and suggested that the earth revolved around the sun.

The Church said the opposite that the earth was the centre of the universe and made the grave mistake of opposing the astronomers. It forever limited their credibility and ceded the physical world to science.

When Isaac Newton, using the findings of the astronomers—If I have seen further, it is by standing on the shoulders of giants—published his Laws of Motion and Gravitation to explain planetary motion mathematically, the problem was solved. The universe had been explained. And it was mathematical.

Two hundred years later, his theories were modified by Albert Einstein. He completely shook the world with his Theory of Relativity, that time itself was relative. A second was no longer a second. Time was no longer absolute as it was in Newton's laws. It is only noticeable at speeds close to that of light. At everyday speeds, the laws of Newton were still applicable. But Still!

Ten years later, in 1915, he published his second monumental breakthrough, which changed the understanding of gravity. In Newton's world, it was a very weak, attractive force that existed between all objects but was only noticeable between very large ones such as planets. Einstein's theory of General Relativity showed it was a gravitational field, not a force, and was emitted by the planets in a solar system.

It causes light, which normally travels in straight lines, to bend in the gravitational field of large masses. In 1919 during a total eclipse of the sun, scientists observed a small amount of light as it passed by the sun. Their results showed that the light had bent exactly as predicted by Einstein's theory.

In 1929, the American astronomer, Edwin Hubble showed that the universe was expanding, which, if extrapolated backwards, meant that it had a beginning; a single point, or singularity as it is called. This was calculated to have occurred some fourteen billion years ago when it exploded in the Big Bang that started the process that has resulted in the universe we see today.

At the singularity, the mass was infinite and the volume was zero, values which Relativity couldn't handle. Einstein's theory could only be used after the Big Bang had occurred. A new theory was needed to explain the critical first few microseconds of the universe.

The answer came from a very different way of looking at things. Quantum theory developed in the early part of the twentieth century to explain how sub-atomic particles moved. But it was based on uncertainty and unpredictability. Pretty much the opposite of how most people perceived science and scientific progress. But a quantum universe required that all the natural laws and particles be redefined in terms of quantum theory. This was done for all but gravity and its fundamental particle the graviton.

To solve this problem a new mathematical model, called string theory, was developed. Sub-atomic particles are vibrating strings of energy. And different vibrations determine whether it is a particle of matter, a particle of light (photon) or a particle of gravity (graviton).There were different versions of string theory, but they were combined, in the 1990's, into M-theory. This, it was claimed, explained how the universe had come into

> *being from nothing and expanded into the world we
> see today. This was the holy grail of cosmology. The
> universe explained from within the universe. No prior
> input needed. The Theory of Everything.*
>
> *No strings attached!*

Hampton added a summary:

- *Newton explains the motion of the universe.*
- *Einstein modifies with his Relativity Theories. They **explain gravity** but cannot be applied to the big-bang singularity.*
- *Quantum Field Theory, which can be applied to the singularity and can explain all particles and forces, **except gravity**.*
- *String theories which attempt to bridge the two. It is a mathematical model which cannot be tested with existing equipment.*

M-theory, also known as the Theory of Everything, unifies the different string theories

The first day ended with a comment that Hampton thought was significant. One of the theologians in the group declared his incredulity:

"Forgive me but this 'theory of *nearly* everything' is beginning to sound like a conjuring trick. First the Greeks thought that everything could be explained by *Logos*, then Newton came up with his explanation, but that wasn't quite right. So along comes Einstein to add relativity to the mix. That was okay for a while, but not entirely, so they turned to Quantum physics. And finally Strings. What will you come up with next? Are you sure God isn't just yanking your chain?"

Even though it was said in jest, Hampton recognized the validity of the statement. *M-theory*—the so-called Theory of Everything—was not so much a single theory, rather a composite of Relativity, Quantum and String Theory. And String Theory was not even a theory in the scientific meaning of the word; it had not met the test of experimental proof.

What is certain is its uncertainty. It still defies our attempts to explain it in a single unified theory.

Chapter 32

Hotel Monterrey
Sanlucar, Spain

Morse drove the Peugeot back to the main road and looked around for somewhere to stay. Tomorrow he would buy the gear he needed and use the rest of his stay to ask around about the Chateau; who lived there, how old, the comings and goings, and so on. He drove to Sanlucar found a small hotel. It was now late and he still hadn't eaten so he ordered a salad and a steak from room service. It was good, he ate it and then turned in.

The next day he made a list of what he would need for his visit to whatever was inside the fence. It took him several hours and visits to five different stores, but he eventually got everything he needed, although the tranquillizer gun and darts were difficult to find. He organized everything in the Peugeot, with the back seats folded down. He covered it all with a tarpaulin.

By the time he got back to the hotel it was 5 p.m. and he set the alarm to 8 p.m. and lay down on the bed and was quickly asleep. His internal clock woke him five minutes before the alarm went off and he climbed out of bed and showered. He put on a black tracksuit, and black rubber soled shoes and left the hotel via a back entrance to avoid prying eyes. He trotted down the road to his car so that anyone who did spot him would just assume he was a jogger. Once in the car he drove back to the access road but before turning into the clearing, he switched off the car lights, and drove quietly to the back and parked. Using only a small penlight he took some black makeup and rubbed it onto his face and hands; with his tracksuit and black tuque he would be all but invisible. He took a bag from the car, containing a package wrapped in foil, the tranquilizer gun, and darts. Taking advantage of the thick cloud which blocked out the moon, he made his way as silently as possible to the same spot at the edge of the tree line. There was no sign of the

Dobermans as he undid his package to reveal four large steaks. He threw them one at a time over the fence and the dogs came running, detecting either the noise or the smell. They came up to the meat but didn't eat it. They had been well trained and when they became aware of his presence they bared their teeth. He fired the gun four times and the dogs began to stagger and after about a minute they fell over, each of them with a small dart sticking out of their flanks. Based on the information he had been given they should sleep for at least two hours, maybe three depending on their size and these dogs were big so he decided that two hours was his maximum.

He went back to the car and returned with the rest of the equipment in a black bag and carrying an extension ladder on his shoulder. Taking the multi-meter out of the bag, he clipped it to the fence; it registered fifty volts, not enough to kill a man but enough to prevent him from trying to climb it. Next he took the ladder and opened it up fully to its twenty-foot height. He tied a length of rope to the top rung then leaned it against the branch of the tree he had spotted earlier. The ladder was hinged in the middle so that it could be used either upright or bent. This was going to be the tricky part; he felt a nerve in his cheek twitch.

He pulled on a pair of thick black rubber gloves, and with the bag over his shoulder he climbed up the ladder until he was close enough to grasp the branch. He tested its strength and swing himself onto it. He sat for a while, with one leg either side, until he had his balance. Carefully he moved along it getting as close to the fence as he dared and then carefully positioned the ladder so that the bottom was three feet from the fence on his side. He pushed the top rung, allowing the rope to gradually slide through his hands. Lowering it slowly he was able to manoeuvre it until it was bent in the shape of a letter 'A' with the feet on either side of the fence, but not touching it.

He moved along the branch until he was directly above the ladder and slowly moved one foot to the top rung. By shifting his position, he was able to place the full weight of his body on that foot. The bottom of the ladder on the inside of the fence moved slightly, then settled and held firm.

Carefully he climbed down the ladder, stopped, and stood still, listening for any sound. Nothing. So far so good.

He checked his watch; it was half an hour since he had drugged the dogs. He walked over to them, they were sleeping soundly, and picked up the steaks, removed the darts, and placed them back in his bag. Pausing to make sure he had his bearings, he headed for the point where the road disappeared behind the trees. Once there he kept his body out of sight and cautiously poked his head out. He almost gasped in surprise. The place was massive, protected by a solid wall. Above it towered the roofs of several buildings; it wasn't just a château as he'd thought but a huge compound that could house a small army of people. *'What was it?'* he wondered, *'the private residence of a billionaire? Some kind of conference center? A monastery?* Given who he had followed here, he ruled out the last one!

He stayed in the trees and moved closer until he had a clear view. He took out his night glasses and trained them to where the road ended at the main entrance. There were two massive gates about eight feet high set into the wall.

Just to be sure unwanted visitors got the message, the wall was topped by what looked like razor wire. He moved the glasses to the gates and saw two spotlights that he guessed were motion sensitive. He couldn't see any security cameras, but he was sure they were there. The gates looked like steel and would require powerful motors to open them. The place was built like a fortress, impregnable and certainly not visitor friendly.

To the left of the gate, set in the wall was a panel but even with his night glasses he couldn't see it properly, the angle was wrong. To get a better view he needed to be on the other side of the road with the floodlights on. This meant crossing the road where he would be exposed to the cameras. If they were being monitored, as he was sure they would be, they would see him.

He didn't know the range of the motion sensors. To be safe, he went back to a point where the road was hidden by the treeline and made a dash for it. He waited and was relieved that no lights came on.

He made his way through the trees to a spot where he had a good view of the panel, but he still couldn't see it well enough, he needed to activate the floods. As he was looking around for something large to throw, the problem was solved for him. He heard the noise of someone moving through the undergrowth to his right and he immediately pulled out his revolver and stepped silently behind the bole of a large tree. A raccoon with two babies in tow emerged, sniffed the air, caught his smell, and wandered diagonally across the road, away from him. When the three of them were halfway across, the lights came on. The raccoons took off at great speed and making sure he was well hidden from the spotlights which were sweeping the area he pulled out his regular binoculars and focused them on the entrance. The panel was now visible, it consisted of a keypad and what looked like a keyhole, but it was difficult to be sure without getting closer. Above the gates, there was a large metal plate with the letters 'CΦC'.

He looked at his watch and saw that he had thirty minutes left. Once those lights went off, he needed to head back. He had to wait another ten minutes until they did, then he retraced his steps. The dogs were still sound asleep and he was back in his car, all his equipment safely stowed before the two hours were up. He drove along the access lane onto the main road and back to his hotel in Sanlucar.

Once in his room he opened his notebook and entered a description of the place; its semi-hidden location, how to get there, the size, the letters and symbol above the gates. He included a full description of all the security measures including the Dobermans, who right now were probably waking up with a serious hangover.

* * *

Castillo de Chipiona

Balinska was in his room getting ready for bed when the phone rang. "It's the security guard, I have the info you wanted."

"That was fast. Go ahead tell me what you've got."

"I checked the plate and found out it was registered to Avis at San Pablo. It's a silver Peugeot and it was rented at yesterday at three o'clock and I got the rental details from someone I know who works at Avis. According to his driving license, his name is Leonard Morse and his address is in Hampstead."

When he had finished, Balinska said, "I don't recognize the name, and I think Hampstead is in London. Not much, but thanks."

"There was one other thing," the guard said, "when I was talking to the desk jockey at Avis he told me that the guy spoke as if he knew you. He said he would see you at the hotel when you arrived."

"Did he get a description?"

"Not a very good one; he was wearing sunglasses and a hat with a wide brim that hid most of his face. He's fairly tall, close to six feet. He had an athletic build and looked very fit. He couldn't see the color of his hair or if he even had any."

"Which hotel?"

"She didn't know."

"What about accent and language. Did he speak Spanish?"

"Don't know. Their conversation was in English and he spoke it without an accent, according to the car jock."

"Anything else?"

"No."

"Is he still out there?"

"No, he doesn't show on any of the cameras, although the motion lights were triggered earlier but it was a raccoon and her cubs."

"Leave it for now but if he shows up on any of the monitors let me know no matter what time it is. I'll sleep on it, for now, see if it makes any more sense in the morning. Goodnight, and thanks."

* * *

Hotel Monterrey, Sanlucar

Morse woke refreshed. He showered and dressed went down to the dining room and ate a leisurely breakfast. Then he drove into the center of town and began to make inquiries about the *Chateau.* He tried local restaurants, bars, the library and the town hall. It didn't take him long to discover its name was 'Castillo de Chipiona'. That explained what the C's in 'CΦC' stood for, although the Φ was a mystery, possibly a Greek letter. The buildings were ancient and belonged to the church. It had been abandoned and unused and was in danger of collapsing, then about twenty years ago renovations began including repairing the wall around the compound and adding the new fence on the exterior of the property. The work was done by a local building contractor who informed him that the building, inside and out, was restored completely to its original condition down to the smallest detail. Money was no object. Once the work was completed a large staff, cooks, maids, security guards, secretaries moved in. No-one seemed to know what took place behind those walls. Or they weren't telling.

That evening he ate at a local restaurant. He ordered Ecsalivada salad and a seafood paella called Arros Negre, and the traditional dessert, creme brulee flambé.

When in Spain . . .

Excellent as the food was the best part of the evening came at the end of his meal as he was sipping his coffee. A man from one of the other tables came over and introduced himself. "Buenos Noches Senor, my name is Sandor Nadal and I was told you were looking for information about the *Castillo*," he said, almost in a whisper.

"Yes, I am. Please have a seat Señor Nadal."

"No that would not be wise. It would be safer if we met somewhere private, tomorrow."

"Well, we could meet at my hotel."

"That would be safer. I will come about ten tomorrow morning."

Morse wrote the name of the hotel and his room number, on a napkin and said he would look forward to talking to him.

Next day at exactly 10 a.m. Señor Nadal arrived and over coffee he told about his experience with the *Castillo.* "I own a construction company and do a lot of work on the villas and chateaus in the area. My company had a contract to renovate the Sotano, the basement of the Castillo, which is very unusual in itself since buildings in this region don't have them. When I went to inspect it, to see what work needed doing, it looked like it probably did 500 years ago. There were several rooms, some of them with crumbling apparatus in them."

"What kind of apparatus," Morse interrupted.

"I'm not sure, but I'd guess they were probably used for torture. Which explains why one of the conditions of the contract was that we were not allowed to discuss what we saw with anyone."

"Is that why you were so secretive last night?"

"Yes, anything to do with that place gives me the creeps. From the cleric who runs the place to the new guy who seems to be in charge of surveillance. He is huge and he made it very clear that if I divulged any information about the *Castillo* then my wife and children might be in danger. The way he said it made me believe it. He even knew their names."

Morse knew he was getting close. He was sure that Nadal was describing Balinska. He wrote something in his notebook before asking, "Did you get any names?"

"Only the Cleric, he signed the initial contract. Let me think." He took a few moments, staring out of the window, as he tried to remember. "Benito. No that's not right."

Morse was tempted to suggest the name, but that would prejudice Nadal's recollection. He stayed silent.

"Got it!" Nadal said, "It was Father Bernado."

The name of the Priest that Charpentier had mentioned! This tied Balinska to Bernado! The man he wanted and the cleric that Charpentier was after. He controlled his excitement and asked, "What happened next?"

"A few weeks ago their maintenance manager called and said they were having some electrical problems in the Sotano. Since we had done all the wiring including the main fuse box, he asked if I could we send someone to find the problem. I said I would and arranged for my electrician, Milos, to go the next day."

"Did he find the problem?"

"He did, but it was what else he found that was frightening. You now needed a key and a code to open the door that leads down into the Sotano. It wasn't there when we did the original renovations. They sent the head security guard with him. He inserted and turned his key, then punched in a code, being careful to make sure Milos couldn't see. Once they got downstairs, Milos checked the fuse box and saw the problem was in one the rooms in the Sotano."

"Are these the rooms you mentioned, that had the apparatus in them?" he asked?

"Yes, but now they are all renovated. Milos put his voltmeter across the terminals and it showed a short circuit in room 19. To fix the problem, he would need to get into the room. The guard first said no and then said that he would have to check with his boss, to get authorization. He punched in the extension on his phone, but there was no response so he told Milos to stay right where he was and went back up the stairs.

"He didn't know Milos, who thinks of himself as an undiscovered James Bond. He just loves to sniff around looking for clues and while the guard was gone, he checked it out he swore that the place was wired with explosives. He thought he heard noises coming from one or two of the rooms. He was going to take a closer look but heard the Guard coming down the stairs. Evidently the chief enchilada had given the go ahead because he opened the room.

Milos told me that there was a chair with arm straps that looked exactly like the electric chairs he had seen in American movies. Milos suspected that the short circuit came from one the cables hanging down from the ceiling. He noticed a switch on the wall and after explaining to the guard what he was going to do, he turned it on. There was a hum of electricity and as he expected Arcs of electricity flashed between two of the cables. He had to go out to his van to get a replacement and when he returned the guard stood in the room watching him while he replaced the faulty cable. Milos noticed a cupboard in the corner of the room. It looked like a medicine cabinet. He asked the guard to go and pull the circuit breaker for room 19 so he could connect the new cable. While the guard was out of the room he tried to see what was in the cupboard, but it was locked."

What could be in it, thought Morse? From the description of the room, he thought that it must be some kind of torture chamber for electric shock. And God knows what was in the medicine cabinet.

Nadal continued. "Milos replaced the cable and tested it. As he was coming up the stairs, he swore he saw wires running along one of the beams, the type of wire used with 'nonel' detonators, in the demolition of old buildings. He was pretty sure that they ran from the beam to the keypad on the door, but he couldn't get a good look because the guard was right behind him."

"He certainly saw a lot in his short visit. Maybe he should become a spy."

"I'm afraid not. When Milos told me, I didn't pay much attention because he loves to exaggerate. Now I realize that I should have."

"Why what happened?"

The contractor paused, replaying what had happened in his mind. "Milos shot his mouth off one night in a local bar, after several drinks. He told several people that the place was wired with explosives. Three days later he was killed in a car accident. His car went over a cliff into the ocean and it took two days for divers to recover it, with Milos' body still strapped in and the windows closed."

"And you don't think it was an accident?" he said looking at the expression on Sandor's face.

"No. If he had been alive when it went into the sea, he would have undone the straps and tried to open the window. I think he was killed first and then his car was pushed over the cliff."

"And you think his murder was connected to what he saw in the Sotano?" said Morse, wondering who these people were and how Balinska was involved. He knew he was a killer, but why would he be working for a religious outfit in Spain?

"There isn't any other explanation. If he'd have said nothing about it, he might still be alive but I think they thought he knew too much."

"What have the police done?"

"They say they are making enquiries and if anyone has any information they would like to hear from them. No-one, including myself, has stepped forward," he said looking guilty. "They don't want to finish up like Milos."

"Then why come to me?"

"Because from what I heard you aren't official, and can keep a secret. And you want those bastards brought to justice. Milos left a wife and two kids and I feel responsible. I sent him in there."

After Nadal had left, Morse took out his notebook and added the rest of the information to his notes. The next morning he used his case notes to type a full report into his laptop and sent it to Charpentier.

Chapter 33

Tortura del Aqua, Sotano
Castillo de Chipiona,
Sanlucar, Spain

Father Emile was in the Sotano, with his hands and legs manacled. The table to which he was strapped had been tilted so his head was directly under the tap. The retractor was in his mouth and the hood had been placed over his head. He had been stripped naked.

He didn't know where he was or how he got here. He had been working in the office in Munich when the door had been slammed open and someone grabbed him and jammed a needle into his neck. He had lost consciousness and when he woke, he was here in this room. Strapped and manacled; left in the dark and alone. After what seemed like hours two men came in.

Balinska, who was standing to the side, ordered the guard to open the tap to a slow drip. He adjusted the table slightly so that the water fell directly into the Priest's mouth at a steady rate. "Turn off the lights," he ordered the guard then leaned over so his mouth was close to the Father.

He began to speak quietly. "We can stop at any time. Whenever you're ready to tell me the names of the others. We know all about the *Dialogues* and if you don't tell us we'll find out from the others. So why don't you spare them the pain and torture?"

Balinska stood completely still, listening to the choking noises coming from Father Emile. He told the guard to turn off the tap and waited until the sounds of the priest gasping for air had slowed, before he said, "Are you ready to tell us now. Or would you like more of the same. We can go on all day if we have to. If you can last that long." There was no answer. "Very well, turn on the tap," he said to the guard.

The choking noises started again. The guard felt nauseous but daren't say anything. He had been hired as a security guard, not as an assistant to this evil brute. After fifteen minutes, Balinska ordered him to turn off the tap. "What do you say now, Father. Perhaps a prayer? It won't do any good. I don't think He's listening."

But Balinska failed to understand what he was dealing with; a man whose beliefs came from deep within him; a man who would not break.

Even though he could not control his body or his bodily functions; even though this brute might kill him, he would never give in. He was prepared to die; it was part of his faith. If that were the price demanded of him, he would gladly pay it. His life was already forfeit; it was the price of the Cross.

His body was in agony, running on autonomous signals, screaming for survival. He was drowning. *Do something. Anything. Stop the pain. Let me live.* But he reached deeper into his failing consciousness and found the resolve to withstand it. To let him die.

The spirit is willing . . .

"Stop," Balinska called out. The guard turned off the hose and Father Emile's body shook as his lungs struggled to draw in air. Balinska waited, "Now are you ready. We'll get it out of you one way or the other. We have all the time in the world. You don't. In fact, if you don't give us those names, your time is up."

There was no response and Balinska was about to tell the guard to turn on the tap when there was a knock on the door of the chamber. "Hold on," and walked over to the door, opened it and went outside. It was Messi.

"Well. What do you want? I don't like being interrupted when I'm working."

"Too bad. The Archdeacon thought I should tell you straight away. I was looking at the Priest's computer and there are a lot of emails to the same person. I'm pretty sure I know the name and where he's from. So you can leave the poor man alone," he said, as he looked in disgust at what was going on. We already have the name of his colleague.""

"Really. And what makes you think you can tell me what to do. Perhaps I should let the Father go and use you as the patient instead."

"Wouldn't you just," Messi said as he turned and went back and up the stairs. Balinska went back into the room and told the guard he could leave. "He is mine now. This is personal."

Then he looked down at the prisoner and said. "I hope you've made your peace Father. Only one of us is going to come out of this alive."

Forty minutes later Balinska emerged from the room. The table was in a vertical position. Only the straps stopped Father Emile's body from falling. His head sagged forward. On the floor beside the table was Balinska's blood stained switchblade and a club the size of a baseball bat, matted with hair and blood.

When it was obvious the waterboarding wasn't going to loosen his tongue, Balinska had resorted to physical torture. Father Emile's forehead was streaked with blood from a gash on the top of his head. His face was swollen and bruised and his eyes were closed.

His left arm stuck out at an impossible angle and his genital area was stained red. His penis had been severed.

Not that any of it mattered now. Father Emile was dead. The only words he had uttered, through swollen lips, were "May God forgive you."

Balinska knew he had lost and the Priest had won. *He hated that!*

He went up the stairs and knocked on the door of the Archdeacon's office. The secretary called for him to come in and when he saw who it was his face soured, but he kept his voice neutral, "Yes, Señor Balinska how can I help you?"

"I would like to see the Archdeacon. I know he's in."

The secretary pressed a button on his phone, "Excuse me Archdeacon, but Balinska is here and would like to see you," deliberately omitting *Senor*. He continued, "Is it convenient?" He looked directly at Balinska hoping that the Archdeacon would make him wait. Unfortunately, he didn't.

"Yes, Pierre please show in him."

The Archdeacon waved Balinska to a seat. "What can I do for you? I trust you got the message in time. I told Messi to hurry and give you the good news, that he'd found another name." Balinska sat for several moments before explaining what had happened, expecting the Archdeacon to use it to criticize him.

Bernado didn't immediately respond. He knew this was a chance to put Balinska in his place. Establish authority! Or collaboration! Be in charge or be equals. He surprised himself; he chose the latter. "It was a mistake, but in the same situation I would have done the same. We are alike in many ways. We both hate to lose."

Although he said it for the sake of cooperation, he realized it contained more than a modicum of truth. They shared the same perspective on life. It was about winning; removing those who got in your way. Like Balinska he would eliminate them; it was a matter of expediency.

The Archdeacon continued, "This unfortunate accident has to remain between us. I don't think anyone else needs to know. Did Messi see anything when he came down?"

Balinska tried to think back. He remembered how angry he had been, but he had gone to the door. "No, I didn't let him in. I came out of the room to talk to him. Even if he did the Priest was still alive. And I sent the guard out of the room as well."

"Good! Do you think you could put the Priest's body in a bag, and carry it to the incinerator once it's dark?"

"Yes. That would get rid of the evidence permanently. And no-one would be any wiser."

Once they had worked out the details, Balinska went back to his office wondering what Messi had found. He pressed the intercom and a few minutes later he arrived carrying a single sheet of paper. "Alright," said Balinska, "what did you find?"

"I was able to get into Father Emile's computer, his security codes and passwords were easy to figure out. I looked at who he had sent emails to over the last month and I found one in particular that occurred frequently. I've written it down." He pushed the paper across the desk.

Balinska picked it up and looked at the single line written on it.

fathermichael@EspirituSanto.es

"Even I can recognize that it's an email address but how does it help?" Balinska asked.

"Working backwards, it means that it's from somewhere called *EspirituSanto and the es* at the end means it is in Spain. I Googled the name and it's a Monastery just outside Saragossa."

"And the person is Father Michael!" Balinska jumped in, beginning to see the value of the internet and, reluctantly, realizing the importance of Messi."

"Correct. Maybe we should pay a visit and persuade the Father to come with us," Messi said.

Let's run it past the Archdeacon first. He may have someone in the area." He pressed the intercom for the Archdeacon and told him what had happened and gave him the information about Father Michael.

"I'll get in touch with the Regent for that area and see if he can get us any further information."

The next day Bernado called him. "I heard back from the Regent, who is a priest in Toledo, called Father Diego Paz, and he knows Father Michael personally. He is no longer at the Monastery. He retired a few months ago and now lives in Toledo. This Paz is also in Toledo and would be glad to show you where he lives."

The next day Balinska flew to Toledo and met the Regent and together they planned how they would do it.

* * *

Toledo, Spain

Two days later Balinska called the Archdeacon. The operation had been successful. Right now the police were doing searches all over the area so he was going to lie low for a few days before bringing the Father back to the Castillo.

Chapter 34

National Police Headquarters
Madrid, Spain

Before leaving Jose told his secretary where he was going and what had happened. She in turn would notify his boss who would decide if this could be linked to his job at the agency and a possible terrorist connection.

On the drive down the AP-41 motorway, Jose recalled the years he had spent growing up at Santa Isabel. The summers at the monastery seemed to last forever. There was much to do for a young boy; feeding the animals, harvesting and crushing the grapes, picking strawberries and apples. The stream that wandered through the grounds was broad and deep enough for several favorite swimming holes; there was a small stable where he learned to ride and in the nearby village there was a junior soccer team. As he grew older, he discovered he had many of the same interests as his uncle, and he began working in the library developing a knowledge of history and classical languages.

He enjoyed school. It had been lonely at first, but he had soon made friends, both girls, and boys. He got good grades and loved sports. Everything was going well until that awful day.

He was fourteen and during the spring term, Papa Michael came to see him as he often did. Usually, it was on weekends but this time it was a Tuesday. Jose was called out of class and taken to the library where Papa was waiting. "Hello," he said as Jose came over and embraced him.

Jose could tell from Papa's expression that something was wrong. "You usually come on weekends, not in the week. Is this a special occasion?"

Papa Michael looked around at the shelves of books, without actually seeing them. He was trying to find the right words. He finally realized there was no easy way. "I received some bad news yesterday. You know that your father was doing crucial work for our country."

"Yes," answered Jose, looking alarmed. "Has something happened? Has he been hurt?"

"I'm afraid it is worse than that. He has been killed."

Jose didn't say anything but his face went white and he was clenching and unclenching his hands. Finally he said, "How did he die?"

Papa Michael looked out of the window; blue skies with white cumulous clouds and the green of the sports fields. An idyllic picture; not a place to talk of death. In the end he lied, "He was killed in a car accident."

When Jose was older would be soon enough to learn the truth; that his cover had been compromised and he had been kidnapped by the Basque terrorists and executed. They had left his naked body in a church, where it was found by the Priest the next day. Papa Michael had been called to identify the body.

"Would you like to come home for a few days, to the Monastery?" he said, growing concerned that Jose had not broken down, although the tension was evident in his face and body.

"No, Papa. I think I should stay at school." Even as he said it, it didn't sound convincing, but he had developed a tough outer shell to hide his feelings. His mother had left him and now his father was gone.

After speaking to the housemaster, explaining what had happened—a car accident—he gave instructions that he should be contacted immediately if necessary, day or night.

Jose missed his father, terribly, but he never mentioned it. He wasn't a child! He kept it to himself and filled his days with classes, study, and sports. Anything to occupy his mind and his days. It was hard at first but with time it grew easier.

He was subdued and his work dropped off for a few weeks, but he recovered and eventually regained his standing as an excellent student and athlete. He never told any of his school friends, or anyone else for that matter.

By the time Jose finished his education at San Cristóbal, he was fluent in French, German and English. His informal education from the monks had given him an essential knowledge of Latin and Greek, and an understanding of the fundamental principles of wine production. He had learned some other basics from the girls at the school and the ones in the nearby village. From the long hours of silence practiced by the Fathers, he had learned how to concentrate on a problem for extended periods of time; all abilities that were to serve him well.

Papa Michael persuaded Jose to follow in his father's footsteps and go into the law. He enrolled at the University of Barcelona but after two years he decided that he preferred doing to learning. A friend of his father's found him a place in the Madrid police force. He rose rapidly, some said more on who he knew than what he knew and was promoted to Deputy Inspector in his late twenties. At the age of thirty, he was seconded by the counter-intelligence group of CESID, for a special assignment that required fluency in both Spanish and French. Although the job ended successfully, he was constantly at loggerheads with his boss. Even so, he was offered a permanent appointment with the unit, but he chose to return to his old position with the National Police.

Jose braked as he saw the sign for exit 8 to Toledo and arrived at his uncle's house just after 9 a.m. There were already two police officers there. They turned to Jose as he entered, "Hello Jose," said the senior detective who had met Jose a few times before.

"Hello. Nice to see you again. What are you doing here?"

"We got a call from your boss, giving us the bare bones and asking us to check things out. He said you were on your way here."

Jose looked around at the mess. Someone had certainly gone over the place, scattering things everywhere. And, as his housekeeper had told him, his computer had gone. "Did you find anything?"

"Well, maybe something. According to Señora Romano, your Uncle usually walked to the University, leaving every morning at nine o clock."

Jose knew this was true because Papa didn't drive and loved physical exercise. 'God gave me two good legs, and I have an umbrella, so why ride when I can walk.'

The Inspector continued, "She watched him walking along the street when a car drove by and stopped beside him. He seemed to recognize the driver, but he appeared to indicate that he preferred to walk. The driver must have said something that changed his mind because Papa got into the car and it drove off."

"Did she have any details of the car? Color, License Plate?"

"Only that she thought it was blue and quite small. Not much to go on. But we'll start a house to house to see if anyone has any information. What you need to do is phone the local police and file a missing person's report. That should get things moving; they might turn up something."

Jose contacted the local police and gave them the details, omitting anything that would connect it to the National Police. The duty officer took the details and promised he would deal with it immediately, but Jose got the impression that he would file it at the bottom of the list. Limited budgets meant that missing persons were low on the pecking order.

A few hours later he got a return call from the sergeant, "Do you know people in high places?"

"Not particularly. Why has something happened?"

"You better believe it. I just got chewed out by my boss. He was furious that I hadn't made your uncle's disappearance a priority. Who is he anyway?"

Jose considered what to say without making the sergeant suspicious, but, in this case, the truth was a matter of public record. "He was a monk before he retired. Actually not just an ordinary monk, he was the Abbot of the monastery of Espiritu Santo."

"Okay. I wish you'd told me that in the beginning, I would have made it a priority." The annoyance in his voice coming through.

'Right!' thought Jose.

"I'll need a photograph and anything else you haven't told me. It's been given Status Red and it'll go to the national database of missing persons once you get back to me."

"Thanks, I really appreciate it. I know how hard pressed you are," Jose said, trying to soothe his ruffled feathers. Status Red was a top priority and once a person was entered on the database a photograph and the details were sent to every police station in the country.

Señora Romano had gone to stay with her sister so he looked around Papa's house for a suitable photograph, but he couldn't find one.

'Who doesn't keep a picture of themselves?' he thought; perhaps Papa considered them a vanity, one of the seven deadly sins. Jose went and got his laptop from the car. He skimmed through the pictures folder and found several of himself and Papa. The latest one was taken several years ago, but it would have to do. He cropped himself out of the picture, then emailed it to the desk sergeant.

About an hour later as he was wondering whether he should stay in Toledo or go back to his office in Madrid, his mobile rang. It was one of the officers who'd done the house to house. He gave Jose the results, "We checked every fucking house in the area," obviously annoyed at having to knock on every door. "All we got was bits and pieces; some of it helpful, some of it conflicting and some of it out in never-never land. But putting it all together here's the gist of it. Three people reported seeing a blue Opel driving along the street at about 9 o'clock and one of them saw your uncle get into the car precisely as his housekeeper described. One of them said there was someone else in the car, besides your uncle and the driver; a big man with a shaved head. A kid on his way to school said the car was a blue Opel Corsa."

"Did he get the license plate?"

"No, but he thought it might have the letters CS in it but he wasn't sure where, beginning or end. He was sure they were together."

"Have you run the information against the car registration database?" Jose demanded.

"How, when we don't have the license number? We did try to get a list of all blue Opel Corsa's registered to people in Toledo, but we don't have that information on police files. We have someone checking with Opel to see if they can come up with anything," the agent said, obviously frustrated by Jose's tone.

Jose realized that he was pushing too hard and backed off, "Sorry I'm so snappy, but it is my uncle we're talking about."

"Understood," the detective responded, "What happens next?"

"I guess we wait and see what Opel can tell us. How many blue Opel Corsas can there be in Toledo?"

"Well, I'm going back to my office. I'll have my people let you know what happens as soon as we get anything," he said, glad to be finished with an assignment that should have stayed with Missing Persons.

Jose had planned to have someone from the local police force go through the mess in his Uncle's study. But since it was too late to go back to Madrid he decided he might as well start on it himself.

After three hours of sorting and cataloging, Jose had found nothing of any significance. There were all the usual business documents; the lease for the house, insurances, bank books, details of his pension. Letters from friends but strangely nothing that would shed any light on whatever Papa was working on. Maybe that was what had been removed.

He felt light-headed; this always happened when he felt things were out of his control. According to the shrinks, it was a sense of abandonment, from his childhood. They gave him some pills to take, but they didn't do much; he found the bottle much better and he always kept a full one nearby. It had almost destroyed his career and himself. He could use a drink right now, but he'd been dry for a year and he forced himself to focus on what he was doing. Concentrating his mind was the one thing that helped him get past it.

He reviewed the facts; the kidnapping; the break in; the theft of papers and his uncle's computer. He suddenly had a sense of Deja Vu; he'd seen or read about this before and recently, but when, where? He couldn't recall, but he knew his mind well enough to do something else while it worked away in the background. He decided that listing dates and facts in sequence would help. He took a sheet of paper and began writing.

Monday:

Papa had left for the university as usual.
Blue Corsa stopped beside him and offered him a lift.
He seemed to refuse, but the driver had said something
that changed his mind and he got in. There was another
man, a big man in the car, as well as the driver.
Papa doesn't come home

Tuesday:

Thieves broke in while Señora Romano was out shopping.
Señora calls me

Wednesday:

Drive to Toledo; Photo on national database.
Area canvassed for anyone who'd seen what happened;
more reports of Papa getting into a blue Opel

As he reviewed the list, his *eureka* moment kicked in. He'd seen it on the police eBulletin that he looked at every morning as soon as he arrived at his office. Several days ago there had been an item about the disappearance of a priest in Munich. He hadn't paid too much attention. Now he wondered if it might be significant. There was no access to the bulletin over the internet; the information was too sensitive and was only accessible via computers in police headquarters that were hardwired to the network. He would need to phone his office and have one of his assistants look it up. Even this was discouraged and should only be done in an emergency. *This was Papa Michael. That made it an emergency.*

He looked through his list and added several notations on what he needed to do:

> *Visit the University to try and find out what was Papa was working on?*
> *What was so important that they had to kidnap him?*
> *The driver of the Opel must have known Papa; why else would he get into the car?*
> *Someone had to be watching the house to know what time Papa left the house each day and when the house was empty.*
> *Check the police bulletin and find the investigating officer in Munich.*

It was 2 a.m, too late now, he would have to do it in the morning. Fortunately, Señora Romana had made up the day bed in the guest room. He undressed, set his alarm for 7 a.m. and was asleep as soon as his head hit the pillow.

Chapter 35

Charpentier was going over the report from Morse. He had tracked Balinska to a Castillo near Sanlucar, which sounded like an armed encampment. He had done a recon and it was obvious that it didn't encourage visitors; they had the security to prove it. It sounded almost impregnable.

From a local contractor, Morse had found out that the priest in charge was Bernado, the same cleric who had visited Cardinal Karmazin in Rome. Add the third member, Pierre Salodin from the Russian embassy, and what did he have?

He didn't know!

Charpentier jotted down what he did know:

Cardinal Karmazin is from the Ukraine. He was a bishop during the Soviet occupation (Could he have met Salodin then?) The Cardinal is known to be an ultra-conservative and part of the Popes Inner Circle. He regularly meets with Salodin (Why?)

Pierre Salodin, attaché at Russian Embassy in Rome. Is he using Karmazin to get info about inner workings at Vatican?

Father Bernado, Archdeacon at Castillo; meets with Karmazin. (Why?) Castillo sounds like an armed camp?

It didn't help a lot. Nothing definite emerged. What he needed to know was why Morse and Balinska had personal business. Especially now that he is obviously connected to whatever is going on at the Castillo.

He contacted Morse and told him he had to know why he was chasing Balinska. The reply he received did not satisfy him. It said that Balinska was the man's new name, an identity change from Boris Radovic. It explained why Morse had needed the contacts in Ottawa and Toronto. That much was believable but the next part, that Balinska was wanted on a murder charge in Vladivostok, didn't hold up. It may be true, but that was the business of the Russian police, not Morse.

Try as he could he didn't get anything else from him so he gave him a warning. Finish Interpol business before your own. In other words, get to the bottom of this triangle; Salodin, Karmazin, Bernado.

Chapter 36

John Hansen had taken a weekend break and was ready to complete his report. He opened up his computer and accessed the Dialogue database where his report was stored. There was an email asking him to check the communications section of the database.

There was an urgent alert from Kinghaven:

Father Emile had not reappeared and now Father Michael could not be reached. Ian Frazer had reported that he thinks he is being watched. Everyone should be extremely cautious.

He wondered whether he should move to a different location but if they, whoever they were, were keeping an eye on him, they would see him change hotels. Anyway, he thought he would be finished in a day and then he could head home where he would, hopefully, be safe.

He moved the recording to where he had left off.

> *Because of the success of science we tend to accept its findings without too many questions, but there are several that need to be raised. Mathematics is the ground on which science is built. And it is built on logical reasoning, rationality, as it is often called. But how do you prove that rationality is a valid method of proof? You can't use rationality to prove rationality, it's a circular argument. So it has to be accepted on faith, which is no different to believing in God. He can't be proved either. He too has to be accepted on faith.*

*The Current theories of the universe are models, but there is a significant difference between a model and reality. They are not the same thing. A model mirrors **one** particular aspect of reality and places boundaries on it. The limits of the cosmological model are the physical borders of the universe. It cannot make any statements outside of that; it cannot hold any opinion of God or religion, or philosophy since they exist beyond and outside. The phrase 'the universe is mathematical' is seen by many to be accurate. But it is not! What it should say is that 'the mathematical model of the universe is mathematical', which doesn't have quite the same import. It can, and has, been argued that if you use mathematics to probe the universe, then there's an excellent chance that what you discover will be mathematical. Bertrand Russell recognized this almost a century ago. He said, 'Physics is mathematical **not** because we know so much about the physical world, but because we know so little; it is only its mathematical properties that we can discover.'*

*The claim that cosmologists make that they have explained how the universe was created from **nothing** is a spurious claim. Quantum theory uses a 'false vacuum' made up of particles that cancel each other out. That is very different to a real vacuum, that is completely empty. The explanations of String theory are just hypotheses. They still have to be tested against reality.*

There is a further limit to mathematics that comes from mathematics itself. Kurt Gödel was an Austrian mathematician and philosopher. In 1931, he published his incompleteness theorem, which stated that a mathematical system cannot be both complete and consistent. To be complete means that every theorem of the model has been proved. To be consistent means, there are no contradictions in the model. You can have one or the other, but not both. A sort of mathematical uncertainty principle.

Probably the greatest challenge to the Church comes not from cosmology but from the fundamental rule of science, namely that the Laws of Nature are constant, they cannot be turned on and off. They are on 24/365/ forever. Where the physical events of Christianity conflict with this, then theology is stepping outside its own spiritual boundaries and into the physical world. Just as it did when the astronomers proposed that the earth was not the centre of the universe. The miracles, the virgin birth, and the physical resurrection just couldn't have happened the way the Church contends.

Only in the separation of physical and the spiritual is a solution possible. But it requires a theological translation of the physical contradictions to the spiritual universe. Then the disagreement becomes one of perspective rather than contradiction. Whether the Church is able to do this without destroying its fundamental message and meaning in the process, is the ultimate question. And only the Church can answer that.

His job was finished, he had stored the draft report on the database and sent the other *Dialogue* members an email to review it. Before he finished, he deleted the report from his laptop. He looked at his watch. It was late and he had an early flight the next morning. He closed his computer and turned in.

Chapter 37

Office of the Archdeacon
Castillo de Chipiona
Sanlucar, Spain

Father Bernado was sitting at his desk when his phone rang. "Hello. Bernado speaking."

"I'm sorry I wanted to talk to the Archdeacon." the caller said.

"This is the Archdeacon," he replied, realizing that to the Regents that was his title. He had never used the name Father Bernado with them.

"This is Baltic," he said using the convention that they referred to themselves only by the region they represented. "I have some information that I think should be dealt with now rather than waiting for our next meeting."

"Let me get a pen and a notepad," He opened the top drawer of his desk and took out a pad of paper and placed it on his desk. "Go ahead," he said as he picked up his pen.

"A priest in Copenhagen called me yesterday. He is taking a degree in sociology at Andersen University and one of his anthropology courses is taught by a Professor Sorensen. During a discussion, the Professor mentioned that modern research is finding new information on the Judeo-Christian era. In particular they shed new light on Christian communities that sprang up in the Mediterranean region. They were modelled on the teachings of Christ which were passed on by word of mouth. It was called a Sayings Gospel and the Professor claims that it preceded the written gospels and may have been used by the evangelists themselves as one of their sources."

The Archdeacon was writing furiously. "This is very exciting Baltic. What we need now is more information about this Professor; his academic credentials, his address, email and so on. Once we have that we have people who can find out exactly what he is doing. Make it a priority."

He hung up and reviewed the notes he had made. Could this Professor Sorensen be a member of the *Dialogues*? He called Balinska and told him that what had happened. They decided it was sufficiently important that they needed to deal with it as soon as possible.

The Archdeacon called the Regent and told him to make arrangements to be at the Castillo the following day for a meeting at 2 p.m. and to bring three copies of the information with him.

The next day they met as arranged; Balinska, Messi, the Baltic Regent, and Father Bernado. They met in a boardroom adjacent to the Archdeacon's office. Balinska asked the Regent to review the facts.

"All the information is in the folder which each of you has in front of you." He waited while they opened and studied the information. He reviewed the facts and concluded, "I think there is a strong indication that the Professor is either a member of the *Dialogues* or has contact with them."

"What is Professor Sorensen's speciality?" Balinska asked.

"He is a professor of Anthropology. It's there on page two of the notes."

Balinska found it, and even better, it had his address and phone number at the university. "This is good." Surprising everyone—they had never heard him praise anyone before. Balinska continued, "We could pick this professor up and interrogate him, but that might make the others suspicious, especially since we've already kidnapped two of them. Maybe he can lead us to the others, and to where they are keeping their information.

He turned to Messi. "This is where you come in. I need you to tell us what we should do next. And no techno-shit please just plain English."

"Well, I think I've got everything I can from the two computers that we have from the priests. The one from Father Michael is a dinosaur and didn't have any useful information, except the email address of the other priest. They mainly seem to have been in contact with each other. That's the only two contacts that are repeated several times. There are lots of other names but no way of telling whether they are part of the *Dialogues*. If we can either get hold of this Sorensen's computer or better get into his office and insert a Trojan horse we could cross reference all the names."

"I said no techno-shit," Balinska said, then quickly added, "please! What's a Trojan Horse?"

Messi explained how it worked. "I'm going to embed a small program into his computer. It's the equivalent of an electronic bug on a phone. It will send me information on what information he has on his computer. The embedded program is called a Trojan Horse."

The Archdeacon smiled inwardly. Apparently Balinska had never heard of the siege of Troy and he wondered if Messi had either.

He continued, "I could do it by concealing it in an email so that when he opens the email, the Trojan horse installs itself. But if we could get into his office and I can get into his computer it would make it easier. We could also put a bug on his phone at the same time and then we'd be able to capture his conversations as well."

The Archdeacon was watching Messi as he spoke. This new world of computers, coded instructions, bugs, and Trojan Horses. What a strange place it was becoming when we have to depend on geeks, like Messi, to access information. He much preferred the old ways; people like Balinska or the Gestapo, who would rip the truth from them. Then dispose of the bodies. Easier and more permanent.

"And then what?" Balinska asked.

"It depends on what we want to get. I could write the program so it could send back a list of his email contacts or what files he has on his computer."

"Why haven't you written it? What are you waiting for?"

"I can't write it until I know the computer and its location and this is the first I've heard of this Sorensen; also it's not as easy as it sounds. They usually protect their computers with security software that tries to block and destroy this kind of attack. But I have ways to get around them."

"Doesn't sound that certain to me. Maybe the best plan is a trip to Copenhagen so we can take a look at this professor. Sniff around a little. Then visit his office, plant the bug and this horse, and see what else we can find."

"I could download the files from his computer while we're there; might be some useful information."

The Archdeacon, who to this point, had been listening to the two of them interjected, "That sounds like a plan. Why don't you get my secretary to arrange for you to go there?"

Balinska was trying to pin down his dislike or was it resentment, of Messi and the few other *nerds* he had met. They lived in their own strange world, fuelled by drugs; they rarely ate and they never had windows in their offices, as if the outside world was their enemy. He knew they needed Messi for now, but watch out once this was finished. He would have him then.

Pasty faced little prick!

Chapter 38

Andersen University
Copenhagen, Denmark

Something was wrong. Marius Sorensen could sense it. He was certain he was been followed. At his home, on the metro, at the University he couldn't shake the feeling. The previous day as he was walking along Fredensgade to the restaurant where he ate dinner he turned quickly and thought he saw someone duck quickly into an alleyway. He ran back, ignoring the puzzled looks of the other pedestrians, but there was no one there. *Did he imagine it?*

He wondered if he should start eating at another restaurant, but this was his favorite; he knew the staff by name and they knew him. He was a creature of habit, he liked his routine and was loath to change it. With his waiter, Albert, he discussed soccer, the local leagues and the chances of Denmark making it to the World Cup. It was hard to believe that Albert had once been a promising player. Now his ample girth made him waddle rather than walk.

After he had eaten, Marius took some papers out of his briefcase and went over them. He reviewed the list of names. They were the speakers that he hoped to persuade to present papers at the conference he was organizing.

After dinner, he left the restaurant and began walking back to the university. The streets were relatively quiet; the rush hour over, but he could definitely hear footsteps behind him. He quickened his pace; the steps quickened. He moved faster, almost at a run. His pursuer kept coming, he could hear him gasping; not in good shape for an assassin.

Marius reached the corner, turned right and flattened himself against the wall. He grabbed his briefcase, solid leather with metal edges, ready to hit his pursuer. As he turned the corner, Marius swung the briefcase with all his strength and struck the man full on the chest. As he went down, he saw who it was. "Oh my God," Marius yelled, "I've killed him." It was Albert, the waiter from the restaurant. "Why didn't you shout, call my name or something?"

Albert tried to speak, but he couldn't get his breath. With all the running and the blow to his midriff, it was several minutes before he could answer the question. "I . . . called you . . . but you didn't hear me and . . . then . . . I couldn't get enough breath . . . to yell," he gasped, between great gulps of air.

"Why were you following me anyway," Marius asked.

"Because you . . . forgot your . . . credit card."

Marius helped him to his feet. "Do you want me to call an ambulance? You should probably get an X-ray to be sure nothing is broken."

"No. I think I'm okay. I have quite a cushion of protection."

Am I becoming paranoid? Marius asked himself. *Chasing shadows? Attacking overweight waiters.* But he still couldn't shake it. He was sure he was being watched.

Two days later he went to his favorite bar on the Stroget. Every Thursday he stopped by the Irish Rover pub for his pint of Guinness, a taste he had acquired during a year he had spent as a visiting professor in Dublin. He was sitting at the bar and had just taken his first sip when the young man sitting next to him lost his balance. He was stepping down from the bar stool and fell heavily against Marius, knocking him backwards. Fortunately, the man behind grabbed him and stopped him from hitting the floor. The young man apologized profusely, but no harm was done. Marius turned to thank the man who had caught him, but he wasn't there. Someone was just leaving the bar. That must have been him. He was big with a shaved head.

The next morning when he arrived at his office and reached into his pocket for his access card, it wasn't there. He tried all his other pockets. Not there either. He had never misplaced it before. He went over to the security office. "Morning Keys," he said, using the nickname of the security officer. He didn't know his real name and doubted if any of the other professors did either.

"Morning, Professor. What can I do you for," he said with a chuckle.

Marius explained that he had lost his card. "I can't imagine where I left it," he said waiting for Key's mini-lecture. He got it.

"Tut, Tut Professor. You realize how dangerous that can be. It not only gives access to your office but also to all common areas of the university. I'll have to cancel that one and issue a new one." He went over to his computer and placed a blank card into the slot and typed a command, looking at a message on the screen. "I see you were burning the midnight oil, last night."

"What do you mean?"

"According to the security system you entered your office at 1:05 a.m. and left at 3:23 a.m. Here see for yourself," he said and turned the screen around so that Marius could see.

"How strange. I was home, asleep."

"Well, it's possible, I suppose, that the security system isn't working properly, but I've never had a problem with it. You'd better check your office to make sure nothing was tampered with," he said handing Marius his new card.

Once in his room, he looked around. He saw immediately that the items on his desk had been moved. He was particular about the organization of his desk, obsessive almost. Everything—In Basket, Out Basket, Desk Diary—all had to be aligned to each other. And they weren't; the inbox was out of position and not lined up with the edge of his desk and the angle of the screen on his desktop had been changed. He had marked two small lines between the monitor and the computer. They had to be to be lined up otherwise an arthritic joint in his neck gave him hell. His filing cabinet was unlocked. It was possible that he had forgotten to lock it, but not likely. He checked inside. All looked undisturbed. He checked his files and everything seemed to be there.

He picked up his phone to call Keys but after the embarrassment of losing his card, he had no wish for another 'Tut Tut' session. But he was convinced more than ever that something was wrong and he was beginning to suspect that it was connected to his involvement in the *Dialogues.*

Before leaving Copenhagen, Balinska told his operator, to keep tailing the Professor and to file regular reports with him at the Castillo.

Chapter 39

27 Calle de Sola
Toledo, Italy

When he woke up, Jose wondered where he was. Then he remembered that he was at Papa Michael's. He showered made coffee and toast and was about to set out for the University when he realized he did not know where it was.

He went into the study, still a mess despite his efforts last night to organize it, and found a guide book for Toledo containing a city map. Next he located a phone book and looked for an entry for the University. He found a listing for the Universidad de Castilla-La Mancha, but there were several entries below it, one for each faculty. He decided that Humanities was the best bet reasoning that his uncle would most likely be researching religion or philosophy; law being a long shot. He considered phoning first, but he knew that all he would get was an automated menu, followed by several submenus and eventually a person who didn't have the information anyway. He decided that it was probably faster to go to the Humanities building, find the reference library and talk to the librarian. He wrote down the address—it was on Plaza de Padilla—and located it on the map. From his uncle's house on Calle de Sola, the distance was less than a mile.

He set out doubling back every so often to see if he was being followed. He didn't see anyone, so either they were professionals or they had decided they had what they wanted and further surveillance was unnecessary. After losing his way twice and being directed back by passers-by, he reached the Plaza de Padilla. He asked his way to the library and found the main desk. The librarian was a pleasant looking woman, in her mid-thirties he guessed, with blonde hair streaked with grey highlights, or grey hair streaked with blonde highlights, he never could tell the difference. Her face was cute rather than attractive, soft eyes and a mouth that was set in a smile.

"Excuse me, Ms. Alverez," he said, reading the name on her badge. "I wonder if I can ask you some questions."

"That's why I'm here," she said with a smile, putting down the book she was cataloguing, "What is it you want?"

"I believe my uncle, Father Michael, was using the library for a research project. I was wondering if you knew him or what he was working on."

"Yes, I know him. He's such a sweet man, everyone liked him even the students, which is quite unusual. I don't know the exact details, but it had something to do with religion. He was usually here every day; in fact he always sat at that table in the far corner. It's close to the stacks containing Philosophy and Religion. The students always left it vacant for him, they nicknamed it Tuck's Table."

"What does that mean, Tuck's Table?" he asked, wondering if she was trying to be funny.

"Obviously you are not up on English folklore," the librarian replied.

"Now I'm even more confused."

"Don't you remember the story of Robin Hood and his merry men in the Forest of Sherwood? There was a monk called Friar Tuck." She paused and smiled, obviously enjoying herself. "Most of the time your uncle wore everyday clothes but every so often he would come dressed in his monk's habit. He said it was a way of reminding himself of his place in God's plan.

"The first time he came dressed that way one of the students called him Friar Tuck and the name stuck. That's why it's called Tuck's Table; only he was allowed to sit there."

"Okay; makes sense, sort of," Jose said, wondering how she managed to talk and smile at the same time.

"We haven't seen him for a couple of days. Has anything happened?"

"Nothing serious; he's not been well," he lied, deciding not to alarm her with the real reason and also hoping to avoid having to identify himself as a police officer. "The reason I'm here is to pick up some books. He gave me a list, but I've misplaced it. I wonder if you can remember any of the ones he was using."

"I can't tell you the ones he got from the bookshelves if you need that information you could ask one of the library assistants at the check-out desk. They re-stack the shelves and may remember the ones that were on his table. Our most valuable and rare books are kept in our restricted reference section. It's not open to the general public, only to those who have registered and been approved."

"How is that done?"

"Just the usual way. By completing several forms, stating the nature of the research, supplying references, academic and financial, pledging your first born. Just the usual. It's reviewed by several committees. The whole process won't take more than four weeks. Or I could give you a temporary pass. It will cost you a cup of coffee, though," she said with a smile."

What was this? A librarian with a sense of humor? And is she hitting on me? She was better than cute; closer to attractive.

"Okay, it's a deal. But you may have to wait for that cup of coffee. I may have to go back to Madrid."

"Promises. Promises. You men are all the same." she said filling out a temporary pass and handing it to him, before adding, "You won't be able to take the books with you. They aren't allowed out of the library. Remember I'm always here to help," she said and flashed him a smile somewhere between an offer of literary assistance and 'I'm looking forward to that cup of coffee'.

With the pass clipped to his lapel, he went through the door marked 'Restricted Reference Section'. He identified himself and asked the librarian if he could give him a list of the books his uncle, Father Michael, had requested. The assistant said, "You mean Friar Tuck," and gave him a smile. "I'm not supposed to give out that information but if you can show me that you're related, I'll overlook the rule."

Fortunately, Papa had registered as Michael Rodriguez so Jose gave him his driver's license and the names matched. The assistant said it might take a few minutes but if he took a seat, he'd print out a list as soon as he had time.

About fifteen minutes later he walked across and handed Jose a sheet torn off from the printer with a list of the titles on it:

Apology of Origen
The Wisdom of Sirach: *Translation*
Antiquities of the Jews: *Flavius Josephus*
Q: The Earliest Gospel: *John S. Kloppenborg*
The Gospel of Thomas: *(From Codex II)*

"The librarian asked him, "Would you like me to get the books for you?"

"No, thanks. Not right now. I need to study the list for a while."

Jose didn't recognize anything on it. He needed to find out what they were. He remembered that Father William at the monastery had worked with his uncle in the library. He might know.

He folded the list and put it into his pocket then made his way out of the library. He stopped by the main desk. "Thanks, Ms. Alverez for all your help. I'll be back and I'll buy you that cup of coffee and you can tell me about Robin Hood and all his merry men."

"I'll look forward to it."

He clipped the list of books to the notes he had already made and added a memo to ask Father William about it. He reviewed the other items then used his mobile to call the local police station and the detective in charge of the case. He gave him an update on his visit to the library and told him he was about to head back to Madrid. Trying to be diplomatic he added, "Thanks for all your help and I wonder if I could ask one last favor. Could you get Uniform Branch to check with the neighbors to see if anyone noticed anyone or any car hanging around recently? Someone must have been watching the house. How else would they know my uncle's routine and when the house was empty?"

"Will do. Once I've got the information I'll send it to your Madrid office. Drive safely."

"And let me know if you get anything back on the Opel."

Although it was past seven when he reached Madrid, he drove straight to his office. He logged on to his police computer and searched the database for the article on the disappearance of the priest in Munich. Once he found it he printed it on the office printer; he still preferred reading a paper version to an electronic one. The details were sketchy. His name was Father Emile and he shared the parish house with two other priests, Johann, and Ulrich. It was Father Ulrich who reported the disappearance. The name of the detective in charge of the investigation was Franz Millar. Jose looked at his watch, it was after eight, but maybe the detective worked long hours. He picked up the phone and dialed the Munich number listed. It rang several times and then there were several clicks as the call was transferred, then a voice, "Hello, service desk."

Jose explained the reason for the call and asked how he might contact Detective Millar.

"He's already left for the day, he'll be here in the morning. He has a staff briefing at eight. You could reach him then or I could take a message and put it on his desk."

"Thanks," Jose replied I'll call him in the morning." With that, he hung up and made a note in his calendar. He thought for a while trying to decide on a course of action. It was becoming apparent that if he were to get to the bottom of the disappearances of Papa and Father Emile it would require his full concentration. Fortunately, his casebook was nearly empty although he knew there was a narcotics smuggling investigation headed his way. His best guess was that he had about two weeks before that happened.

The next morning he made an early appointment to see his boss, Captain Ricardo Rico, known throughout the department as Richie Rich. He had more than once cursed his parents for baptizing him with that name. As Jose walked into his office, he stood up and reached across his desk to shake his hand. The captain was tall, towering over Jose, who himself was pushing six feet. Looking immaculate in his captain's uniform, he cut an impressive figure.

"Morning Jose; sorry about the monkey suit but I've got a press conference in thirty minutes about the ETA terror attacks. What's the latest on your uncle's disappearance?"

"Well, that's what I wanted to talk to you about. It's going to take several days to get to the bottom of it."

Jose reviewed all the facts he'd uncovered during the last two days, concluding with "I need to take at least ten days to try and get a handle on exactly what's going on."

"Don't you think you're too close to this Jose? This is not just your uncle this is your second father, the man who brought you up much of the time," the Captain replied. He had worked with Mario Rodriguez when Jose was still an infant and knew the full details of his childhood. "How can you stay objective? What are you going to do if you find out who did this? If Father Michael is hurt in any way, you're likely to lose your temper. And that would be the end of your career. We buried the last incident but one more and you strike out."

He was talking about an incident eight years ago when Jose was interviewing a suspect in a child murder inquiry. Everyone knew the man was guilty. A long list of priors, including assault and GBH, but he knew how to stymie the interrogators and after three days they still hadn't got any admissions from him. On the fourth day, Jose lost his temper and grabbed him in a choke hold, "Come on you little piece of shit. After what you did to that little girl you don't deserve to live. Maybe I'll finish it now, save the courts the time and money."

By the time the other detectives rushed into the room, the perp was almost blue. It took two of them to pull Jose's arm away. "Holy fuck, Jose calm down. He's not worth your career."

There was an internal investigation that concluded that the marks on the prisoner's neck were caused when he tried to hang himself with his belt in his cell. Jose was officially cleared, but a note was placed in his file with the details of the incident.

"I know Captain. I learned my lesson; since then I've kept my temper in check. I'll do this by the book."

"If it were anyone else, I wouldn't allow it, but your family and mine go back a long way. I'm going to cut you some slack, but I want a report on my desk first thing every Monday morning. And if I hear you're cutting any corners then I'll yank you off the case. Understood."

"Yes, Captain; thanks," Jose said knowing that the Captain was referring to the years he and Jose's father had spent together during their early years on the force. They had graduated from the academy the same year and spent their first ten years in the same division before his father had decided to go back to school to take a law degree.

Jose went back to his desk cleaned up a few outstanding items and checked his emails. He looked at his watch, 10:30 a.m. He dialed the number for Franz Millar, in Munich. The detective answered on the second ring. "Hello, Detective Millar here. How can I help?"

"This is Detective Rodriguez with the Madrid police. I'm working on the disappearance of a priest in Toledo, named Father Michael. I was checking the database and found out that you had a similar one."

"Yes, about a week ago," Detective Millar replied, "and please call me Franz."

"Okay Franz and I'm Jose. Tell me what happened."

"We got a call from the housekeeper that one of the priests, a Father Emile, had not returned to the parish house last Thursday and hadn't been seen since."

"How many lived in the parish house," Jose asked.

"There were four altogether. And don't quote me on their titles, I was never a guppy cruncher." Franz said then realized that since Jose was Spanish there was a good chance he was a Catholic. He quickly added, "No offense Jose."

"None taken. But I should tell you that the Priest, who disappeared in Toledo, is my uncle. And since we're going to be dealing with church people it's probably a good idea to avoid the more colorful descriptions," Jose said, frowning. He hadn't heard that expression in years; the Catholic tradition of eating fish on Fridays.

"Agreed. To get back to the parish house. There are the housekeeper and three priests. One of them was away at a seminar and the other Father Ulrich, the curate, had some kind of viral infection."

"When did she call?"

"Two days after he disappeared. I asked her why she hadn't called earlier and she said that sometimes priests visit outlying parishioners, without telling her, and don't always make it back the same day."

"What about files and computers," Jose asked?

"I was just getting to that. I went out and met with Father Ulrich, who was still a little shaky. Each priest has his own room in the parish house and I checked each one. They were a little messy, it's possible someone may have gone through their possessions but according to the curate nothing was missing. I asked him about documents, papers, appointment books and so on."

"'Oh,' the Father said, "'all that sort of thing was kept in the church office.'"

"Was there one office or did they each have their own?" Jose asked.

Franz checked his casebook. "Just one office for the three of them but only Father Emile had access to the computer. We got the key to the room from Father Ulrich; what a mess, documents, files everywhere and the computer had gone."

"Sounds familiar," Jose interrupted thinking of the mess in his Uncle's office. "Were you able to decide what had been taken, besides the computer that is?"

"We sealed off the office, but I've had to wait almost a week before I could get a team in to dust the place and do the forensics; remember this is not high profile. We got the Curate to help in identifying many of the documents, but he wasn't a lot of help. They tested for fingerprints and turned up three main sets, which matched the three priests."

"How do you know? Are they on file?" Jose asked.

"No. We checked them against the dabs in their rooms. There was one other interesting print. On the desk beside where the computer had been, there was a metal letter opener with a piece of plastic hanging from the tip. It looked like someone had snagged the finger of a latex glove on it and then grabbed the letter opener and in the process left a print of their index finger."

"Anything else?"

"Yes, but rather than talking on the phone can you fly up and we'll go to the Church office together. It's still a mess and sealed off; a fresh pair of eyes might turn something up that we've missed."

"Good idea. I'll get the secretary to book me on a flight tomorrow." Jose asked, hoping that the print might lead them to whoever had done this.

"I'll pick you up at the airport. Have your secretary fax me flight details and times."

"How will I recognize you when I arrive?"

"I'll wear my green Tyrolean hat with a red feather and my lederhosen. Just joking about the shorts but look for the tallest guy there, last time I checked I was pushing six foot six."

Chapter 40

Computer Center
Castillo de Chipiona
Sanlucar, Spain

Messi was uploading data from the USB drive that contained the files from Copenhagen. Much of it was encrypted and what wasn't, didn't relate to the *Dialogues*. He was aware of Balinska prowling behind him. He turned towards him and said, "You prowling around isn't going to speed things up. Just take a seat and wait or go back to your office and I'll call you when I find something.

Balinska gave him a grimace, "I'll be in my office," and left.

It was another two hours before he found it; a non-encrypted contact file with names and locations. *Thank you! Thank you!*

He printed out the list of fifteen names and compared it to the lists he had got from the other computers. He got the match he was looking for. Besides the names of the Priests, there were three other names on all the lists. He called Balinska. "I think we have the names of three more members of the *Dialogues*. Remember—"

Balinska cut him off. "Bring them to my office." It came out like an order, so he quickly added, "If that's okay." *He was really going to have to hold on to his temper or he would kill the nerdy bastard.*

Messi took his time getting to his office, just to underline the point and handed him a sheet of paper with the three names.

Balinska looked at the names, angry that hackers like Messi were becoming essential.

He read the names:

John Hampton	University of Toronto
Professor Ian Frazer	University of Sheffield.
Michael Kinghaven	University of Stockholm

"I think we're onto something." He said with a smile that looked more like a grimace. "No point pulling them in yet. I'll put a tail on them to see what and who they lead us to."

"How? Do we have people in all three places? Isn't it expensive?" Messi asked.

"I think that's my call. But to answer your question. Yes, it is expensive but Bernado has deep pockets and can afford it."

Balinska didn't say anything for a few minutes, thinking what came next, before saying, "I think it's time we took a look at the other side of this business. This far we've concentrated on finding the people. It's time we looked at finding and destroying whatever information they've got stashed away somewhere. That's your speciality. See if you can crack that database or whatever it is you do.

The next day Messi was scrolling through the files on Sorensen's machine when he noticed a journal entry that the Professor was planning a trip to Montreal to go fishing." He called Balinska and told him.

"Fishing! Did you say fishing?"

"Yes. That's what it says."

"It has to be a cover for something," Balinska said, looking out of the window at the car park baking in the scorching sun. "Who the fuck flies all the way to Canada to go fishing?"

"That's what it said."

"Okay, get me the details, dates flights, times and I'll alert Pierre Molatov, he's our guy in Montreal."

They now knew six of the *Dialogues*. Molatov would track Sorensen once he arrived in Montreal. That might turn up more of them. And he could see what else he could extract from the Monk.

He called Bernado and gave him an update. When he had finished the Archdeacon said, "Before you start, I've something to show you. Meet me in the Sotano."

When he got there, the Archdeacon was waiting. "It's in here," he said as he opened the door of Room 19, then stepped back to let Balinska see what was there.

"What is it," he asked, "it looks like a dentist chair."

"It is but straps have been added to keep the patient from moving. See the cables coming down from that box on the ceiling."

Balinska looked up and saw them hanging from what looked like an air conditioning unit.

"They can be attached to any part of the patient's body and the dial on that console in the corner can be used to adjust the voltage. If they're attached to the frontal lobes, they can be used to affect their memory. With sufficient electricity they can erase it. There are truth drugs in the cabinet over in the corner. They can be given first to increase the potency."

"Better not tell Messi or he'll want to try them," Balinska said as he walked over and opened the cabinet. Scopolamine, Sodium Thiopental, LSD. Balinska stood still visualizing the patient strapped to the chair after an injection of one of the drugs as he slowly increased the voltage. Water boarding and now this.

There really was a Santa Claus

"Where did it come from?" he asked.

"It was designed by my father and I had it built from the design that was in his notes."

"What did he do?" Balinska asked.

The Archdeacon was obviously proud of him and took the chance to tell Balinska everything; his medical practice in Berlin before the war, the experiments in Auschwitz. And his enduring belief in the Third Reich.

Like Father like Son. Both frickin Wierdos!

Chapter 41

True to his word, as Jose came out of the arrivals hall, in Munich, Franz was towering over everyone. And just to be sure he couldn't be missed he had a feather protruding from his hat that must have been at least thirty inches long.

Jose walked up to him, "You must be Franz," he said looking up at the feather.

"That's me," he said with a smile. "Never fails."

They walked to Franz's car, which was illegally parked with a card on the dash stating 'on official police business' and a parking ticket tucked under the wiper blade. "I don't know why they bother. They know we'll have it voided."

Jose stood back and looked at the car, a fairly new BMW 330i. "Is this a police car?" Jose asked, thinking about the beat up Peugeot he usually got from the motor pool.

"Of course," Franz answered, "BMW are the standard patrol cars of the police force. Don't forget Munich is the headquarters of BMW. In fact I'll point them out; they are on our way."

From the airport, they took the autobahn into Munich, driving through farmland, each field a perfect rectangle. But as Franz pushed the speed up to 240 k/h, Jose lost interest in the scenery. He liked fast cars, but this was too fast. If they hit anything, they would be instantly vaporized When they reached the outskirts of the city he slowed his speed to a more reasonable 120 k/h.

"Thank God. I was petrified. Do you always drive that fast?"

"That's the main advantage of the autobahn, there are no speed limits."

"Then why are slowing down, not that I want to go any faster. This speed is just fine."

"In and around cities and other congested areas there are posted speed limits. Many people think we should have those speed limit's everywhere, but the car lobby makes sure that doesn't happen. If the speed is limited, they won't sell as many of their big and expensive Mercs, Bimmers and Audis."

From the airport expressway, they took the ring road and then wound their way south on Lerchenauer Strasse. Jose was trying to get his tongue around the umlauts when the towers of the BMW headquarters came into view. Franz pulled to the side of the road so Jose could get a good look.

"It was built in 1972. The tower is made up of four cylinders, side by side, to represent the inner workings of a four banger."

"You're quite the tour guide," Jose said, "What else should I know?"

"Well, since you ask, did you know what the BMW symbol represents a propeller, from their origins as a plane manufacturer? After the war, they only survived by making pots, pans, and bicycles and assembling the Italian designed Isetta microcar. If you look past the BMW building, you'll see another famous, or more accurately infamous, set of buildings."

Jose looked where Franz was pointing at what looked like the top of a giant marquee. "I see it, but what is it?"

"That's the Olympic park from the 1972 games, unfortunately mainly remembered for the massacre of the Israeli athletes by Palestinian terrorists."

"Oh my God. I'd forgotten all about that. I was still a kid, but I can remember watching it unfold on TV."

"It was a black stain on our city and country especially at a time when we thought we were finally emerging from the horrors of the Second World War. And a severe blow to the reputation of the Munich police."

"Enough of this Franz, let's move on and concentrate on the present. Let's try and find out who is kidnapping these priests."

They drove the short distance to the church of St. Sebastien on Karl-Theodor Strasse. Franz said, "I've asked Father Ulrich to meet us at the church and to try and remember anything that might help."

When the church came into view, it looked fairly new and covered almost the whole block. Jose later learned that it had been built in 1929 but almost entirely destroyed by fire bombs in 1944. It was restored in 1964 and an office, parish hall, and a church school had been added since.

Father Ulrich was waiting for them and pointed them to a parking spot across the road. He led them into the church and unlocked the door to the office. As they entered the office, Father Ulrich said, "It's exactly as you left it, inspector, no one has been in here since. By the way, I found this in the parish house," and he handed Detective Millar a green bound book.

"What is it," he asked.

"It's the appointment book. It's usually kept in the office, but one of the others must have taken it back with them. I thought it might help."

The detective skimmed through it and noticed several entries for the previous week. "This could be extremely useful. Thank you. I'll need to hold onto it until the investigation is over. Is that alright?"

"I thought you might want to, so I made a copy of all the entries for the next several weeks."

Jose turned towards Father Ulrich and asked, "Do you know if Father Emile was working on anything special."

The curate produced a letter-sized notebook and gave it to Jose, "I found this on his desk in his room and thought it might have some significance."

Jose opened it and saw it contained page after page of copious notes, much of it unintelligible to him, but what he could understand were scientific references. Some referring to scientists—Einstein and Newton—others relating to scientific theories—gravity, relativity, quantum mechanics.

It would take some time to fully decipher and he would have to find someone with the appropriate expertise to do it. For now he needed to see what he could glean from an inspection of the office.

"This could be invaluable Father. Thank you," Jose said to Father Ulrich, wondering about the curates motives. Entering Father Emile's private room and removing personal possessions! Was he just being helpful? Or keeping an eye on him?

Jose looked around the office. The room was about fifteen feet by twelve feet, with bookcases on three of the walls. Half of the books were still on the shelves but one of the bookcases was completely empty and files and books were scattered all over the floor. It looked like the thieves had been looking for something in particular, but it would take a lot of work to sort everything and even more work to find out what was missing.

Franz pulled on latex gloves and gave a pair to Jose, who put them on. They went over to the desk and Franz pointed to the outline of a letter opener. "This is where they found it. Our boys took it back to the lab and dusted it. They checked it against the database but didn't come up with anything, so they've sent it on to Interpol to see if they can get a match. Hopefully, we'll have the analysis back from the lab by tomorrow."

"Let's hope it's positive and gives us a perp. I'm just going to wander around to see if anything strikes me as interesting."

Over the years, Jose had developed a sixth sense that told him when he was on the verge of something that might break a case open. It always caused an empty feeling in his stomach.

"Who discovered the break in?" Jose asked Father Ulrich.

"I did, but not until three days later. I'd been sick at the time of Father Emile's disappearance. The housekeeper had reported him missing, but it wasn't until I was back on my feet and came to the office that I found out that it had been broken into."

"So we don't know for sure when this happened. We have to assume that it was the day that Father Emile disappeared, but there is a three-day gap, so we can't be a hundred percent sure."

Jose continued to work his way around the room and as he got closer to the door, he felt the empty feeling in his stomach. He moved the loose books and papers and then he saw it protruding slightly from under a book. It was a piece of plastic, about two inches square. Jose picked it up. On one side, there were the symbols CΦC and on the reverse $f9$ and *f12*. There was a small circular hole in the top left corner that looked as if it should have a key hanging from it. He placed it an evidence bag.

"Any idea what they mean?" asked Franz.

"Well, the symbol between the two C's is the Greek letter 'phi,' roughly equivalent to the English letter 'f', but I've no idea what *f9* and *f12* represent."

On the drive from the airport they had decided that since Jose had been assigned full time to the case and Franz was expected to fit it in with his other cases, it made sense for Jose to coordinate everything. They spent another hour looking around the office. Jose gathered all the loose sheets together, and with the white square of plastic and the appointment book placed them in his briefcase.

"I think that's all for now," Franz said to Father Ulrich, "but don't let anyone in here until we tell you that we've finished with our investigation. We'll send some officers in to look through the rest of it, in the next few days."

Franz and Jose headed back to the police headquarters on Ettstrasse and to Franz's office on the second floor. They sent the white card to forensics. While Franz looked through his messages and emails, Jose looked through the sheets he had brought back with him. He didn't see anything that made any sense, so he filed the rest and turned his attention to the appointment book.

It was filled with dates and times of meetings mainly related to church affairs. Most of them were local, in the Munich area, but he found an entry for Aug. 30: *Dialogues Stockholm.*

By now it was 6 p.m. and Franz asked, "Are you ready to get something to eat. By the way when are you heading back?"

"My flight back is tomorrow afternoon and I still haven't checked into my hotel. Maybe you could drive me there and then we could grab a bite. I'd like to come back and finish going through all this stuff. But if you've got plans or a family waiting I can take a cab."

"Neither, let's grab a bite at your hotel and then come back and finish off here."

The next morning they reviewed the results of their work. Not much of any relevance. Jose had found one other sheet of paper that referenced the '*Dialogues*' they had a possible fingerprint and the card. That was about it; not much to go on.

Just then the phone rang and Franz picked it up, "Millar here." He listened for a moment and then hung up the phone. "Good news, they've got a package from Interpol for me downstairs. Fingers crossed."

Franz was back inside ten minutes and placed the package on the desk. He opened it and pulled out a printed sheet as well as a smaller sterile pack with the letter opener and latex in it. Franz read the letter, "There was a match to a set of prints from some gang-related murders in Toronto, a year or so ago, but they have no definite information who they belong to. There was a memo on file from the investigating detective that he thought a thug called Boris Radovic was involved, but no definite proof. And there is a record that he died a few months ago."

"So he's not our man?"

"Apparently not."

"Shit!"

The report from forensics on the white square of plastic arrived later the same day. It had been handled by so many people that it was impossible to get any clear prints.

Chapter 42

426 Clarke Avenue, Westmount
Montreal, Quebec

Tom McDonald didn't have any classes today so he and Cindy Preston, his girlfriend, had burned the midnight oil, and then some. They were both professors at McGill University in Montreal. His speciality was Anthropology and Cindy was an IT prof who ran the McGill computer network.

He'd switched off the alarm but the phone ringing at 7 a.m. woke him. He rolled over to get it, but Cindy already had it. It was for her anyway; the computer network had crashed. She dressed and left in a hurry. He went back to sleep and woke 3 hours later.

It was already hot and humid; steamy was a better description. The forecast high was close to 30°C with humidity to match. This was summer weather, July or even August, certainly not mid-September. *Perhaps they are right, we are in the middle of a climate change.* He decided he didn't want breakfast, just coffee and he would pick that up at the corner. His old Forester was showing its age, but it had the best air conditioner of any car in its class. As soon as he had turned the key he switched it to Max. But even in the short time it took to ramp up and suck out the moisture, his forehead was dripping and his shirt was sticking to his back. So much for the nearly cold shower he had had an hour before. Of course if he'd left at his usual time, early in the morning, he would have avoided the worst of it.

He drove from his apartment along Sherbrooke. Traffic was light the rush hour had come and gone. He reached McGill and turned into his parking spot. He sat for a moment with the air conditioning still blasting. It was about 50 yards from his car to his office and he was trying to decide which would generate the least amount of heat. To race from his car and cover the distance in the shortest amount of time, or to walk slowly and hope that he would be under the *sweat* threshold. There was probably a scientific formula that could be used, something to do with entropy and thermodynamics, but his field was anthropology and he was a Canadian. So he did what Canadians have done for generations. He compromised and walked at a brisk pace. It didn't work. By the time, he reached his office he was hot and sticky again.

He turned the a/c to full and placed the garbage can by the door about six feet from his desk. Then he sat down and began sorting through his mail. Anything from book publishers asking him to recommend their latest offering to his students were scrunched into a ball and given the benefit of his once renowned finger roll shot. Those from companies telling him about the latest gizmo that would make his courses so much easier suffered a similar fate. Most of them entered the garbage can without even touching the rim. They evidently didn't appreciate the purpose of a university education. It wasn't supposed to be easy. It was meant to be hard. It was supposed to make you think. It was supposed to make you go and do some independent research in the university library.

Once he had sorted and dispatched the *trash* he was left with three envelopes personally addressed to him. Two of them were from other universities, advising him of teaching opportunities. Not because he was pre-eminent in his field but because they sent it out to everyone on the *list*. Available, for a price, from companies who compiled them from conference attendees, magazine subscriptions and surveys disguised to look as if your opinion mattered. Then they made a fast buck selling them. They quickly joined their ilk in the garbage can. He was happy where he was, doing what he was doing.

The third one looked interesting. It was postmarked Copenhagen so he guessed it was from his friend Marius Sorensen. He opened the envelope scanned the letter. It was a request to give a paper at the annual conference of the *Society for the Advancement of Anthropological Research* – SAAR for short—sounded like a disease. One more acronym that he could do without.

He blamed computers for their proliferation, but then he blamed computers for everything. They were supposed to make life simpler; they made his more complex. Grading student's essays was always painful, now, in addition to teeth grinding grammar, he had to check to see if they had been plagiarized from the internet.

Instead of just giving the marks to a secretary he now had to enter them into the *computer database,* which sounded like some dark abyss, inaccessible to mere humans. Then the computer typed the marks into a letter under the university letterhead and another machine addressed and stamped an envelope, folded the letter and inserted it. He wasn't sure if it actually licked and sealed it. Probably. And, of course, the secretaries who had performed this function previously had been made redundant.

Eventually, if one projected this to its logical end, all that would be left would be computers and students. And one had to wonder if the students were actually necessary.

He looked through the conference topics; he didn't really want to do a paper, but he and Marius had known each other for several years now so he would have to do it. What had begun as a professional acquaintance had developed into a personal friendship when they discovered they both shared a passion for fly fishing. They arranged once or twice a year to attend the same academic conference provided it was located in an area where the trout were plentiful. And since Montreal and Copenhagen had an abundance of trout streams and rivers, they always managed to travel to one or the other during the year. This year they were planning on trying the rivers in and around Drummondville in the Eastern Townships. Marius was flying to Montreal next week for a few days fishing then flying to Toronto to present a paper at a conference organized by York University.

At the bottom of the letter, there was a scribbled note;

> *Something strange is happening here. I have a feeling that I've been followed and that my computer has been bugged. Don't send emails to the university. If you need to email me, send it to my personal email. I'll explain everything when I see you next week. And when I picked up my office phone to call you, there was a faint click that I'd never heard before.*

Tom leaned back in his chair wondering what had happened. Marius was a pretty down to earth Dane not given to flights of paranoia. He looked up his phone number but discovered he didn't have his cell, just home, and office. He dialled the home number, but Marius wasn't there. He left a message telling him he had received the letter and asked Marius to call him back.

Next morning, Tom had just woken when the phone rang. It was Marius. "Sorry to call so early, Tom, but I wanted to catch you before you left for the office. I got your message and I need to update you. It's suddenly got worse."

Tom interrupted. "Hold on Marius where are you calling from?"

"On my mobile."

"Okay, why don't you tell me what's happened."

Marius told him about the *Dialogues* and about the strange things that were going on, including his office access card being stolen as he was now convinced it had. "And two members, both priests, have gone missing. One was a physicist as well as a priest and the other was researching early Christian texts."

"Could it be an attack on the Church?" Tom asked, wondering if there was a simpler explanation.

"I don't think so. There have been other reports that something strange is going on. John Hampton from Toronto is certain he was followed from the airport on his way home. And Ian Frazer, from Sheffield, thinks someone is watching his house."

"It sounds like something's going on but are you sure they're not just coincidences?"

"I wish that were true, but there's been too many for it just to be chance. What I really called for was to see if you think we should call off my visit next week I don't want to involve you in any of this."

"You surely are joking. Give up our fishing just because there may be a little danger afoot. I want you to know, *laddie*, that my ancestors fought alongside Robert the Bruce at Bannockburn. The McDonald Clan never backs away from a fight." But after he had hung up, Tom McDonald wondered what was going on.

The crowd in the waiting area at Trudeau Airport was getting larger. An Alitalia flight from Rome had arrived twenty minutes earlier and the arrivals hall was getting very crowded. Tom McDonald was having trouble seeing the passengers as they began to emerge.

It was even harder for Pierre Molatov. He kept looking at the photograph and description of Marius Sorensen that he had received from Balinska, as well as the flight and time. The flight had been delayed in Amsterdam and didn't land at Dorval until 6 p.m.

There was a break in the crowd and Molatov saw him just as he was leaving the customs hall. As he came out a man with thinning hair detached himself from the group and moved forward to meet him.

"How was the flight, Marius?" Tom asked taking a suitcase and leading him towards the exit.

"Long. I was nearly four hours in Schiphol, which was perhaps as well because my departure gate was at the opposite end from the arrival gate. I wish there were a direct flight from Copenhagen. Anyway enough of that. How are you and what are our plans?"

Molatov was close behind. He didn't know whether they would take a cab or if they had a car. To be sure he didn't lose them, he had an airport limousine waiting. He had told the driver to be ready to go as soon as he came back. McDonald and Sorensen walked to the short term car park,

Molatov got into the limousine. "Move up so we can see the exit from the parking garage, and then follow them. Don't make it obvious. There's a hundred dollars in it for you providing you don't lose them."

Tom worked his way through the airport traffic, before saying, "I thought we'd get a quick bite and then let you get some sleep. How long have you been travelling?"

"I left my house at 8:30, 2:30 a.m. Montreal time and it's now 7 p.m. That's a long day, even by my standards."

"It's a long day by anyone's standards. You must be exhausted. So why don't we drive straight to my place and while you unpack I'll fix us something to eat. Then you can tell me what's been happening."

Marius was having trouble staying awake, said, "If that's not too much trouble I'd appreciate it. I'm not that hungry anyway, and I'd sooner wait until tomorrow to fill you in."

The limousine followed them as they drove west across Sherbrooke and into Westmount, where they turned right onto Clarke Avenue. Molatov told the driver to stop at the bottom and wait. He watched the car turn down the ramp of an apartment building.

"Okay drive up," he told the driver. He made a note of the address then told his driver to take him back to his hotel. Back in his room he went to work on the computer. Using the car registration, which he had written down, together with the address, it didn't take him long to find that his name was Tom McDonald. Since he knew, Sorensen was a professor in Copenhagen he did a quick check of the faculty at McGill. He found McDonald's name there as well He checked his watch, 8:30 p.m., which made it 2:30 a.m. in Spain, too early to call Balinska. He would wait until midnight before calling. He shut down his computer and went downstairs to get dinner.

Next morning, after breakfast, each with a cup of coffee, Tom asked Marius to give him more details about the *Dialogues* and who he thought was behind all the cloak and dagger stuff.

"I don't know and that's why it's a concern, especially the disappearance of the two priests. I'm beginning to think they were kidnapped or something worse."

"But who would want to do that? From what you've told me all that you're doing is pulling together research that already exists. How could anyone be bothered by that?"

"I agree, but it's as if someone out there is trying to stop us."

"But who?" Tom said, looking at his friend, still thinking that he may have got things out of proportion. "Are you thinking of stopping? What about the others? Do they feel that way?"

"Not at all. If anything it's made everyone more determined. Apparently somebody out there is worried by what we're turning up and that has made it more important than ever that we finish it."

"Well, you can count me in. Whatever I can do." Tom said, then regretted it. He still didn't believe that it was anything serious and he had enough on his plate right now. Besides a paper he was giving, the publisher was on his back to finish the first draft of a book he was co-authoring.

"Well I do need some help but I think it is taking advantage of our friendship."

Tom could see that Marius was hesitant to ask, and he thought of saying no, but he knew he couldn't. "What are friends for? Go ahead and ask."

Marius described the database and the network that had been set up and how he was concerned that if someone had managed to get into his computer, they might be able to corrupt or destroy the database. "What we need is a second site as a backup."

"And you'd like that to be McGill?"

"Yes, if possible. I realize it's asking a lot. The last thing I want to do is cause problems, so please say no if it does. I'll fully understand."

Tom smiled. "You haven't met Cindy have you?"

"No. I've spoken to her briefly on the phone when she has answered it. Where is she anyway?"

"Away for a few days visiting her mother but she'll be back tomorrow, and you can meet her then. What you don't know is she's director of the McGill computer system networks so she can probably fit you in."

After that they talked about the conference, then left to go to Le Baron on St. Laurent to check out the latest fishing equipment.

The next day they met Cindy for coffee at 'Beavertails' across from McGill and Marius explained how their system was set up and why he needed a backup in case anything should go wrong.

"But you keep backup tapes don't you, off-site, in case of fire or other disasters," Cindy queried.

"Yes the data administrator looks after it but the company we use, *SafeWithUs* is well known and so is their location."

"Well so long as it is just backup I can fit you in but not online access; we're having trouble coping with existing demands from students and faculty."

Marius had secretly hoped that they could duplicate the system in Copenhagen, including online access, but it was obvious that wasn't going to happen. Instead, they agreed to set up a secure data line so that a backup of the Copenhagen system could be sent once a day.

The next day Pierre Molatov called Balinska and updated him. He had already told him, in his previous report about Tom McDonald and

Sorensen. Now he added that there had been a meeting between those two and a third person, a woman, in a coffee shop. Sorensen had given her a small package. "I was able to get a photograph of the three of them, and I'm checking who she is and should know by tomorrow."

"Thanks Find out everything you can about her and her connection to the other two and, if possible, what was in the package. She must be at the university, but we need to know exactly what she does and who she is. And put a twenty-four hour tail on them, I want to know everywhere they go and who they meet. Keep calling me every day, same time, with an update. And include the photo."

It took Molatov two days to get all the information; her name was Cindy Preston, and she was a professor at McGill. He discovered that Preston and McDonald were living together, McDonald and Sorensen were both anthropology profs and Preston was in charge of the computer systems at McGill.

He got a call, at 5 a.m, from the investigator who was tailing them, to say that McDonald and Sorensen were loading equipment into an SUV, under the cover of darkness. Molatov told him to stay with them and phone him with a report every hour.

The SUV took Sherbrooke to Papineau, then south on the Jacques Cartier Bridge across the St. Lawrence and then north on Blvd. Taschereau and onto AutoRoute 20. They stayed on it for the next sixty miles as it snaked its way into the heart of the Eastern Townships. At Drummondville, they turned south on Route 143 past Saint-Nicephore before turning left onto a small dirt road. The operator decided not follow them immediately, there was no other traffic, and he would be easy to spot. He continued down 143 for a few miles, made a U-turn and drove back to the dirt road. The SUV was nowhere in sight, so he followed the dirt road until he saw it stopped by the side of a cabin on the bank of the river. The two men were unloading their equipment: fishing rods, a large food cooler, and two holdalls. It looked like they were here for a few days of fishing. The road followed the river, and he continued along it until he was out of sight of the cabin. Then he stopped and tried to phone Molatov but there was no service, and he had to wait until he got back to Saint-Nicephore.

"Shit," was Molotov's immediate response; then he added, "keep tailing them until you're sure that the fishing is not just a cover and that no-one else joins them."

That night at midnight Molatov called his boss and gave him his report. The investigator had confirmed that the two professors had spent the whole day fly fishing. Balinska was disappointed to learn it was just a fishing trip, but his interest picked up when he heard that Preston worked in the computer department.

"Say that again."

"Okay," said Molatov, "she is the Director of Computer Systems at McGill, and she lives with Tom McDonald. Didn't you get the photograph I emailed it to you this morning?"

There was a shuffling noise as Balinska checked the papers on his desk. "I've found it. Messi handles my emails, and he must have put it on my desk with all the other ones. Keep up the surveillance and call me tomorrow."

After he had hung up, Balinska looked at the photo. The three people were clearly visible, but their faces were not very clear, although he recognized Sorensen, who was passing a package to the woman. He wondered if Messi could enlarge it so they could get an idea what was in the package. He called him and asked him.

Ten minutes later Messi called back and told Balinska that the package was the size and type used for magnetic tapes used to backup computer systems. "My best guess is that Sorensen had a backup of the *Dialogue* system and was giving it to the woman so she can make another backup."

"Hole in one, Messi, you've nailed it. The woman is called Cindy Preston, and she runs the computers at McGill. So Sorensen is handing her a backup of the system to store on their computer. Right?"

"That makes sense but why would Sorensen be giving it to her. We know from our visit to Copenhagen that he's an anthropologist, not a techie."

"Well, maybe that's what we need to know. See if you can find out."

Balinska was feeling good. Now there were seven! Or eight if you included the woman. He broke his own rule and wrote their names on a pad of paper.

Father Emile	*Munich; deceased*
Father Michael,	*Toledo; in Sotano*
John Hampton,	*Toronto; being followed*
Ian Frazer	*Sheffield, being followed*
Michael Kinghaven	*Stockholm, being followed*
Marius Sorensen	*Copenhagen, friend of McDonald*
Tom McDonald	*Univ. of McGill, Montreal*
Cindy Preston	*Computer Center, McGill*

Dialogue database probably in Copenhagen
Backup at McGill

And soon he would be able to have them join him at the Castillo, with a one-way ticket to the Sotano. Including a woman. He had heard that LSD makes them quite erotic. Something to look forward to.

Everything was coming together. If Messi could destroy their data, he would bring the rest back here. That would be an end to it. He didn't know how many there were but once the rest realized what had happened, they would call it a day. If they knew what was good for them!

Now that Sorensen had given them the Montreal link, he may as well be brought in. He called Molatov and asked him to find out Sorensen's travel details. It would be easier to take him in Copenhagen. Once Balinska had him, he'd make him talk and tell him where their data was kept and how many copies there were. And this time he'd make sure to keep him alive long enough to get the information.

* * *

Kastrup Airport, Copenhagen

His flight touched down at 11 a.m. After collecting his luggage, he wheeled them outside and looked for a cab. Before he could find one, a uniformed chauffeur approached him and asked, "Professor Sorensen?"

"Yes, why?"

"I have a car waiting for you. It's over here," he said pointing to a long black Cadillac parked at the kerb.

"But I didn't order a car," he said becoming a little concerned.

The chauffeur, who was a big man, grabbed him by the arm and pulled him towards the car, opened the rear door and pushed him inside. There was another man in the back seat, who leaned over and closed the door before saying, "Relax professor were going for a little ride." As he saw the look on his face, he added, "Actually it's rather a long ride, so relax and enjoy." He took a syringe from his pocket and jabbed it into Marius' neck. Within ten seconds, he was unconscious.

The chauffeur collected Marius' bags and put them in the trunk, before starting the car and beginning the long journey to Seville. Once they were clear of the airport the man in the back seat pulled on a white coat, which had been in a bag on the floor. The chauffeur opened the glove compartment and removed a set of papers. They authorized the transfer of Stephan Jorgensen from the Amager Hospital in Copenhagen to the Hospital San Juan de Dios in Seville. There was also a passport with Marius' photograph, in the name of Stephan Jorgensen.

Chapter 43

Charpentier was looking at the latest report from Morse. There were two problems mentioned: How was Balinska involved? How could they get into the Castillo?

They were probably the same question, or at least opposite sides, of the same issue. From what he had heard about him, knowing how he was involved would probably be enough to get a search warrant; and getting inside would almost certainly lead to finding out Balinska's role. Trouble was they couldn't solve either!

He wondered if Balinska appeared in the database. Maybe someone else had run into him. He opened the search engine and typed in 'Balinska'. It didn't take long. No hits. Nothing. So much for that.

Then he remembered something. When he had insisted that Morse explain what his 'personal business' was, he revealed that the character he was chasing was called Radovic but had changed his name to Balinska. He entered the name Radovic and got three hits.

The first was a copy of the outstanding warrant for murder, from Vladivostok, together with prints found at the scene. Unfortunately, they didn't match any the Russian police had on file. There was a note attached to the warrant that his last known residence was Canada.

The second hit was a request, from a detective in Munich, for a fingerprint match. There was a partial match with the ones from the murder scene in Vladivostok but no name. They had sent the request to Canada. They had come up with a match to prints taken in a kidnapping and murder in Toronto. The name Radovic was mentioned as a possibility; it could not be proved since they didn't have his prints on file. They couldn't even find him.

The third hit sounded strange. It was a reply from Canada that in searching records for Radovic they had found a death certificate for him.

All three responses had been sent to Detective Millar, who probably had closed the investigation. Millar didn't know that Radovic was still alive with a new identity.

Charpentier found the address for the detective and sent an email explaining the identity switch.

Chapter 44

Computer Center
Castillo de Chipiona
Sanlucar, Spain

Messi had started the job of finding where the *Dialogues* kept their data. What he was looking for were websites that appeared on both computers. He began by looking at the information from the *Trojan Horse* that was monitoring the internet activity on Sorensen's office computer. Comparing the cookies with those on Father Emile's captured computer, would show him which ones they both visited.

> *Put simply, in Balinska speak:*
>
> > *Whenever a computer connects to a website, the website leaves a' cookie' behind. The cookie contains the location of the website and how to get there. This makes it much faster, the next time the computer requests that website.*

He compared the cookies on both computers. He found the following match.

> *On Sorensen's computer:*   *cookie:msore_000@au.cop.dk*
> *On Father Emile's:*   *cookie:ecald_000@au.cop.dk*

The he found the internet address of the website *au.cop.dk*:

> *Every website has an address, consisting of four numbers. For au.cop.dk it was: 217.116.232.205*

Next Messi used another app that showed that *217.116.232.205* was the address of a computer in Copenhagen that provided Internet Services to its clients. One of them was Andersen University.

There was a registry called RIPE NCC, for Europe and the Middle East that listed information about databases.

This could be it; would the Dialogue database be listed?

He carefully typed *'dialogue'* and pressed Enter. A few moments later a mass of database names spiraled down his computer screen. There were scores of *dialogue* databases registered. Too many to check them all.

Most of them contained the word 'dialogue' as part of the longer names, such as *Dialogue Reports* and *Registry of Dialogue Conferences*. Only a few were called *Dialogue*. Messi stopped for a moment and rubbed his eyes which were aching from staring at the computer screen. He needed a break, but he was too close now.

An hour later, working on autopilot, he found it. A *'Dialogue'* entry that pointed to one of the addresses allocated to Andersen University.

He checked the faculty list for the university and found that one of the anthropology professors was none other than Marius Sorensen. This had to be the one he was looking for.

He made sure everything was logged and went back to his room to have a deserved rest and an even more deserved smoke. Maybe even some nose candy.

Four hours later, he returned, feeling refreshed from a nap and relaxed from the candy. He went over his notes. He felt confident now that the *Dialogue* database was on one of the computers at Andersen University.

Messi now knew where to start looking. Now all he had to do was hack his way in. This was the fun part.

> *Every time a computer connects to an external device or service, such as a printer or the Internet it connects through a port which can be seen on the sides or back of a computer. The internet uses a cable that connects a port to a modem. If the connection is wireless, it uses an internet card inside the computer to connect*

to the modem, which in turn connects to the Internet. Whichever way it is done every connection opens up a two-way channel in and out of the computer.

A hacker first finds out which 'ports' are open and then figures out how to send a small program—called a script—he has written through one of those ports. The script is designed to send information back to the hacker, on what is inside the target computer. It can also change or destroy some or all of the data inside it.

One of the most common ways to get the script inside the computer is to hitch a ride on an application that already has a port open. It is like hitching a ride on a freight train. Once you find an open door, you can jump in and close it behind you. When you reach your destination (inside the computer) you open the door and jump out.

Some applications have glitches in them known as vulnerabilities (open doors). Once the hacker finds a glitch, he can embed his script in the program, which carries it into the computer.

Messi used something called a port scan gave to see which 'ports' were open, on the computer and which applications were using them. Then he looked at the list looking for one that had a door open.

He found one and use it to get his *script* inside the computer. His *script* had been written to look for the *Dialogue* database, by searching for the word DIALOG.

The name could have been encrypted so when it didn't find it, it rearranged DIALOG, one shift at a time:
[for a shift of +1, D→E, I→J etc.]

> *EJBMPH*   *(shift +1)*
> *FKCNQI*   *(shift +2)*
> *All the way to*
> *JOGRUM*   *(shift +6)*

When it failed, he tried negative shifts and finally got a match with a shift of – 4; ZEWHKC

Code match found, beginning at 5D09AD

This was the starting address where the match started. Beginning there he dumped [printed] 16 letters:

ZEWHKCQAIAIXANOO

When he applied a shift of + 4 it became:

DIALOGUEMEMBERSS.

He had it! He had found it! In a similar moment of discovery, some Greek dude had yelled 'Eureka' and run through the streets naked. Messi not to be outdone yelled, "Shit! Fucking Shit!" and pumped the air with his fist.

He dumped out the next 256 characters and converted them to text:

WNERKWBKJNRJAKNQFHIIIAEIAJNJIKSA
ACWAIIPEKAWAONAC213V11GQIWJANHNZTEK
KAHAOLICJAZWNYWUXNUOLDYGOOYWN
PJDOJAVEHWHHWLKNHN1LEQJE1W2NZOLP

String after shift of 4

ARIVOAFONRVNEORUJLMMMEIMENRNMOWE
EGAEMMTIOEAESREG213Z11KUMANERL
RDXIOOELESPMGNEDARCAYBRYSPHCKSSCARTN
HSNEZILALLAPORLR1PIUNI1A2RDSPT

He looked closely at the characters, but nothing obvious jumped out at him. The door opened and Balinska came into the room. This was abnormal; Messi's office and room were in a building on the opposite side of the compound from Balinska and the Archdeacon. Usually, they simply phoned him when they needed him.

"You're up and about early, what are you doing."

Messi looked at his watch, it was 5:30 a.m. "I haven't been to bed I was up all night trying to access the server where they keep the *Dialogue* information."

"And did you?" Balinska asked.

"Yes. I found it on a server at Andersen University in Copenhagen, where Sorensen is a prof. I'm sure this is what we're looking for and incidentally I think it confirms what we suspected, that the tape Sorensen gave the women in Montreal was a copy of this database."

Balinska stood thinking for a moment, realizing how close they were. "What happens next?"

"Hopefully I can find their passwords which will let me go in and delete all their information, names, dates, research notes the whole ball of wax."

Balinska thought, *Ball of Wax. Again!* Then he asked, "Can you wipe it out. All of it? Then I can remove the rest of them. Mission accomplished."

"It certainly looks like it, but right now, I need to get some sleep. I've been staring at codes and ciphers for the last twelve hours and I'm seeing gremlins in front of my eyes. Once I've hit my bed for a few hours, I'll finish cracking the code. But no interruptions!"

"Understood. How about a meeting at five o clock this afternoon, which should let you get a few hours' shut-eye and finish smashing the code."

Messi was about to correct him, but he was too tired. Balinska walked back to his own office and phoned the Archdeacon to give him the news.

Balinska felt disappointed. He realized how much he was enjoying himself and how much he wanted it to continue: the challenge, the chase, the Sotano. Then the water treatment followed by a session in room 19. Maybe he could wipe out all memory of the *Dialogues* and then erase the people as well. Wouldn't that be something?

Maybe I'll check if Father Michael is feeling thirsty!

He laughed at his own joke.

Chapter 45

Room of the Apostles
Castillo de Chipiona
Sanlucar, Spain

As he entered through his door, all the Regents stood and waited for him to speak. He took his time and looked around the room. They were all present and he acknowledged each one individually.

After they had recited the Creed he told them to be seated and once they were, he began. "Welcome to our monthly assembly. This is a very important meeting; for the first time you will be able to hear a live report from one of the *Dialogue* conferences." A murmur of interest ran round the room as he said this. He waited for it to subside then continued, "First let me give you a report on our progress, so far. As you know, we already have three of the *Dialogues* in our custody. Just a few days ago our computer expert identified three more and also told me he is close to getting access to their network. Once he does that he will be able to get all their names as well as destroying the information they have collected. Our mission will have been accomplished. "I must compliment Baltic for giving us the information that pointed us in the right direction." He paused allowing the Regent for the Baltic to enjoy his moment.

"What you are about to hear is an overview of a recent meeting of the *Dialogues,* read by one of their members. Some of you have met Senor Balinska," there were some murmurs, hard to tell whether they were favorable or not. "He obtained this recording. How he did so is not relevant. What you are about to hear is about the origins of the Biblical Gospels. I must warn you that what you will hear is both blasphemous and heretical. These people are Apostates. *The Devil's Disciples!"*

He walked over to a small table containing a computer. Messi had set it up before the meeting ready to play. He pressed the start button.

Hello.

This recording is an abbreviated version of a meeting at the Kingsbridge Conference Center, approximately thirty miles north of Toronto. It was organized by the Dialogue group and was attended by six of its members. It took place over two days, and the full recording is available should anyone wish to hear it in its entirety. The discussion focussed on the origins of the canonical gospels, the first four books of the New Testament.

Up until the fourteenth century, the Biblical record was accepted as the word of God, unchallenged and unequivocal. The Renaissance that began in that same century created a new freedom in art and literature. The scientific revolution that paralleled it liberated man's understanding of the laws of nature. Together they gave rise to new ideas and new confidence in man's ability to explain the world around him. This brought about an assurance, sufficient to begin to challenge the authority of the Church.

In the eighteenth century, the Biblical accounts of the life of Jesus were examined and scrutinized. What, until now, had been taken as absolute, was dissected and debated. Nothing was sacrosanct, not even the Bible. A new approach had been developed that was used to provide a new and different explanation, in particular, a fresh look at the man they called Jesus.

The intent was to see him as a man, not a deity; to strip away the religious veneer and examine the man behind the myth. A new tool was used called 'form criticism.' It broke the Bible stories into their different forms— parables, letters, pronouncements— and placed them in context to establish what exactly the writer was trying to say? And when they were written!

Using this technique, scholars were able to show that the gospels were made up of two very different structures; the sayings of Jesus, and a narrative of his life and crucifixion. Also, they claimed that the gospels should not be taken literally because the authors had an underlying purpose; what today we would call a hidden agenda.

The Archdeacon stopped the recording at this point. "This is a suitable time to break for lunch. This afternoon we will have our usual meeting with your regional reports. Tomorrow morning you will hear the rest of the recording. That will give you time to absorb what you have just heard."

He listened to the conversations as they ate lunch. Snippets he heard, convinced him he had done his job. Their loathing of *Dialogues* was now based on hard evidence that they were trying to destroy both the Church and the Gospels.

Chapter 46

Room of the Apostles
Castillo de Chipiona
Sanlucar, Spain

"Good morning. I trust you slept well. Yesterday you heard how the *Dialogues* are trying to undermine our Church and our beliefs. Today you will hear how they are attacking the very foundation of our faith." He turned the recording on.

> *It is generally agreed that the Gospel of Mark was the first one written, around 70 CE, and that Mathew and Luke used much of Mark's gospel in theirs. However, there were also many verses not in Mark (mainly sayings of Jesus). Religious scholars proposed a two source explanation for this; that Mathew and Luke copied from Mark's Gospel, but they also had had access to an earlier document that was not available to Mark. And this document contained the other sayings of Jesus.*

> *This document has never been found. Either because it was a sayings gospel, passed on by word of mouth or because once it had been incorporated into Mathew and Luke's gospel, it was no longer needed. It has been recreated by reverse engineering and is known as the Q document, from Quelle, the German for the word source.*

> *Scholars from many universities studied the document and proposed that the contents of Q could be subdivided into three stages. Each phase had occurred at different times. The first one, called Q1 contained 'wisdom*

sayings' of Jesus; his parables, and rules for living. The second,, which came later is very different; made up of apocalyptic statements about the end of the world. It is referred to as Q2 and seems to make Q1 redundant. If it is all about to end giving out rules on how to live seems a little pointless. Q3 elevated Jesus to the Son of God.

In Q1, there is no mention of Jesus as Messiah or anything that makes him God-like. But there is evidence of communities springing up that tried to follow the teachings of Jesus, what today we might call communes. They were called the people of Q1. But something was missing. These early believers were Jews, just as Jesus was, and a fundamental part of Judaism is a belief in the coming of the 'Mashiach'. Scholars believe that the pronouncements of Q2 were an attempt to rectify this by recasting Jesus as the Jewish Messiah.

In the Jewish faith the 'Mashiach' will be a great political and military leader, descended from King David, but he will be a man, not a god. And the first gospel, Mark's, agreed with this. It originally ended at the empty tomb, which suggests that Jesus was a man who was crucified and died. End of story!

His resurrection and His appearances to the disciples were added later. These additional sayings, called Q3, elevated Jesus from a man to a deity; from the teacher of Q1 to the prophet of Q2 to the son of God of Q3.

Who was the real Jesus? Christians insist that He is in all of Q, but it is Q3 that is the basis of the Christian faith. The resurrection is the foundation of their belief, the triumph of good over evil, the salvation of the soul.

Proponents of Q think he was a man whose wisdom sayings are in Q1. They insist the evidence shows that

Q2 and Q3 were added later to satisfy the requirements of the Jewish and Christian communities. There was no resurrection. The story of His life ended at the empty tomb.

The Archdeacon turned the recording off. "Now you can see the dark intent of their work. They would even tear away our Lord's resurrection. But they will not succeed. We have them in our sights and we will soon make them answer for their heresy. Like those who denied out faith five hundred years ago, they too will burn in hell."

There was a chorus of assent from the Regents. They would oppose this evil with every fiber of their bodies. Father Bernardo waited. He did not speak. He didn't need to. Their fury was evident in their expressions. It was almost physical, a tangible, palpable anger that filled the room.

He had done what he had set out to do. He had focused their minds. Given them a target at which to direct their hatred. Enough but not everything, that was the secret; only what they needed to know. Sufficient to bend them to their task. No more.

There was a final section. The Archdeacon had deliberately removed it. It would not help, it would only confuse. He took the player back to his office and listened to the last part once more, before destroying it.

In 1945 at a place called Nag Hammadi, in Egypt, a local farmer found a sealed earthenware jar that contained thirteen leather-bound documents written on papyrus, dating back to the second century. They were probably buried by monks from a nearby monastery because they contained non-canonical books that were considered heretical at the time.

One of the documents was the gospel of Thomas, which no one knew existed. It contained only the sayings of Jesus with no narrative; over a third of them could be found in Q1. There is no mention of the crucifixion or the resurrection, neither is there any mention of Jesus as the Jewish Messiah. It added strong support to the theory that Q1 was genuine but Q2 and Q3 were added later to shoehorn it into Jewish belief and Greek culture.

But the evidence for Q is not overwhelming. There are scholarly objections that have to be considered. One of the arguments against it is that if the sayings were so important, why weren't they committed to paper, why were they only passed on by word of mouth? And as everyone knows word of mouth is inaccurate; it is embellished as it is told and retold until the message has little resemblance to the original. In rebuttal proponents of Q point out that since the sayings were incorporated into the Gospels of Matthew and Luke, it had served its purpose and was no longer necessary. This theory is supported by the record of Papias the Bishop of the Christian community in Hierapolis. He began to collect sayings of Jesus but only from people who had heard them from the apostles themselves. Papias recorded them in a five-volume book, which tragically has been lost; only fragments remain. Many scholars identify this book with the Q document."

But all of this is conjecture, what lawyers call circumstantial evidence. It does not carry the full weight of factual evidence.

Perhaps the most damaging argument against Q is the validity of form criticism itself. Especially the method of dividing the stories of Jesus into small pieces. This separates the individual text from the context that frames it. It's a little like cutting the Mona Lisa into a hundred rectangles and studying each one separately. You could consider in detail the brush strokes, the pigments in the colors, the type of canvas used, the age of the paint and so on. But you would completely miss the most important aspect of the painting that can only be appreciated by looking at the picture as a whole. It

is only when viewed in its entirety that the full beauty
and meaning is revealed.

*The critics of form criticism, make the same observation.
It is only when viewed in its entirety that the full meaning
and majesty of Christ's life, death and resurrection is
revealed.*

Chapter 47

Room 19, Sotano
Castillo de Chipiona
Sanlucar, Spain

Father Michael was naked and fastened to the 'electric chair' in room 19. His wrists were strapped to the arms and a belt around his chest prevented his body from falling forward. His ankles were strapped together and fastened to a bracket at the bottom of the chair.

Balinska had subjected him to the 'tortura del aqua'. He didn't expect to learn much. He already knew most of what the Priest could tell them anyway. But he wanted the satisfaction of 'breaking' him.

After half an hour, the only words the Father had said were "Why are you doing this?"

"To get you ready for room 19, Father. The water is just to soften you up."

He had two of the security guards carry him to room 19 and strap him to the chair. He dismissed the guards.Now there was just the two of them.

"Alright, Holy Father let's begin with a truth serum. Maybe an injection of scopolamine might help you to talk . . . If not we'll try a few jolts of electricity."

This was the moment that Balinska loved. This power over someone else; to decide if they would live or die."

He went over to the cabinet in the corner of the room, removed a vial of scopolamine and filled a syringe. He injected it into Father Michaels upper arm then sat down to wait for it to take effect.

Not much happened, except the Father seemed drowsy and he kept opening and closing his eyes as if he was having trouble seeing.

After fifteen minutes, Balinska couldn't wait any longer, he was eager to try the electricity. He stood up and attached two of the electric cables to Father Michael's temples, one on each side.

"Now I'm going to fry your brain a little. When you're ready to do what I want, just move your fingers."

Father Michael tried to look at Balinska, but his eyelids were too heavy and he felt dizzy; everything was spinning around him.

Balinska went over to the side of the room and sat down in front of the voltage regulator. He turned it on and set it to twenty volts. *He would start small and increase it gradually. Like a cat with a mouse.*

He looked at the priest and closed the switch. Father Michael's head jerked backward. Balinska turned it off then on again with the same result. He repeated this six times. Next he set the regulator to thirty volts and flipped the switch. The result was the same, but more pronounced. The Priest's hands never moved. It didn't matter. Balinska didn't care about the confession now. This was too satisfying to stop.

But he knew that if he continued increasing the voltage he would soon destroy the Father's brain and that would be the end. Which was not what he wanted! It would last longer if he ran the shock through the body rather than the brain. He removed the connectors from his temples and attached them to each hand. Then he repeated the process.

This time the priest's entire body jerked. He lost track of time, slowly increasing the voltage to prolong the pleasure and the pain.

He was amazed that the old man's body could last this long. Ninety volts! He increased it to one hundred and flipped the switch. Father Michael's body shuddered violently then sagged back into the chair. His head fell forward onto his chest, not moving.

Chapter 48

Computer Center
Castillo de Chipiona
Sanlucar, Spain

Antonio Messi was sweating. He had the meeting with Balinska in three hours and he had promised him that he would have cracked the code by then, but so far he couldn't see any pattern in the coded text.

ARIVOAFONRVNEORUJLMMMEIMENRNMOWE
EGAEMMTIOEAESREG213Z11KUMANERLRDX
IOOELESPMGNEDARCAYBRYSPHCKS
SCARTNHSNEZILALLAPORLR1PIUNI1A2RDSPT

Then he saw it; 128 characters could be the output from a matrix of 8x16 or 16x8 with DIALOGUEMEMBERSS as the key.

He tried 8x16 matrix, arranging the text in eight rows of 16 characters, but nothing jumped out at him. It was 4:54 p.m. He was out of time. Picking up his notes he headed for Balinska's office.

"So Antonio Messi tell me that we've got them by the short and curlies and all we have to do is throw the switch."

Messi looked at him. "Not yet but I'm close and need a little more time."

Balinska was furious. He had told the Archdeacon that Messi had found all their names and was ready to destroy the data. Now he looked like a fool. He controlled himself; "Okay Antonio. I know you've been burning the midnight oil to get this done, but you told me you would have it solved by now. How much longer do you need? What about tomorrow at 10 a.m. that should give you time?"

Back in his office Messi rearranged the code into 16 rows with 8 characters in each row.

ARIVOAFONRVNEORUJLMMMEIMENRNMOW
EEGAEMMTIOEAESREG213Z11KUMANE
RLRDXIOOELESPMGNEDARCAYBRYS
PHCKSSCARTNHSNEZILALLAPORLR1PIUNI
1A2RDSPT

A	R	I	V	O	A	F	O
N	R	V	N	E	O	R	U
J	L	M	M	M	E	I	M
E	N	R	N	M	O	W	E
E	G	A	E	M	M	T	I
O	E	A	E	S	R	E	G
2	1	3	Z	1	1	K	U
M	A	N	E	R	L	R	D
X	I	O	O	E	L	E	S
P	M	G	N	E	D	A	R
C	A	Y	B	R	Y	S	P
H	C	K	S	S	C	A	R
T	N	H	S	N	E	Z	I
L	A	L	L	A	P	O	R
L	R	1	P	I	U	N	I
1	A	2	R	D	S	P	T

Then he added the key vertically

D	3	A	R	I	V	O	A	F	O
I	8	N	R	V	N	E	O	R	U
A	1	J	L	M	M	M	E	I	M
L	9	E	N	R	N	M	O	W	E
O	12	E	G	A	E	M	M	T	I
G	7	O	E	A	E	S	R	E	G
U	16	2	1	3	Z	1	1	K	U
E	4	M	A	N	E	R	L	R	D
M	10	X	I	O	O	E	L	E	S
E	5	P	M	G	N	E	D	A	R
M	11	C	A	Y	B	R	Y	S	P
B	2	H	C	K	S	S	C	A	R
E	6	T	N	H	S	N	E	Z	I
R	13	L	A	L	L	A	P	O	R
S	14	L	R	1	P	I	U	N	I
S	15	1	A	2	R	D	S	P	T

Then he rearranged the rows in the order of the key.

A1	J	L	M	M	M	E	I	M
B2	H	C	K	S	S	C	A	R
D3	A	R	I	V	O	A	F	O
E4	M	A	N	E	R	L	R	D
B5	P	M	G	N	E	D	A	R
E6	T	N	H	S	N	E	Z	I
G7	O	E	A	E	S	R	E	G
I8	N	R	V	N	E	O	R	U
L9	E	N	R	N	M	O	W	E
M10	X	I	O	O	E	L	E	S
M11	C	A	Y	B	R	Y	S	P
O12	E	G	A	E	M	M	T	I
R13	L	A	L	L	A	P	O	R
S14	L	R	1	P	I	U	N	I
S15	1	A	2	R	D	S	P	T
U16	2	1	3	Z	1	1	K	U

There it was, clear and exact, staring him in the face.
He compared it to the list of names they already had:

> *Emile Calderon, Michael Rodriguez, John Hampton,*
> *Ian Frazer, Michael Kinghaven, Marius Sorensen, Tom*
> *McDonald, Cindy Preston.*

McDonald and Preston were not on it and LCRAMNER and
MSEVENSEN were new names. But he had enough information to
begin his attack. He could check the others later. He noted the names
and what he thought must be the passwords.

User Name	Password
jhampton	*excell12*
mkinghav	*royal123*
msorense	*mermaid1*
ecaldero	*olympus1*
mrodrigu	*espiritu*

This would let him get into the data and maybe they would finally
realize how important his skills were. Without him, they would still be
playing cops and robbers. He sat looking at the list enjoying the moment.

But something was bothering him. He didn't want to discredit
himself and he certainly wouldn't say this to the other two but in terms
of encryption algorithms, this one was from kindergarten. Any hacker
still in his diapers could have cracked it.

He phoned Balinska to give him the news, but he wasn't there. Messi
did not bother leaving a message, they already had a meeting scheduled
for tomorrow; it could wait until then. Leaving an access point open
so he could get back in, he closed everything down after saving his
working files.

The next day Messi was up early anxious to see if the username and
codes worked. He opened the laptop they had taken from Munich and
typed the address of the server in Copenhagen. He scanned through the
front page on the server and went to the main menu.

Near the bottom he found an entry for *Dialogues* and clicked on the link which got him the login screen:

Login Screen

user name: _____

password: _____

He entered ecaldero and the password olympus1 then pressed the Enter key; the main Dialogue Menu was displayed.

Dialogue Menu

Christian Origins
Cosmology
Gender Issues
Communications
Administration

Messi looked at the menu, and clicked on the Administration link and got a message

You don't currently have permission to access this Folder

He was half expecting this. If the *Dialogue* system checked the incoming IP against the IP of Kinghaven's computer, the system could go into lock down and force a scan and disinfection. He should have told them to get Kinghaven's machine, but it was too late now.

He logged out and then logged in again, this time using Kinghaven's username and password. As he feared, when he hit enter he got a warning message:

Warning: This computer is not registered to this
address. Do you want to Continue?
YES   NO

No turning back now; he
clicked the YES button and
was into the Administration
screen:

Messi let out a sigh of relief.
Almost there. He clicked
on 'Update System' and
the Update Menu appeared.

Administration Menu

Restore Data only from Backup
Restore System from Backup
Backup Data only
Backup System
Update System
Print System Log
Edit Users and Passwords

Update Menu

Christian Origins
Cosmology
Gender Issues
Administration

This was what he needed. He would corrupt the first three selections by placing a script in each of them. Every time anyone accessed one of those screens, the script would change the data slightly, not enough for anyone to notice. After a time, however, all the small changes would add up and the system would be useless.

IT WAS GOING TO WORK!!

If he had not been so tired, he would have done a happy dance. He made a note of where the code was and logged out. Strange but his elation was tinged with regret that he was destroying someone else's work; his satisfaction came from hacking his way in, proving he was better. Leaving a message behind.

That was enough for him. But he had agreed to neutralize the data, so he began to jot down a list of the necessary steps ready for the meeting, then went back to his room and lit up a joint.

Chapter 49

Papal Apartment
Vatican City

Cardinal Karmazin was shown into the Papal apartment and while they were waiting for coffee to be brought they discussed the general state of the Church. Karmazin gave him the latest news from Ukraine and the rapid growth in church attendance after the Soviets had withdrawn.

Once coffee had arrived and all the servants dismissed they moved on to the real purpose of the meeting.

"I am pleased," Holy Father, "to report excellent progress. There are already three of the *Dialogues* in the Sotano at the Castillo."

"Good news, Cardinal. What about their reports; the research they have already completed?"

"Even better news; the computer expert has gained access to their data and is now planning how to destroy it."

"If he has access why hasn't he destroyed it?"

"I asked the Archdeacon the same question. Apparently it's not that straightforward. They make daily backup copies, in case of accidents. He has to know their location so he can destroy those at the same time."

The Pope took a sip of his coffee while he decided how to express his concern. He wanted it finished before any of it found its way back to him. He cleared his throat and looked directly at Karmazin. "I was expecting this business to be wrapped up by now. When will they be ready? How soon can it be done?"

Karmazin didn't like the tone of the questions. It sounded as if the Pope was panicking. "Is there a deadline? If so let me know and I will convey it to the Archdeacon."

"No, and I apologise if I gave that impression. I am just anxious. I don't want to start the reforms we've discussed until the *Dialogues* are closed down. Keep me informed. I think in future you should send me a progress report. There are eyes and ears everywhere in the Vatican. We don't want anyone becoming suspicious."

"Indeed not," the Cardinal answered, becoming suspicious himself. *Is the Pope backing away leaving me to take the blame if things go wrong?* "I always think face to face meetings are safer. No notes or incriminating reports to come back to haunt you. But, of course, I will submit reports to you on a regular basis if that is your wish."

"You may have a point. Let me think about it. You have performed a very great service to the Church. *We* are very grateful."

'How grateful?' Karmazin thought as he left. *'Grateful enough to leave me holding the baby?'*

Chapter 50

St. George Campus
University of Toronto, Canada

He was in his office, marking papers when the phone rang.

"Hello," he answered, "John Hampton."

"Hello, John, it's Michael Kinghaven. Sorry to trouble you but I've had some disturbing news; have you got a few minutes?"

"Yes, of course," he said putting his marking pen down.

"I've just had a call from the data security people in Copenhagen. They can't contact Marius Sorensen, he seems to have disappeared. They reported it to university security, who checked with the airline and customs. They confirmed that he flew to Montreal last week and then to Toronto for a conference of some sort. The airline verified that he was on the flight back to Copenhagen, and his bags were collected, but he never made it home. We tried to check if he cleared customs, but they don't release that information without some kind of authorization."

John Hampton looked out of his window at Hart House and the clock tower. It had been an enduring part of his life since he was a student here. How had he got mixed up with all this cloak and dagger stuff? Too late to back out now.

"What can have happened to him? This is the third member of the group to disappear. And I'm sure I was followed from the airport. It's a good job we're nearly finished."

"That is the other reason I called you. Data security told me that they think that someone may be trying to hack into the *Dialogue* data on the Andersen computer. They reported unusual activity, and they want to remove it from the server, afraid that it might bring their whole network down."

"But the system is backed up isn't it?"

"Yes, they have a backup of the system in the university as well as one off-site at a security company called *SafeWithUs.*"

"So what is the problem? It seems like the system could be recovered from one of the backups if something goes wrong."

"Not as safe as it should be. *SafeWithUs* are well known in Copenhagen and where they keep their onsite backup system is also known. They have had some problems, some data was compromised, but they say they have found and corrected it. But given the people we are dealing with, whoever they are, they don't want to take a chance."

"Okay, but they still have Montreal. Why can't they use that to restore Copenhagen?"

"That was the idea, but McGill are getting cold feet. They are saying that *Dialogues* is not university related, and they're running out of space, too many demands for computer access. They are looking for an excuse to get rid of it."

"I see the problem, but what is it you want me to do?"

"This is an imposition and if you want to say no, I'll understand. Could we put the system on one of your servers? As you said, the project is nearly over, so it would only be for a short time."

"Would you still administer it?"

"I could so long as your data security people can give me access."

"That might be a problem or at least take several days to get clearance. Maybe I could install it in my protected zone. The system can't be very large, and I seem to have more space than I need."

"That would be a huge help, John. If you're sure about it, we should move as fast as we can."

* * *

Castillo de Chipiona

The Archdeacon was in his office discussing with Balinska and Messi, how they would proceed. "I understand that you have found a way to destroy their computer system," he said.

"Yes, I found usernames and passwords," Messi answered, "that will let me access their system and delete it. We have to destroy their backup at the same time. Timing is critical. We need a detailed plan of when to do it."

The Archdeacon, who had surprised himself by learning some of the terms of this 'strange new world,' said, "I think a backup is a copy of the system, in case something goes wrong."

"Exactly! There are usually two backups, one on-site, in the computer facility, and another off-site in case the computer facility itself is damaged."

In the Archdeacon's world, everything was recorded on paper. "Won't there be paper copies of the information?" he asked.

"There shouldn't be. There are strict instructions on the database that no paper copies are allowed. And there's a Control setting that prevents any printing. But we'll make sure there aren't any. I'll add it to my checklist."

"So what happens next?"

Messi was enjoying himself. Most of his work was performed in isolation. Which was usually the way he preferred it. But explaining it to someone else, gave him a feeling of importance. "We have to find out where all the copies are kept, both on and off site and destroy them at the same time. Otherwise, they can recover from the backup. We only have one shot, because once security realize they have been hacked they'll lock the system down."

"Makes sense," Balinska said, "but how do we kill all of them at the same time?"

Messi wondered if he was talking about the people or the data. Both probably. "I think I have a solution. I go in and corrupt the *Dialogue* system so that every time they use it, it will make changes to the data. These changes will be so slight that at first it won't be noticed, but by the time they realize something is wrong, their data will be meaningless. Also when they back up their system, the copies will also contain the corrupted data. They won't be able to use the backups to recover."

"How do you corrupt the data?" asked the Archdeacon.

"By inserting a script, that's a small program, which will gradually alter their index system."

The Archdeacon realized that he hadn't grasped as much as he thought, said, "Sorry to interrupt again, "but I want to try and understand this. What did you just say? One thing at a time please."

"Computers use index systems to keep a record of where everything is, just like a card index system in a library. If the index is corrupted, it points to the wrong data and the information in the system becomes meaningless. The system still works and at first all that will happen is the information they retrieve will contain some incorrect data. It may not even be noticeable, or the users will think they made a mistake. But over time the errors increase and when enough users start reporting strange results, security will take a look. But by then it's too late for them to recover. My script program is designed to not only make changes, but to duplicate itself as well, so they occur faster and faster. I can set the time it starts and how long it takes to make their system meaningless."

"Don't computers have security systems to stop people getting in and doing this?"

"Yes but there are ways around it and, in this case, I've found a loophole that I can exploit."

"Why not just delete all their data and then when they back it up all they have is nothing." said Balinska.

"Because when you delete data in a computer, it isn't actually deleted, it's just no longer accessible. It's still there and there are programs that can recover it. And deletion would be immediately detected and they could restore the system from the backups."

Balinska had been skeptical of Messi and his computer hacking. Now he realized that Messi sitting at his 'frigging' computer, thousands of miles away could destroy the *Dialogue* system with the push of a key without a head being busted or a gun fired. The world was changing not, in his opinion, for the better, but he'd better get used to it or get out of the way.

"Okay, tell us what we need to do."

"If I start the script late at night there won't be a lot of users, so chances of detection are reduced. Then we have to be sure that it has been backed up, so the copy contains the errors. Andersen University does an in-house backup at 11:30 p.m. so the system must be damaged beyond repair by then. They do a complete backup, immediately after that, and it is picked up by the security company at midnight. I've got a tentative schedule worked out, but I need to fine tune it."

"How do you know the time?"

"When I hacked into their system, I found a schedule of activities for the system, containing the times and locations."

A buzzer on the desk phone went off, and the Archdeacon reached for the intercom. In an angry tone, he said, "What is it, Pierre? I left specific instructions that we were not to be disturbed." He listened to the reply and then said, "Send it in at once." He hung up and told them that mail marked urgent had arrived for Balinska from Montreal.

"That is probably a report I've been waiting for." As he said this, there was a knock on the door and the Archdeacon's secretary came in and handed it to Balinska. He opened it and took a two-page letter from the envelope, read it through and then gave it to Messi. As he was reading it, Balinska said to the Archdeacon, "It's a report from Pierre Molatov in Montreal. It confirms his suspicions that there is another copy of the *Dialogues* in Montreal, but I'll let Messi explain."

Messi read it through carefully before saying. "Good this is what I needed to complete the schedule. Who sent it?"

At this point the Archdeacon broke in, "Could you please tell me what you are talking about," he said.

"Pierre Molatov, my operator in Montreal, saw Cindy Preston and Marius Sorensen in a restaurant together and saw him hand a package to her. He sent a photograph of the two of them as he was handing over the package. Messi enlarged it and was pretty sure it was a copy of the database."

"Not exactly," Messi interrupted, I recognized the container as the type that is used to keep backup tapes in."

"Right, and Molatov checked her out and found that she was in charge of all computer systems at McGill. I told him to follow up, and that is his report. What do we do now to take care of that as well as the copies in Copenhagen?"

"According to this, they create the Montreal backup every day at 1 a.m. using a dedicated data line from Copenhagen. McGill backs up their whole system, including the *Dialogues,* at 10 p.m. Montreal time.

It goes to an offsite location run by a security company called . . . " he looked at the report, "SecuriteQuebec."

"So," Balinska said, "what do we do about it?"

Messi answered, "I think we should take a break for a couple of hours so I can add Montreal to the schedule."

"That makes sense," said the Archdeacon, "why don't you call us when you're ready."

* * *

Computer Center, Castillo de Chipiona

Back in his office Messi began listing the steps needed and in what order they would occur. After an hour, he had an initial chart, showing each step and who controlled it, himself or the university. For steps 4 and 5 he added the Montreal time, using a 6 hour time difference.

Steps	Who	Time (Mtl)
1. corrpt online Cop	Messi	10pm
2. BkUp Onsite Cop	U	11:30pm
3. BkUp off-site Cop*(SWU)*	U	12pm
4. Copy to Mtl	U	1am (7 pm prev day)
5. bkup; off-site Mtl*(SQ)*	Mtl	4am(10 pm prev day)

The first four steps fit together perfectly, by 1 a.m, all copies, as well as the online system, would be corrupted except for the copy off-site in Montreal. The location of the security company was 3457 Rue Peel. It would be 4 a.m. before the corrupted copy got there. So there was a three-hour gap, between steps 4 and 5, when the copy at SecuriteQuebec would still be correct, even if it were the previous day's copy. It wasn't likely that anyone would be using the system at that time and uncover the errors, but it would be safer to eliminate the possibility. And he could leave that to Balinska. Elimination was his stock in trade.

Messi deleted step 5 and added step 6 to replace it.

Steps	Who	Time (Mtl)
1. corrpt online Cop	Messi	10pm
2. BkUp Onsite Cop	U	11:30pm
3. BkUp off site Cop(*SWU)*	U	12pm
4. Copy to Mtl	U	1am (7 pm prev day)
~~5. bkup; off site Mtl(SQ)~~	~~Mtl~~	~~4am(10 pm prev day)~~
6. destroy copy at SQ	Balinska	1:30 pm (7:30pm prev day)

He called the other two and they spent two hours reviewing it in detail. Balinska would arrange for the offsite copy in Montreal to be destroyed at 7:30 p.m. local time. They decided to do it two days from now.

Chapter 51

Back in his office Jose looked at the list. He had started it just after Papa Michael had 'disappeared'—he didn't want to admit that he had been kidnapped—even though all the evidence pointed to it. Since then they had received information back from Opel on Corsas sold to people in Toledo and had narrowed it down to a list of three.

> *Monday:*
>
> *Papa had left for the university as usual.*
> *Blue Corsa stopped beside him and offered him a lift.*
> *He seemed to refuse, but the driver had said something*
> *that changed his mind and he got in*
>
> *Tuesday:*
>
> *Thieves broke in while Señora Romano was out shopping*
>
> *Wednesday:*
>
> *Señora calls me*
>
> *Thursday:*
>
> *Drive to Toledo; Photo on national database.*
> *Area canvassed for anyone who'd seen what happened;*
> *more reports of Papa getting into a blue Opel*

list from Father Emile's office

Plato, Galileo, Newton, Einstein, Heisenberg, Hawking
Gravitation, Relativity, Quantum Theory. String Theory.

Owner of Blue Opels in Toledo

25 of them; narrowed to 3, a professor; a priest, an
accountant.
Registrations are 4576STV, 3762DCS, 8745ANG resp.

The list of books Father Michael used in library:
Apology of Origen, The Wisdom of Sirach, Antiquities
of the Jew:

Q: The Earliest Gospel, The Gospel of Thomas
plastic (key) card
CΦC on one side
f9, f12 on other

He picked up the phone and punched in the number of the Monastery of Espiritu Santo. It rang several times; nothing was done in a hurry by the monks, and when it was finally answered, he asked for Father William. He then waited several minutes until he heard the familiar voice, "Hello, Father William speaking. How can I help you?"

"By agreeing to let me come and visit you tomorrow."

"Jose, it's so good to hear your voice, and I would love it if you came to see me. It has been too long; you are always welcome." Then his tone changed, "Is this about Father Michael's disappearance, everyone here is apprehensive."

"Yes it is, and I'm worried too and I need your help. I want you to look at some of the items we've found to see if you can shed any light on what they mean. You were very close to Papa so you might recognize some of them."

"I'm not sure what a poor monk who has hardly been outside the monastery can tell you, but I'll be happy to do what I can. Especially since it means, I can see my favorite nephew." He always referred to

Jose as his nephew, even though they were not related. During the years growing up at the monastery, Father William was the one he turned to if Papa wasn't available or if he was angry with Papa because he wouldn't let him have his own way.

The next morning it was warm, and he put the top down on the Jaguar and followed the AutoRoute towards Zaragoza and then the ring road around the city. He picked up the E-7 and a few minutes later he left the AutoRoute and followed the small road alongside the river.

Once he had left the town behind the landscape became familiar; he had cycled all around the area when he was a teenager. Where the river widened he spotted a favorite swimming hole and just behind it a thick grove of olive trees that provided a screen from prying eyes. Delfina Alvarado, a little plump and 3 years his senior, had been there before and was more than willing to show him the way.

Where the river bent to the east the dirt road, a lane really, only wide enough for a single car, curved off to the north. Jose slowed the car to a crawl to try and avoid hitting the suspension on the bumps and potholes, and four hundred yards later he passed through the archway to the monastery. He stopped for a few minutes and breathed in the memories of his childhood; carefree days and happy memories.

Father William was waiting for him, having seen and recognized the car from the second floor of the main building where the road was visible in the distance. "Any news?"

"No nothing new but I want to show you what I have and maybe you can see some connections."

"Very well let's go into the refectory, it will be empty at this time of the day, and we can have some coffee while we talk."

Once they had their coffee, Jose described what had happened to Papa and to Father Emile. He took the list he had prepared from his satchel and placed it in front of Father William who studied it for a few minutes before saying, "There are some things that I see. Father Emile's list is about cosmology. It contains the names of scientists and the theories they developed to explain the universe."

"Amazing, but how do you know this?"

"A lifetime spent studying ancient and modern philosophy. Remember up until a few hundred years ago scientists were called

Natural Philosophers. But most important for your inquiries is that they attempted to explain the universe scientifically and without recourse to God. I'm sure it could make many devout Christians angry, which might be part of why Father Emile has disappeared."

"Do you really think anyone would do that just because of some scientific theory?"

"Maybe not if it was only one instance but now look at what Father Michael was studying. They are all about the origins of Christianity and the early church communities. Most date back to the first few centuries after Christ, but Q is a product of modern scholarship over the last two centuries and gives a very different interpretation of how the Gospels were composed. These religious scholars suggest that there was a collection of the sayings of Jesus, which were used by the apostles in writing their gospels. Maybe Father Michael was studying it; again a topic which would be vigorously opposed by the established Church."

"Do you think the Church is trying to close them down?"

"Possibly, if this was the Inquisition, but hard to believe in this day and age. I very much doubt that the Church would resort to kidnapping priests to protect its views."

Jose, who had jotted down the information that Father William had given him, said, "Well, you never know. Thank you, Father, you've given me something to think about."

"I've not finished yet, Jose. There are a few more items that I think I can help with. As you know, I know nothing about cars, I prefer to get around on my old bicycle, but I have seen a blue car coming in and out of the monastery. The owner is a priest called Father Diego Paz who used to come here to use our library. As a result I think he got to know Papa."

"Did he know what Papa was researching?"

"No. None of us did. Papa was very secretive about his work."

"And you are sure that the priest drove a blue car."

"Yes of that I'm certain. Another strange thing is that his parish was close by in Zaragoza but when Papa retired and moved to Toledo, Father Diego moved there shortly afterward."

Jose suddenly sensed the empty feeling in his stomach. Father Diego Paz must be the owner of the Opel. "Really. That would explain a lot,"

He made a note to check up on the priest as soon as possible. "Is there anything else?"

"The symbol and markings on the card do you know what they are?"

"Not really. I recognize the Greek letter phi, but nothing else."

"There is another interpretation. That symbol Φ was also used to represent the divine proportion, sometimes called the Golden Ratio."

"What was that?" Jose asked.

"I'm not sure of the details, but it is a ratio, something to do with the length and width, and proportion. Buildings that are constructed to that ratio are thought to be more esthetically pleasing than any other. It occurs naturally in the spirals you can see in nature; for example, the center of a sunflower and in the shell of a mollusk. It was used in the construction of many well-known buildings: the Great Pyramid in Egypt, the Parthenon in Athens, and the Taj Mahal. And I seem to recollect a reference to a Chateau in the Sanlucar region built in the sixteenth century that used those proportions."

"Father you are incredible. Your mind is a living encyclopedia!"

"It's amazing how much the mind retains. But I am sure that the monastic life is part of the reason. Peace and tranquility leave the mind free of stress and the trivia of everyday life. You should try it sometimes, Jose."

"You're right, but I don't know how to slow down, and certainly not until I find Papa. Well, thank you again this has been extremely valuable."

Jose decided to drive to Toledo to find the priest and the blue Opel. It had to be the car that picked up Papa and the other person in the car could have been the kidnapper. From what he had learned he was beginning to put things together. A group of researchers has found alternate explanations that run counter to the Church and the Vatican. And someone was determined to stop them. It was very hypothetical, but it had the three essentials, motive, means, and opportunity, and it would explain the disappearance of Papa Michael and Father Emile. The priest with the blue Opel must be connected in some way, and he was the only lead he had. Let's see how he stands up to the third degree.

He phoned the inspector in Toledo, who had been in charge of the disappearance of Papa. He was a little antagonistic that his 'real" case load was being interrupted again. But once Jose explained that they were now sure this was a kidnapping he was more helpful. "Remember the list of blue Opel's that we got back and then narrowed down to three people. One of them was a priest. Did you ever get a name and address?"

"Hold on I'll check." A few minutes later he came back on the line, "You're in luck. One of our detectives looked it up, but no-one actually followed it up. We were hit by two murders and the Father's disappearance got put on the back burner. Anyway, here's the address." He read it out, and Jose wrote it down.

Father Diego Paz, San Juan de la Cruz, Calle Reino Unido, Toledo

He reached Toledo in three hours, but it took him another hour to find the church. It was getting dark when he arrived, but there were lights showing from inside. He went in and found the church empty. As he walked towards the front a priest came out of a door at the side and asked if he could be of help. Jose asked him if Father Diego was around, and the priest showed him to the Church office where Father Diego was working at a desk computer. The priest introduced them and left.

As soon as Father Diego heard that Jose was from the police, he closed his computer and the expression on his face changed slightly, enough for Jose to notice. The priest was small, dark featured with a beard.

Jose began by going through the details of the disappearance and the connection to the blue Opel. "Did you give Father Michael a lift that day?"

"Yes," the priest replied in a surprisingly deep voice, at odds with his short stature, "it had started to rain, and I was going near the University."

"How did you know he was going to the university?"

The priest avoided eye contact when he replied. "Because he went there every day. Remember I have known Father Michael for several years both here and in Zaragoza.

"What was he working on?" Jose probed.

There was an undertone of anger in his reply. "I don't know, he never confided in me."

Jose sensed it and knew that he should choose his words carefully, or he might just clam up. But he was tired, it had been a long day, and he was certain he was lying. "Isn't that surprising, you know he goes daily to the university, and you have known him for several years and yet you don't know what he was working on."

"I didn't know him that well. I used to see him in the library at the Monastery. That's all."

"That doesn't make a lot of sense. You knew him well enough for him to get into your car, and after he had moved to Toledo, you relocated from Zaragoza. Almost as if you were following him."

"I don't like the direction this interrogation is taking. You are treating me like a suspect."

Jose picked up on the words *interrogation, suspect*. "Why would you call it an interrogation? And why do you consider yourself a suspect? I never used those words." Before Father Diego could reply, he said, "I'm merely trying to get at the facts. Let's talk about the other person in the car. Who was it?"

"Another priest who was visiting from Ocana. I was taking him to the railway station."

"Could you describe him?"

"Why?" He was becoming evasive. Jose knew he was close to losing him!

He still pushed him, trying to get him angry, in the hope of getting him to say more than he intended. "I need to see if the description I got from some eyewitnesses was correct?" Jose lied.

The Priest's face was turning red. "Are you doubting my word, Inspector?" He was close to the breaking point.

"If you say so. All I'm trying to do is establish the reliability of the witnesses."

The priest didn't answer because, He didn't know if Jose already knew who the person was. If he gave the wrong description, he would be caught out.

"Are you having difficulty remembering?" Jose pressed.

"No, I just don't like your tone. Alright, I'll tell you but no more questions. He was a tall man in his mid-thirties, very muscular."

"Well my witnesses must have got it wrong, none of them mentioned he was a priest. Two of them got a good look and didn't see a dog collar."

"Perhaps he wasn't wearing one; I don't remember."

'Don't remember,' the phrase that often came out when suspects had something to hide.

Jose knew that he needed to back off before the priest decided he wanted his lawyer present. "Thank you, Father, you've been a big help. One last question which entrance to the library did you take him to?"

"I didn't take him all the way there I dropped him off a few blocks away, and he walked the rest of the way."

"I thought you said it was raining, which is why you picked him up."

"It must have stopped by then. I don't remember!"

Again.

"It would really help us if you could remember exactly where you dropped him off. You see he never made it to the library that day so something must have happened between the library and where you dropped him off."

"I'm not sure but I think it was somewhere on Calle San Clemente," he said naming a street that was well known and close to the university.

"Thank you for your time Father. Here is my card in case you remember any other details. Give me a call on either of those two numbers."

The priest looked at the card and said, "This means you're with the Madrid police aren't you a little far from home?"

"Yes indeed but I have a lot of experience working on kidnap cases, and I guess the Father was pretty important. As you know, he was the Abbot of the Monastery."

"And it seems to me that you're on a witch hunt and treating me like a suspect. If you have any evidence why don't you charge me?"

'I'd love to, and once I have enough dirty laundry to hang you out to dry, I'll have you inside faster than you can say, Hail Mary.'

Jose walked back to his car and looked at his watch. It was already 7 p.m. and getting dark, no point in trying to get back to Madrid tonight. *I'll sleep at Papa's house, I still have the key.* Then he had thought; he still hadn't bought that librarian a cup of coffee, maybe she'd settle for dinner instead. He looked in his satchel and pulled out his casebook and quickly found her card. She answered on the third ring. "Hello," he said, "I'm looking for someone who can tell me something about Robin Hood, over dinner. I hope you haven't eaten."

"No, I haven't and with an invite like that I wouldn't admit if I had. Where are you?"

He told her, and she gave him directions. He got lost twice but eventually found it and she was waiting for him. She had been *cute* when he saw her in the library, but now she looked quite stunning, in a short black dress that accentuated the curves of her figure. Over dinner, he told her about growing up at the monastery and that in fact 'Tuck' was his uncle and he told her a little about his father and how he had become a detective. She in turn, told him about herself where she grew up, near Sanlucar, and how she married young and divorced early, moving to Toledo to get a fresh start. After dinner she invited him back to her apartment 'just for coffee' she insisted. But 'just for coffee' changed to 'well maybe for breakfast as well'.

Jose woke early and slipped quietly out of bed, went to the kitchen and made coffee and toast and found orange juice in the fridge. He ate his own breakfast and then made up a tray and carried it into the bedroom. "Good morning, Señorita Isobel, room service."

She sat up in bed still warm and sleepy. "You shouldn't have," she said taking the tray from him and placing it on a side table, "but first things," first she said dragging him into bed.

An hour later Jose made a fresh pot of coffee and was looking over his notes when Isobel emerged and looked over his shoulder. "I've seen that symbol before," she said, "pointing to the letter phi, "on a building near where we spent our family holidays when I was a child."

"Do you remember where?" he asked, excitement in his voice.

"We always went to the same place, a small hotel in Sanlucar. My father was a keen sailor, and he would take us out in his sailboat not too far from shore. I remember sailing past these old buildings, they were huge, and there was a wharf running along the front of it. One day we docked there and looked in through the gates. There was a metal railing all around, and many of the buildings looked like they were falling down. I imagine they have by now. Over the gate were some letters and that symbol. I remember it because I had just started taking Latin and Greek at school, so I recognized it."

"Do you remember the name of the place or where it was?"

"Not really. We sailed down the coast away from the river. I might be able to find it from a boat, but I doubt if it's still there. It will have been pulled down by now. I only saw it once from the road. We were cycling, and we passed the entrance. It had the same sign."

"I don't think it has fallen down, and I need to try and locate it. It's worth a try." He explained to her that the letter was also a symbol for the golden proportion and that Father William believed there was a building near Sanlucar that had those specifications.

He checked his phone for messages and saw there was one from Franz Millar in Munich, asking him to call as soon as he got the message. It had been left at 11 p.m. last night. Millar must have been working late but why didn't I get his call. Then he remembered he had turned off his phone. He called the number, and Franz answered. "Guten Morgen, Jose. How are you and where are you?"

"Very well Franz and I'm in Toledo. You called pretty late last night. It must have been important."

"It was. How come you didn't answer?"

"I'd turned off my mobile."

"Let me see. You're in Toledo, and you told me about a very attractive librarian that lives there. You turn off your phone. I think I'm beginning to get the picture."

"Enough of the pleasantries, Franz, what do you have for me?"

"A message from Interpol. They've had a reliable communication about a place called, let me see, Castillo de Chipiona."

Jose wrote the information in his notebook and Isobel was looking over his shoulder. "That's it," she cried.

"Do you know it," Franz asked.

"No," said Jose, but a very attractive librarian does. Do you have the specific location?"

"No, there was no address specified but whoever sent the info to Interpol found the place by following a character called Balinska. And there was a note attached that Balinska is Radovic and Interpol suspect it's a case of identity theft. I contacted the Canadian authorities, actually the Assistant Commissioner did, I don't have the clearance, and they got back to us this morning. Andre Balinska died in 1951 when he was only two years old."

"My God, Franz, things are coming together."

"Wait, there's more. There's a death record for Boris Radovic and two weeks after that a passport was issued to Andre Balinska. So now we know why we were told that Radovic was dead when his dabs went to Ottawa. But be careful, Jose, the report also says the place is like an armed fortress and the main building is wired with explosives."

"What? Just what are they doing there? Thanks for the heads up. I'll be careful and keep you posted."

"What's happening?" asked Isobel.

"How about a day or two at the seaside, where you spent your vacations as a child?" Jose answered, then wondered if it was safe to take her; 'armed fortress' was how Franz had described it. Too late now, but he added, "It could be dangerous so I might need to drop you off somewhere safe if I think you could get hurt."

"Just try, Mister, there's no way. This is the most fun I've had for . . . ever!"

She packed a bag and fifteen minutes later they were on their way. That's something else I like about her; he thought to himself, she packs quickly and compactly. She only needed a small suitcase, the size of a carry-on. Just as well, the trunk on the Jag was pretty small. Jose entered Sanlucar into the GPS and checked the distance; three hundred and sixty miles. It was going to be a long drive, but the roads were nearly all highways, perfect for the Jag.

He got out and opened the trunk and came back with a blue police light which he attached to a bracket on the car. He followed the directions out of the city and once on the highway he turned on the light, this was police business and pushed the accelerator until the speedometer showed 100 mph. Isobel, who until now had been quiet, asked, "Are you sure a car this old should be going at this speed especially when you're on the wrong side of the car."

"It may be old in years but not in miles and it's kept in top condition by the police mechanics. But you're right about the steering wheel being on the right side. It's not a problem on highways, but there are a few sections of two-lane roads where you're going to have to tell me when it's safe to pass."

"I said I liked fun, but that might be too much fun."

He looked at her and smiled.

"Keep your eyes on the road," she yelled, then added, "you can look at me all you want when we get to wherever we're going."

The car was built for speed and even when the speedometer showed one hundred miles per hour, it didn't feel excessively fast and the suspension was tuned to perfection. They only saw one police patrol and when he saw the flashing blue light he just waved as they flashed by. They reached Seville in just over three hours and bypassed the city, then followed the GPS instructions onto A-471 and into Sanlucar.

They found a small hotel, booked a room and had their bags taken up while they ate an early dinner at the restaurant. As they ate, Jose went over the plans. "Tomorrow we'll rent a boat and take it down the coast to see if you can recognize it from the sea. If you do, I'll be able to get a fix on the coordinates, and then we can try and find it from the land side."

After dinner, Jose made arrangements to hire a motor boat for the following morning then called Franz, who was still in his office. He explained where they were and what had happened. "Do you think Interpol would give us the contact who supplied the information?" he asked.

"I can contact them and see, but it will probably be tomorrow before I can arrange it."

"Okay, that will be good. We're hiring a boat tomorrow to see if we can find the place from the ocean side."

"I noticed you said we, is your library assistant with you?"

"That's really not your business but, in this case, I'll tell you she is helping me with my inquiries," and he explained about her seeing the place when she was a child.

"Sounds like mixing pleasure with business. Don't forget the business part."

PART THREE

Chapter 52

Computer Center
Castillo de Chipiona
Sanlucar, Spain

Messi was nervous now that the moment had arrived. It always seemed straightforward on paper but in reality there were always unexpected complications, the backup times could be changed, the transmission to Montreal could fail plus myriad other issues. He put them all out of his mind and concentrated on the things that could be controlled. In fact, his only role now was to plant his script into the database and let it corrupt the data and the index file. Beyond that, he had to wait with everyone else until they got confirmation, from Pierre Molatov. He went over his script and checked the user id and password.

He looked at the clock. Still five minutes. Balinska came into the room, "Everything ready," he asked. His voice had an edge to it; even Balinska was feeling the pressure.

"I'm just waiting for the clock to tick down, and I don't need any interruptions."

Balinska knew the *kid* was right; there was nothing he could do. "I'll be in my office if you need me. Good luck, we're counting on you."

After what seemed an age the clock ticked down, and Messi accessed the server in Copenhagen and followed the links to the *Dialogue* system. He logged in, found the administration module, and selected the 'Update System' option. He consulted his notes from before and scrolled down until he found the code he wanted. He first copied it to his laptop, for future use if necessary, then pasted his own script in its place. The code was re-entrant and was used every time someone accessed one of the menus. Just to be sure he exited the Administration module and logged into the 'Christian Origins' module. He looked briefly at the content, and then he went into the 'Cosmology' module and got a warning that the data requested was out of range. Already his script was working. After glancing at the content he was tempted to read more of it, it looked interesting. But he knew the rules; get in and get out as fast as possible, covering your tracks as you went.

The script was in and activated, all he could do now was wait until they heard from Montreal that the copy at SecuriteQuebec had been destroyed. It was going to be a long three and a half hours. He phoned Balinska and the Archdeacon and told them that the script had been introduced successfully.

* * *

Computer Center, McGill University

The systems operator at McGill was running the jobs listed on the schedule. He looked at the clock on the wall; he was running late by about thirty minutes. The next job on the list was the download from Copenhagen. He was about to set up the files when he heard the explosion. It was close enough to rattle the windows and loud enough to penetrate the reinforced walls of the computer center. From the window he could see the smoke and flames only a few blocks away; it looked close to SecuriteQuebec. Picking up the phone he dialed the number. There was no answer, so he followed protocol and called the hotline. This time someone picked up.

"Hello, SecuriteQuebec hotline."

The operator told him what he had seen and heard.

"Yes, there has been an explosion at our office on Peel but we don't know how extensive it was or how much damage it did."

"From here it sounded like it might have taken out half the block. Is there anything else I need to know?"

"Until we get information from the Fire Department I don't know any more than you do so I can't give you any advice. Sorry."

Next on the emergency procedures list was to close down any programs that were running and send out a systems message to any users informing them that the computer center was closing down. He dialed Cindy Preston's cell phone to advise her of what had happened.

She listened to him and then told him she was coming over and should be there in half an hour.

She drove along Sherbrooke and tried to turn north on Peel but it was blocked by police cars, and she could see the smoking buildings and the firemen pouring water on the flames. She got out of her car and explained to one of the police officers who she was and that the company they used to store their data was located at 3457 Peel.

The officer checked her notebook before she replied, "From what we've been given, it looks like it could have been one of the buildings involved. All the ones in the block 3453 to 3467 have been damaged as well as some of the buildings on the other side of the street."

When she reached the Computer Center, she checked the log and said to the operator, "Good, you didn't start the download from Copenhagen. I don't know why but I've had a bad feeling about that system since we got those warning flags a few days ago and now this. I'm going to remove it from our system altogether. I think they are planning to move it to Toronto anyway, I received a request from their coordinator, Kinghaven last week to send them a copy. We were supposed to send it after we received it from Copenhagen but I'm going to have to tell them that we only have the one from yesterday, and we'll send them that. Then I want you to call Copenhagen and cancel."

* * *

St. George Campus, University of Toronto

The two of them, John Hampton and one of the computer operators, were in the control room of the university's computer center. It was 8:15 p.m. and Cindy Preston had called ten minutes earlier and advised them of the explosion at SecuriteQuebec and her decision to cancel any further involvement. Then she added, "I don't think you've been exactly honest with me about your system. You must have known there were problems."

"I didn't have anything to do with setting up in Montreal, wasn't that Professor Sorensen from Copenhagen?"

"Yes, it was but I'm still pretty angry that no one followed up to tell me that there might be some danger involved."

"I'll apologize Cindy, but don't you back up all your data, not just *Dialogues*, at the offline facility, it could have been some other files they wanted to destroy?"

"It's possible, but I doubt it. *Dialogues* is the only new system we've had in the last few weeks, and we got some warnings a few days ago when we were doing the download from Copenhagen. I'm just glad we didn't allow them to have online access. Okay, I'll have the operator set it up to transmit our in-house backup to you but remember what you're getting is one day old, whatever was changed today won't be there. And once you're up and running, let me know so I can remove it from our system entirely."

"Understood. And thanks. He thought about telling her that Sorensen had disappeared, but it would only add fuel to the fire."

The message *'waiting for McGill transmission'* appeared on the screen and then thirty seconds later, *'Ready to Transmit. Press Enter to commence.* Hampton hit the Enter button, the download started and completed 35 minutes later with no problems.

When it was finished, he called Cindy, "Thanks, Cindy, we've got it. I hope you can recover your other systems."

* * *

Office of the Archdeacon, Castillo de Chipiona

The three of them were sitting in Balinska's office waiting for a phone call. There was not a lot of conversation; they watched the clock and waited to find out what had happened in Montreal. The strain was becoming unbearable. Messi caught Balinska's stare; he looked like he was about to explode. If anything had gone wrong, he knew who would pay. He was desperate for a joint, but he could hardly light up in front of those two.

At 2:15 a.m. the phone rang, and Balinska grabbed it, "Yes who's this?" When he heard the answer, he nodded to the Archdeacon and Messi, who both sat forward in their chairs, holding their breath. He listened carefully before hanging up, his face solemn, and then he jumped up and yelled, "He did it. The bomb went off as scheduled and from the number of fire trucks responding it has almost certainly destroyed the office and its contents.

"We did it. We fucking did it!"

Chapter 53

SecuriteQuebec Offices
Peel Street
Montreal, Canada

Inspector George Simonet was treading carefully through what was left of the SecuriteQuebec facility. It consisted of three outer offices and the vault to the rear. From the initial reports of the office manager and the Fire Chief, he was trying to piece together what had happened. He had lost a day because the site had been closed to everyone by the Fire Chief. They had crossed swords before and the Inspector's argument—every day reduced the probability of finding the perps by twenty-five percent—fell on deaf ears.

Whoever had done it had made sure nothing would be left. Either they didn't know what they were doing and used too much explosive or they did know what they were doing and made sure nothing remained. The cause, according to the reports, had been a large, as much as five pounds of C4 or Semtex, attached to a timer.

The inside of the vault was black and charred. And from the radius of the damage the bomb had almost certainly been placed inside the vault where all the client's data files were kept in thick steel cabinets. It looked as if the bomb had been placed in front of the two used for McGill University. The doors had been blown off, and the heat of the fire had melted the contents. The rest of the cabinets were severely damaged but still intact. Whoever had done it, had got into the vault to place the bomb. Someone, the guard, was the obvious suspect, had let them in or given them the combinations.

There were two Security cameras, one in the outer office that had been smashed and the broken remnants of one in the vault. The Manager's report said that the Guard on duty was found unconscious by the street door of the office from a blow to the back of his head. He was still in a coma in intensive care, given only a fifty-fifty chance of making it. Even if he did, he would be out of circulation for a long time.

There were a lot of questions going through the Inspectors mind. Why had the guard opened the vault door? Why hadn't they silenced him permanently? How had the perp got into the office at all? Was the guard was taking bribes?

Until he could question him, he wouldn't know for sure and from the medical report that was going to be a long time, possibly never. He looked at the sheet of numbers he had been given and dialed the number for Allan Parrish, the Office Manager.

"Mr. Parrish, how are you. I'm Inspector Simonet from the Montreal police, and I have some questions I need to ask. Do you have time now?"

"Yes, of course, although I still can't believe the damage that was done."

"It is a mess I agree, but hopefully we can catch the people who did it. I have your report here, and I've been looking at it. It's pretty thorough, but I need to get a little more detail. You say that the vault could only be opened by people who had the combination and whose fingerprints were recognized."

"Yes as I told the Fire Chief, you had to first dial in the combinations, four of them, one for each bolt lock and then insert your finger into the fingerprint reader. The system then matches your fingerprint with the ones on file."

Which meant that the Guard on duty had to have opened it. Unless he was missing a finger.

"So everyone who was authorized had to record their fingerprints. Where did you keep those images?"

"On one of our data files and, of course, in the fingerprint recognition software."

"Are they still available?"

"I doubt it, but I haven't had a chance to see what is left and what has been destroyed. The Fire Chief won't let us back in until his people and the police forensic team have finished."

"Tell me about it! Who had the combinations?"

"Only a few people; myself, the assistant manager and the security guards."

Simonet was looking at what was left of one of the vault doors. "What about the locks on the steel cabinets inside the vault?" he asked.

"They required two combinations, kept by different people."

"How did that work?"

"The drivers who picked up the clients' tapes had one, and the three shift supervisors had one each. So when they came back from their pickup, the driver would dial in his combination and one of the shift supervisors would dial in the other."

The Inspector was probing some of the debris with his foot but thinking that the security guard could have been persuaded to open the vault, but he didn't have the combination to open the steel cabinets. Which would explain why the cabinets were unopened and why they had used as much explosive as they had? They had to be sure that the cabinet contents were destroyed.

"Who else would have been inside the vault beside the people you've mentioned?"

"Potential clients who wanted to see where we kept the data; we show them the vault and the steel cabinets which are constructed from half inch thick steel."

"Anyone gone round recently?" the inspector asked.

"Yes there was a man from the provincial government who wanted to see our facility, they were looking for somewhere to store their employee data. We were excited because it would be a very lucrative contract."

"Do you remember his name, address, which part of the government?"

"Only his name, Henri Leforet, the other details have probably been destroyed."

"Anything else?"

"There was something that the driver reported a couple of days ago. He thought he was being followed on his pickup route; the same car on two successive days. He wasn't entirely sure, so we didn't report it, but now I wonder if it was connected."

"Did he give a description of the car? I suppose a license plate would be too much to hope for."

"No," the manager replied, "he told me that it was dark brown, a sedan, probably European, but that was all."

"What about the security guard who was on duty. What do you know about him?"

"All our staff have to undergo extensive security checks, and if there's the slightest evidence of any problems, and that includes, criminal, financial or personal, we don't hire them. Guy Walberg that's his name has been with the company for ten years, longer than I have, with no problems whatsoever. He's a married man with two young children."

"Well thank you you've been very helpful if you think of anything else, please call me." He gave him his phone number and then went through the facts, in his mind, trying to develop an outline of what might have happened.

The explosion had occurred at 7:30 p.m. and everything pointed to the Security Guard. He had the codes and the finger to open the vault, but he couldn't open the cabinets on his own. And why was the bomb placed in front of the McGill cabinets? He needed to talk to someone at McGill to find out what was on their tapes. He had one further look around and asked the forensics team when he could expect their report. As expected it would be at least three days, by which time the perp could be on the other side of the country or the world.

Simonet drove back to his office and asked his assistant to find out if the Provincial Government had a Henri Leforet on their books. He had a strong suspicion that either no-one of that name worked for the government or if he did, he had an alibi for the date and time. Then he started looking through the list of employee names; he had been given. Despite the Manager's assurance that all the employees had pristine backgrounds, he sent the names off for financial and criminal checks.

The video from the front office showed a man entering. His hat shielded his face and a few seconds later the tape went blank. Three days later he got back the forensics but other than a set of fingerprints on the cabinets and vault door there wasn't much. An interview with the staff at McGill didn't yield a lot. One of them had heard the explosion and seen the smoke and flames. When questioned he said that the files contained mainly student records and a backup of a system they kept for a group in Copenhagen. As far as he knew they were doing research in anthropology.

The only other suspicious fact came from the phone records. At 7:15 p.m. someone had made a call from the SecuriteQuebec office to a mobile number owned by a Gina Leberg. It took a further two days to find out she was the wife of Guy Walberg. It had been so much simpler when they had the same last name.

Simonet interviewed the wife twice, but all he got was that her husband had called her just after dinner and asked about the children if they were they alright.

When the Guard finally came out of the coma, and he got to interview him, a strange thing happened. His boss, Captain Morrisseau, came with him; he said there had been some similar crimes, and he wanted to see this Guard for himself.

Walberg's story was much as Simonet figured it would be. He suspected it was all lies. He had heard a noise from the outer office and when he'd gone back to investigate there was a man there wearing a mask and a hat, with a gun pointed at his head. He put a bullet into the CCTV and then forced him to open the vault and stay in the outer office. When the man was finished, he told Walberg to go ahead of him and the last thing he remembered was a blow to the head. The Guard also explained that he had made the phone call to his wife. The phone company records showed he had only done that once before, and that was over two years ago.

The inspector wanted to cross-examine him, but the doctors wouldn't let him. By the time the Guard had recovered, Simonet was up to his neck in the corruption scandal into the construction industry in Montreal. His boss told him to put the SQ file in with the cold cases and get back to it when he had the time. Simonet knew that wasn't going to happen.

Chapter 54

Hotel Monterrey
Sanlucar, Spain

The weather was cooperating, it was cloudy but no wind and no rain in the forecast. Ideal for taking a boat out on the ocean. Isobel's only experience had been on her father's yacht and that had been twenty years ago. Fortunately, Jose was proficient. When he was with CESID, he had tracked high-speed launches running arms shipments, from Morocco across the Strait of Gibraltar, into Spain. He had quickly learned how to maneuver the powerful catamarans they used to intercept them.

After breakfast, they drove to the harbor where he had rented the boat, a twenty-four foot Searay, with a 350 hp inboard. It took Jose half an hour to familiarize himself with the controls and another thirty minutes to take it out with the rental agent to make sure he could handle it in the ocean. He used the charts to set a Southwest course that would keep them 150 yards seaward of the shoreline.

By 10 a.m., they were on their way, just a couple of vacationers, out for a day on the water, with a packed hamper provided by the hotel. The sea was calm with small waves, and Jose cut through the light swell at low speed. Isobel was out of sight, in the cabin, watching the shoreline through binoculars. Just before noon she called out, "Got it, that's the place, although it must have been completely redone, but the sign over the gate is the same; that Greek symbol *phi*. What do we do now, Captain?"

"What any two carefree vacationers would do. Time for a swim and then a little lunch."

He cut back the motor, checked the depth, thirty feet, and dropped the anchor. From the cover of the cabin, he took the glasses and looked at the place. Isobel was right, there was the sign CΦC over the main entrance. It did indeed look like a fortress, two massive gates about six feet high with a wall of the same height, and on either side two security cameras. Running along the length of the building, from one end to the other, at least 300 yards, he estimated, was a large dock and tied up at a berth was an ocean going motor launch. "That's an expensive boat; either they have some very influential visitors arriving by sea or they need to be ready to make a quick escape through the back door. Now let's have that swim. Did you bring your swimsuit?"

"Afraid not, bra and panties will have to do."

"Sounds good to me," he said as he stripped down to his underpants, and dove over the side. Isobel followed suit and for fifteen minutes they swam in the warm water. When they got back to the boat, Isobel asked, "What happens now?"

"A little lunch, and then some skulduggery."

"I like the sound of that!"

They sat on the prow of the boat and opened the hamper and slowly ate their lunch both of them feeling that they were being watched. They limited themselves to one glass of wine while they planned how to get a closer look.

"Here's a plan that I hope will work. There's a light onshore wind, and the tide is coming in. If I raise the anchor a little, it will drag, and the boat will drift in towards the dock. Once it's about fifty feet away, I'll set the anchor to stop it drifting and then I'll go over the back. Hopefully, I can swim far enough underwater to reach the dock, and if I stay close to the fence, I'll be out of the sight of those cameras."

"What do you want me to do?" Isobel asked.

"Create a diversion. Anything you can think of. Okay. Ready?"

Jose raised the anchor, and they sat on the prow pretending to finish the wine and appearing completely unaware that they were drifting. When he estimated they were close enough, he set the anchor, filled his lungs, and slipped into the water from the back of the boat. He was a powerful swimmer, even underwater, and neither of the cameras picked him up. Isobel had reached into her bag and smothered sun tan lotion slowly and deliberately over every part of her body. Then she rolled onto her stomach and removed her bra.

"Hey Mario, come and look at monitors 5 and 6."

"Wow, great shape. Come on baby, roll over."

By looking sideways, she could just see Jose's head appear at the side of the dock. She rolled over supporting herself with her arm so that she was stretched out with the front of her body facing the Castillo but holding her bra up with her hand.

"Come on baby drop it. Show us what you've got."

Jose slowly pulled himself up until he could see the security cameras. Good, they were both pointing at the boat. Isobel must be putting on quite a diversion. He moved so that he was at the side of the dock and up against the fence before pulling himself up, pretty sure that the cameras couldn't see him. He looked back at the boat and realized why the cameras were pointing that way. He just hoped that her diversion didn't prompt someone to come out to get a closer look.

He worked his way along the wall to the edge of the gate, where he thought he had seen some kind of entry system. He was right, there was a slot for a key and at the side of it a keypad, covered by a sheet of clear plastic. His guess was that once the key was inserted and turned the plastic cover would retract, and you could punch in a security code, probably those numbers on the back of the card they had found. But without the key he couldn't test it. Still some further planning needed but at least he had found the place, and he had the feeling that Papa Michael was in there.

He took a deep breath and made it back to the boat, without notice, Isobel continuing her display. He climbed up the ladder at the rear of the boat and said, "That certainly was an effective performance, Lady Godiva."

"Oh, so now when it suit's you, you remember English folklore."

Back at the hotel, Jose had just finished showering, Isobel was still in bed when his phone rang. He checked the number; it was Franz, "Hello Franz, what did you find out?"

"It took a while, Interpol is like any other bureaucracy, maybe worse because there's a whole level of secrecy added on top. Anyway, I eventually got transferred to the right person, although I never found out his name, just that he was in charge of Interpol Integrated Inquiries, whatever that is. He questioned me to make sure I was who I said I was and then took down your number and told me someone would get in touch with you, possibly today but more likely tomorrow."

Franz was correct, contact was made the next day but at four in the morning. "Did I wake you, inspector?" the voice at the other end said.

"Yes, actually you did," said Jose, still half asleep and looking at the clock to see what time it was.

"Good, I always feel that it's an advantage when your quarry is half asleep, and their brain is still addled."

"Okay, point taken but who the hell are you?" snapped Jose, his mind beginning to clear.

"First a few questions to make sure you are who you purport to be."

Purport? Who was this guy, an English professor?

This was followed by a mini interrogation that showed he had done his homework. When he was satisfied, he said "Very well Detective Inspector Rodriguez, you passed the test. My name is Morse. Now, what is it you need to know?"

Jose explained that he was trying to find his uncle, Father Michael and a priest from Munich, Father Emile. He also told him about the card they had found in Father Emile's office. He added that yesterday they had found the Castillo from the ocean side and wondered if Morse could help them find it on the land side.

"Yes I can help you, and you can probably help me. It appears we are both looking for the same character but for different reasons." He avoided mentioning why and Jose knew better than to ask.

"I have two problems," said Jose, "I need to locate the Castillo from the land side, and I need to get a search warrant to get inside."

"I can help you with the first but not the second, at least not yet. I have a lot of stuff on this Balinska, but none of it is strong enough to hold up in court and not enough to get a warrant."

Morse gave Jose road directions to the Castillo but warned him about the security system, including the Dobermans, then asked, "Did you get close enough to see their entry system?"

"Yes, it requires both a key and a code. I'm sure that once the key is inserted, the cover on the keypad opens, and you enter your code." Jose told him about the card he had found."

"That checks out with what I learned from a local contractor," telling Jose what he had learned about the Sotano. Then he asked, "Do you think the numbers on the card are the code?"

"That seems like the obvious conclusion, except they are both preceded by the letter *f,* and the keypad is only numeric."

"Strange, why don't you tell me what they are and I'll see if they make any sense to me."

Jose gave him the two codes then added, "Let me know if you have any brain waves and if you get any information on Balinska that might persuade a judge, to give me a search warrant. How do I contact you? I don't suppose you're going to give me your phone number."

"Correct, the fewer the people who know about me, the better. If you need to get hold of me, use the same procedure. Get your friend Franz to contact Interpol and they'll get hold of me. They've been told it's urgent."

Jose hung up and tried to think what to do next. From what Morse had told him he was even more convinced that his Uncle was in the Sotano, and God knows what they were doing to him. The place sounded like a medieval torture chamber.

If they've hurt him, I'll kill every last one of the bastards. It was more urgent than ever to get inside the place!

Chapter 55

Office of the Archdeacon
Castillo de Chipiona
Sanlucar, Spain

The three of them were sitting in the Archdeacon's lounge, each with a glass of scotch and a cigar. Balinska would have preferred Vodka and Messi a joint, but they could hardly refuse the Archdeacon's hospitality.

The Archdeacon had a generous wrist and Messi had drained his first glass in one gulp and was halfway through his second. He was wasn't used to alcohol; he preferred a different poison. But this was a special occasion. He was feeling no pain and having trouble pronouncing their names, *Arshdeacon* and *Bawinsky*, He swallowed the rest of his scotch and took a long pull on his cigar and immediately went into a violent coughing spasm. Once it subsided, he was about to try using their first names when the phone rang, saving him from making a complete idiot of himself.

The Archdeacon answered it and handed the phone to Balinska, "It's Pierre in Montreal, he needs to speak to you urgently."

Balinska took the phone, and as he listened his face turned red, then purple and a vein on the side of his head was visibly throbbing. He slammed the phone down and turned to Messi. "Apparently you fucked up."

Messi was still practicing his speech in his head. He didn't realize that Balinska was talking to him until he picked him up by his collar and lifted him off his feet. He held him a few inches from his face before yelling, "LISTEN CAREFULLY, YOU DRUNKEN PIECE OF SHIT." That got his attention partly from the loudness and partly because the choke hold was turning his face purple; he couldn't breathe.

Balinska continued, "That was Molatov in Montreal. He has just heard from his contact at McGill. Apparently the bomb went off on time, but before the transmission from Copenhagen started; they heard the explosion and canceled it as a precaution." As he said this, he let go and Messi, gasping for air, dropped to the floor and just lay there.

Messi tried to say, "so what does that mean," but all he could manage was "Sho wash . . ." Then he passed out.

Balinska grabbed him, hauled him to his feet, and turned to the Archdeacon. "It's no use trying to talk to him in his condition; we need to get him into a cold shower."

The Archdeacon picked up the phone, dialed a number and spoke briefly to an assistant. A few minutes later two men arrived, loaded Messi onto the stretcher and as they were leaving he said, "Sober him up and make it hurt." Once they were gone, he turned Balinska, "It's going to be an hour or so before they've finished with him, tell me what's happened."

"Well, as I said, the transmission was canceled, so the backup copy in Montreal was not corrupted. It is a day old but still good. I think McGill had already decided they didn't want to continue with it, and this was good reason to dump it. Before they did, they sent a copy to the University of Toronto. So as of now Toronto has a clean version, one day old, but it will be easy to update it."

"How do we know this?"

"I'm not sure, but I think Molatov is paying a grad student, who works part-time in the computer lab, to feed him information."

The Archdeacon took a sip of his scotch before saying, "So we're no better off, the data still exists, and now they will be even more cautious. How did this happen and where do we go from here?"

"I know what you're thinking, and I am as well. He's smart enough with computers but not at planning. He didn't allow for delays; no Plan B. Now I have to destroy Toronto, and we still need Messi to tell us how we can do it."

The Archdeacon topped up their glasses, before saying, "Rome is still on my back; pushing for results but offering no help. I've had more support from Salodin than the Vatican. I'm supposed to make sure that none of this can be traced back to them. But if this goes wrong and backfires they had better watch out. The media would go ballistic for a story like this!"

An hour and a half later, the two attendants brought Messi back, white as a ghost, with a dazed look on his face.

Balinska took over. "Let me tell you what happened. Apparently the bomb went off before the copy was to be sent from Copenhagen. Your timetable had it the other way round. Here," Balinska waved the schedule Messi had given them in his face. "Look at it. See what it says; Copy from Copenhagen to Montreal at 1 a.m. Destroy copy at SecuriteQuebec at 1:30 a.m. Montreal figured something was wrong and canceled it, so the copy in Montreal is still good, one day missing, but not corrupted. And they've sent it to Toronto, so we are no better off than we were before. HOW THE FUCK DID THIS HAPPEN?"

Messi just stood there not knowing what to say, hung over with a violent headache unable to think clearly. He tried to say something, but the words were jumbled and made no sense.

Balinska cut him off. "Here is what is going to happen. Go back to your office and figure it out. You have one hour. If you don't have an answer by then, it means you are no further use to us, and you will be terminated. Do you understand?"

"Yes," he answered not knowing which kind of termination he meant, and in his present condition, not caring.

Messi left, and as soon as he got to his office, he pulled his stash, rolled and lit a joint and took a long, deep drag. It felt good and calmed him down a little, at least he could think.

If the bomb went off on time but before the transmission it meant that the transmission was delayed. How could he be expected to know that was going to happen? But try telling that to Balinska.

And how had they known about the explosion so quickly? He pulled up a Google map of Montreal and found the two locations, the University, and SecuriteQuebec; they were only a few blocks apart. *Shit!* They would have heard the explosion. How was he going to explain this?

What a frickin mess? He thought of just leaving but where would he go? Balinska would find him. Or he could say that the two of them had had a copy of the schedule and hadn't seen any problem with the timing. As the headache and the dizziness began to subside so did his fear; replaced by his usual tenacity.

He went back and explained what had gone wrong, and before Balinska could interrupt, Messi added, "You both had the plan, and neither of you spotted the danger. It's your fault as much as mine. I did the computer hack successfully you failed to spot the flaw in the timing. So if you want to point the finger point it at yourself."

Balinska went ballistic and was about to grab Messi by the throat when the Archdeacon intervened. "Not yet Balinska. Not yet!"

Chapter 56

Hotel Monterrey
Sanlucar, Spain

After an early breakfast, they got into the Jag and drove down the coast road, following the directions he had been given. As he approached the section where Morse said the clearing was, Jose slowed to a crawl. Fortunately, there was no traffic behind him. Isobel spotted it first, and if they hadn't been looking carefully, they would have missed it. Jose found a spot, a few hundred yards down the road, where he could pull off the road and park the car, so it was hidden from the road. Hopefully!

One of the best things about owning a vintage automobile was that everybody noticed it. One of the worst things about owning a vintage automobile was that everybody noticed it.

They walked back to the clearing trying to stay under the cover of the trees. When they reached it, Jose said, "remember that at the back of the clearing, there's a dirt road that leads to the Castillo. There's also a security camera, so we need to stay down and out of view. In fact, I'll crawl through the bush to see if I can find a spot where I can get the lay of the land without being seen. You wait here."

Isobel looked at the undergrowth and said, "I don't like missing the action, but, in this case, I think I'll go along with your plan."

Jose crawled through the brush and elbowed his way to where the trees ended. If he went any further, he would be visible. He saw the warning signs on the fence that it was electrified and that this was private property. As he was going back, a Doberman approached with its fangs showing.

Back in the car, Isobel asked what he had seen, and he told her, then added, "To get into that place we will need to get a search warrant. And we don't have enough firm evidence to get one and even if we did we'd have to knock the juice out of that electric fence."

At the hotel, there was a message waiting for him, from Father William asking him to return his call. After lunch, he phoned the monastery and asked to speak to him. A few minutes later he came on the line and Jose said, "Hello Father how did you know which hotel I'm staying at?"

"I didn't, and you didn't answer your mobile. So I called your office, and it took about twenty minutes to locate you, but eventually they phoned back with this number."

"I'm sorry I had to turn my mobile off, I was involved in something that required no noise. Has something happened?"

"Remember when you were here, and I said that there was a connection between the golden ratio and a mathematical series of numbers, well I found out what it is. The golden ratio, when calculated, is equal to about 1.618. The numeric series gives you the same ratio when you divide successive terms. And what's really interesting is that the mathematician was called Bonacci, the same as the wealthy merchant who built the Castillo. He could have been a descendant.

"By the way I think those codes you showed me, referred to the same mathematical series and translate into the number 2189."

He wanted to ask how he had figured it out, but he had so much that needed doing he didn't have time. "Thank you for this Father. I'm staggered, as always, at the information you either know or can find out. You're better than Google. You should publish an encyclopedia of astonishing facts. I'm sure it would be a best seller. I promise to come and see you soon."

"Just find Father Michael and then you can visit me together."

"What did he tell you?" asked Isobel after he had hung up.

"That there is a connection between the Castillo, the Golden Ratio, and some number series."

"Over my head," she said. "So what happens next?"

I need to call the local police to see if they have someone who can neutralize that electric fence, but with the security cameras and the Dobermans, we'd be visible before we even got near it. And we couldn't do anything anyway, without a search warrant."

"What Dobermans?" she asked, sounding alarmed.

"According to Morse there are four of them. I only saw one, and it had his teeth showing and a very nasty look on its face."

"Then next time, I'm staying in the car. Attack dogs scare me to death."

"We definitely won't be getting a Doberman then."

"Did you say *we*," she said, with a broad smile on her face, "but a spaniel would be okay."

"Just a figure of speech," he said, but it had been an automatic response, and it surprised him.

They drove back to Toledo, to Isobel's apartment, and next morning Jose drove back to Madrid.

Chapter 57

Balinska and Messi were in the Archdeacon's office deciding what to do next. Time was running out. Balinska had got a report back from Toronto. He opened it. "I had my people do some checking, and the report says the data is stored on the University computer, and only Professor Hampton has access to it."

"How long would it take you to crack their system?" Balinska asked Messi.

"Quite a while. I have to get past two, maybe three, levels of security. One is the University's, then Hampton's, and probably the *Dialogue* database. I have the codes from before, but I'm sure they'll have changed them. I did some digging and the security system at the University was developed in-house which makes it that much harder to hack into. I'd love to take a crack at it, but it might take weeks rather than days, assuming I was successful. I don't think we can afford the time."

Balinska smiled but didn't say anything; the ball was back in his court. So much for all the new techno-shit and nerds like Messi, when it came down to the crunch it was his way, the old way that worked. "There are two options, as I see it; destroy the data or get this Hampton to hand it over to us."

"How?" the Archdeacon asked.

"Since Messi doesn't know how to destroy it, we have to use the second option and get the Professor to hand it over."

"Why would he do that?"

"Because we have something he wants in exchange."

The Archdeacon knew what he meant. "You're talking about a ransom."

"Exactly," According to the report he is married and has two daughters aged twelve and sixteen. And if one of them was to disappear I think the professor might be persuaded to trade in the *Dialogue* system for her safe return."

"Excellent idea," said the Archdeacon, who like Balinska still preferred a direct approach. "How long would it take?"

"A few days. I still have people in Toronto who can do this. All we need to know is the girls' routines. They must go to school every day. We find the quietest part of their route and then lift one of them. What do you think Messi? Any problems?"

"Even if he handed over a DVD with a copy of the system. How do we know that they've destroyed the original and any backups?"

Balinska looked at Messi. "Do you seriously think he would risk the life of his wife or the other daughter by keeping a copy?"

"Especially since we have no intention of returning the kidnapped girl. Her body will be found floating in a river somewhere. Correct?" the Archdeacon asked looking at Balinska.

"Precisely. You never return them. They always remember something about the kidnappers; their appearance, or where they were kept. The only safe way is to kill them."

The next day Balinska and Messi drove to San Pablo Airport. There were no direct flights to Toronto, the best they could do was two changes, Madrid, and Heath Row. They didn't notice that they were followed to the airport by a man in a Peugeot who waited until they had checked in before approaching the ticket counter. He got the information he needed and booked himself on the same flights.

Chapter 58

Jose had gone through the information they had, and none of it was important enough to get a search warrant. Their best evidence, the fingerprints on the letter opener, wouldn't stand up in court, and it would be hard to prove a connection to the Castillo.

They could ram their way in, but he knew if he did that his career would be over. One of the hardest things, in the police work, was that you had to stay within the law while the perps could hide behind it.

Even if he could get a search warrant, they still had to get through the electrified gate and fence to get into the compound. He needed to speak to Sparky.

Edward Mantez was in charge of all things 'electric and electronic', and went by the nickname, Sparky. He worked out of the Seville police headquarters and Jose had met him when he was there trying to find the location of the Castillo. Sparky had been interested in the codes $f9$ and $f12$ on the plastic card. Jose had passed on the other information he had been given by Father William.

Jose phoned him and explained the problem of the electric fence. "Is there any way we can kill the power?" he asked.

"If I can get my van close enough to run cables to it I can short it, either by shunting the power for a few seconds or I can blow the whole circuit. In the first case, their security might assume it was just a temporary fault but in the second they would certainly know something was going on. But from what you've told me we have to take out that security camera first."

Jose ran a finger along the scar on his cheek; an indication that he was tense. "We should be able to do that with a sharp shooter, but even if we do, and I get inside what then? It would be an illegal entry. I need some new evidence, strong enough to get me a search warrant."

He was about to hang up when Sparky said, "By the way, I think I have a solution to the numbers on the key. I'm pretty sure that the code is 2189."

Jose, wrote it down, thinking, 'this is starting to sound like the Da Vinci code.'

Prior to his Monday meeting with his boss, Jose had spent several hours over three days trying to think how he could get enough evidence for a search warrant. It was possible that Morse might come up with something, but he couldn't rely on that. His best—actually only—idea was to try and get into the compound unobserved and take a look around to see what he could come up with. But even he wasn't sure he could do it, especially after Morse's description of their security. When he explained the idea to Captain Rich, the response was short and sharp. "No fucking way!"

Jose took a sip of his coffee while trying to counter the Chief's response. "But if I could get in there, just briefly, I might see something we could use."

"Are you listening? You don't invade a private compound. If you were caught we'd have the press all over us; plus it's owned by the Church. I can see the headlines now! *Police invade Church property.* We'd have the Vatican all over us. I told you at the start of this investigation that you were too close to it, and this is what I meant. Do it by the book. Clear?"

Jose knew his only hope was that Morse would come up with something or he got a lucky break from somewhere else. And just to be sure he was ready he organized an 'attack' unit of vehicles and put them on standby, prepared to go at a moment's notice.

Chapter 59

Heath Row Airport
London, England

Morse had phoned Androv from Heath Row. He was keeping Balinska and Messi in his sights, but he wasn't sure if he would be able to stay with them once they landed in Toronto. He gave him the flight details. Androv already had a photo of Balinska, and he knew the two Toronto addresses, the one in Forest Hill and the apartment on Lawrence Avenue. Since they didn't know which one they would use, he would have to tail them. He also informed him that Messi, the computer geek, was with Balinska. Morse heard his flight called and told him he'd call him as soon as his flight landed at Pearson airport.

Androv arrived at Pearson airport early. He had to circle until a parking spot opened up in the short term parking directly across from arrivals. He checked which arrivals gate the flight was using and walked over. There was a crowd of people waiting as passengers began to emerge, but Balinska was easy to spot because of his size and height. He had a pale, anemic looking man with him, who must be Messi.

While the pair pushed their way through the crowd, Androv headed for his car. As soon as he got outside he saw the black Mercedes. He knew which car he would be following.

They exited the airport onto Highway 427 and then 401 East. His phone rang. It was Morse. He brought him up to speed and told him he would let them know which location they were going to, as soon as he knew.

The Mercedes passed the Allen Expressway and the cut- off for Avenue Road, which they would have taken for Forest Hill. They took the exit for Bayview South and a few minutes later the Mercedes pulled up in front of the Edwardian at 775 Lawrence Avenue East.

The chauffeur opened the doors then carried their bags inside. He stood talking to Balinska for a few moments then drove off.

Androv had parked two blocks further along and took out his phone and called Morse. "They're at the Lawrence apartment. What do you want me to do?"

Morse looked at his watch; it was still on British time. He adjusted it. Seven thirty and already beginning to go dark. "Stay where you are and I'll get someone to relieve you in a couple of hours. I don't expect they'll be going anywhere tonight.

Morse was finalizing his plan and documenting what he knew about Balinska, Bernado, and the Castillo de Chipiona. He needed a document that incriminated them enough to get inside that fortress. What he knew was that Balinska was probably the strong man of the outfit and Bernado coordinated everything with the Cardinal in Rome.

He knew from Nadal that the basement contained a room with equipment for water torture and another with some kind of electric shock machine. That on its own might get a search warrant, but it was a long shot. Detective Rodriguez had information about the priests. Maybe together they could build a case. He called him, and they discussed it. They both agreed that they would need something more than what they had. Morse didn't say anything, but he was forming a plan. If he could get a confession out of Balinska that would tie in the Castillo, it should be enough to get a search warrant. He would have to confirm the information that had turned up in Hong Kong. But if it was correct, it might be enough to force Balinska's hand.

All he said to Jose was, "I might have something on Balinska that could help. Have your team ready. I'll keep you up to date and let you know what's happening. Hopefully, I can make it happen in the next two days."

After they had finished, Morse listed what he had.

> *Rape and murder charge from Russia*
> *Id theft*
> *Kidnapping of Father Emile and Father Michael(?)*

Torturing them in the Sotano; waterboarding and electric shock.
Murder of Milos
Murders in Toronto (?)

If he had to bring this to a court of law, it would take too much time to come up with all the evidence. But Morse knew he had two other aces in his hand. He put it all together in the form of a confession.

Chapter 60

99 Via Crescenzio
Rome

He was reading the letter he had received from Kinghaven. The contents were extremely disturbing.

Two Priests had disappeared, Father Emile Calderon and Father Michael Rodriguez. Now a professor from Copenhagen, Marius Sorensen, was missing.

Bethlehem wondered who was behind it. Surely Pope Aquinas would not condone the kidnapping of the researchers, even if he did disagree with what they were trying to do. But Cardinal Karmazin was a different story. He had grown up during the Soviet occupation of his country, and they removed anyone who they saw as opposing them. From what he had heard the Cardinal admired this *strong-arm* approach.

He decided to wait. Maybe one or more of them would reappear with a simple reason to explain their absence. But he doubted it.

He would get a message to Kinghaven to contact him immediately if anything else happened. And to have plans ready to get the *Dialogue* members to safety if it did.

Chapter 61

Grenville Street
Toronto, Canada

It had been easier than he expected. Messi had found the address on the internet. They had rented the van and followed her until she was on a quiet street. They pulled up just beside her and asked for directions. While she was telling them which way to go, the sliding door opened, and she was grabbed and dragged inside. The whole thing took less than a minute.

* * *

Kings College,
University of Toronto

Androv had been tailing Balinska since he got back from Spain. A green BMW had replaced his Lexus. To make sure he didn't lose him, he waited until he had parked it then clamped an electronic transmitter under the rear bumper. The signal was good for five hundred feet, and it showed as a moving red image on the screen of the receiver in Androv's car.

He followed him to Kings College, on the campus of the University of Toronto. This was the last place he expected Balinska to be. 'What the hell was he doing?'

Balinska got out of his BMW with an envelope in his hand. He opened the back door and took a jacket and cap from the rear seat and put them on; both had the UPS logo. He went into the building. Five minutes later he came out without the envelope. Androv made a note of the address and phoned Morse for instructions. "Stay with him and phone me when he's back at his apartment or somewhere that he'll be for a while. I'll send another operator. Switch cars, yours has the receiver in it. Then check who or what is in that building."

Once Androv was relieved, he drove over to Kings College and parked behind the building. Just to the side of the main entrance was a sign 'Department of Physics.' He went inside just as students started emerging from classrooms on either side of a long hallway. He saw a directory off to the right and went over and looked at it. There was a layout of the building with the names of the lecture theaters. At the far end of the building, it showed some faculty offices.

He waited for the students to disappear either to the exit or the classroom for their next lecture then walked to the end of the hallway. There were five offices with the names of the professors on the doors. This must be where Balinska had gone. He had left the envelope for one of them.

He made a note of their names: Mary Simmons, John Hampton, Shavi Kindoori, Isaak Amisov, Peter Drogma.

* * *

The Edwardian Apartments, Lawrence Ave., Toronto

Balinska went over the rest of the plan in his mind. The kidnapping had gone perfectly, and the girl was now in the basement of a house that was used for distributing drugs. She was a cute little thing, just beginning to blossom. Possibilities? Maybe?

It was now Tuesday evening, and everything was ready to go. Thinking about the girl had given him an appetite. He knew who could satisfy it. 'One of his rich bimbos.' He hit the speed dial and waited until she answered. "Hello Ida, have you missed me?"

"You bastard where have you been? You just disappeared without so much as a word."

"That's what happens with my business. I have to go when I have to go. And I don't tell anyone. That's how I stay below the radar. So do you want to get together? Nice and tight."

"You think you can just call me up when you want, and I'll just come running."

"That's the general idea. I'll be at the Marriott in an hour. But if you're not interested just tell me. I've got a few other numbers in my little black book."

"Bastard. I'll be there."

Chapter 62

King's College Circle
University of Toronto

John Hampton was in the faculty lounge when his wife called. She sounded panicky. "The school just called and asked if Kimberly was sick. She never made it to school this morning."

"Just be calm Anne. I'm sure there's a simple explanation," he said, trying to keep his voice calm, belying his own fear. "What about Marnie?"

Marnie and Kimberly were his daughters. Kimberly was sixteen and in high school; Marnie, who was twelve, was still in junior school.

"Yes. She's alright. I phoned and checked. Do you think I should go and pick her up?"

He looked at his watch. It was half past two. "Yes that's a good idea, but don't tell her why. Make up some excuse. I'll cancel my three o'clock tutorial and come straight home. I should be there by the time you get back with Marnie."

He put a note on his door for his students and then told the secretary that he had canceled his tutorial and was going home.

"If anyone asks, I'll tell them," she said.

As he was about to leave, he noticed an envelope in his mailbox. "When did this arrive," he asked. He had picked up his mail this morning, and there was usually only one delivery.

"A UPS man delivered it about an hour ago."

He opened the envelope and looked at the note.

IF YOU WANT TO SEE YOUR DAUGHTER ALIVE FOLLOW THESE INSTRUCTIONS.

DO NOT CONTACT THE POLICE OR SHE WILL DIE.
BE IN EDWARDS GARDENS AT THE SPOT INDICATED ON THURSDAY AT 5 AM.

BRING THE TAPES WITH THE DIALOGUES DATA AND ALL THE ACCESS CODES.

DELETE ALL OTHER DIALOGUES DATA AND WE WILL RETURN YOUR DAUGHTER.

IF YOU DO NOT YOU WILL NEVER SEE HER ALIVE AGAIN.

AND MAKE SURE NO OTHER DATA EXISTS. IF WE HEAR OF ANY DIALOGUE REPORTS IN THE FUTURE YOUR OTHER DAUGHTER MARNIE WILL DISAPPEAR.

Below the note was a diagram of Edwards Gardens There was a path that led from Lawrence Avenue; part way down was a groundskeeper's hut with an X marked beside it.

He put the note in his pocket, tried to appear calm, and left the office. He didn't want the secretary to think anything was wrong.

When he got home, his wife had not yet come back. He went up to his study and called Michael Kinghaven. He explained what had happened and told him he didn't know what to do.

Kinghaven told him that his daughter was far more important than the *Dialogues* and to do what the kidnappers had said. What Kinghaven didn't tell him was that Marius Sorensen had also disappeared, making it three.

Hampton came down from his study and his wife and daughter arrived a few minutes later. He hugged both of them. "Shouldn't we—" his wife began to say.

"Not yet," her husband interrupted, then turned his attention to his daughter. "Marnie do you know who Kimberly's best friends are?"

"Why?" she said with concern in her voice. "What's happened to her?

Hampton took his time replying, choosing the words carefully, "Nothing as far as we know. She left school early," he lied. "She's probably with a friend. That's why we need to phone them."

He tried to avoid appearing anxious; it was difficult, and he could tell his wife was trying hard not to panic.

Marnie told them the one's she knew. He wrote them down and told her to go to her room and do her homework. Fortunately, this was the regular routine, so Marnie didn't question it even though she felt that something was wrong.

Once she had gone, he turned to his wife, "Sorry I cut you off. I didn't want to frighten Marnie, any more than she already is."

"But what are we going to do? Her feeling of panic was rapidly spiraling out of control. Shouldn't we call the police?"

"Not yet until we've called her friends." He knew if he told her about the ransom note, she would collapse completely.

He found the numbers for the names Marnie had given him and called them. There was no answer from many of them; probably still at work. He asked those who answered if they had seen Kimberley. None of them had, and he was beginning to feel helpless when the mother of Louise Turner told him she had seen something. "Louise isn't home yet. She left early this morning for a band practice, so she wasn't here when Kim called. But I watched your daughter walking along the road, and a van stopped beside her. I couldn't see exactly what happened because she was on the far side. But she must have got in because when it drove off she wasn't there. I assumed it was a parent giving her lift."

"Where was this? Which street?" He wrote down the time and the address.

"Did you get the license plate of the van?"

"No, I'm sorry, I didn't, but I'm certain it was green, and I'm fairly sure it was a Chevrolet." He thanked her and rang off.

He told his wife, and she almost yelled, "Now we have to call the police."

She was clenching and unclenching her hands. It was a habit she had, whenever she was under pressure. He didn't answer but went to the liquor cabinet and poured two large glasses of scotch and gave one to his wife. He knew he was going to have to tell her about the note.

He took the envelope from his pocket and before he gave it to her he said, "Try and keep calm. I don't want Marnie to know."

As she read it, her face went white, and he saw her hand begin to shake. "It's that damn group you're part of, isn't it. Why did you have to get involved?"

She was getting hysterical and was on the edge of breaking down. He walked over to her and held her tight. "Listen we have to think calmly what to do. We have to support each other. We can't fall apart. We need to think carefully about what steps to take."

He knew that he should contact the police. They had teams to deal with these situations. But it was different when it was your child. It blocked all other thoughts. He drank his scotch in one gulp and poured another. It burned his throat and started him coughing, but he felt the warmth in his stomach and it calmed him a little.

"Drink the whiskey, Anne," he said, "it will help calm you."

"What are we going to do?" she asked. "We can't call the police now. They'll kill her if we do." Then she went hysterical and yelled so much that Marnie came into the room to see what was wrong. "It's Kim, isn't it? Something horrible has happened to her hasn't it? Is she dead?"

"No, Marnie," her Father answered, "nothing like that. She's just late home from school, and we're not sure where she has gone.

Anne was trying hard to regain her composure. She went over and poured herself another drink.

John Hampton looked at his wife and daughter wondering what to do. Maybe his wife was right; maybe he should wait. But for how long. Today was Tuesday. There was only one day before the deadline. Just waiting and doing nothing was going to be impossible.

Chapter 63

Eaton Center Marriott
Bay Street
Toronto, Canada

He was sitting in his car with his eyes fixed on the lobby of the downtown Marriott hotel. It was ten on Wednesday morning, and he had followed Balinska there the previous evening. He had been relieved by the night operator at midnight but came back at six o'clock. There had been no sign of him. Androv slipped the doorman a fifty and found out that this was a regular rendezvous but not for the last few weeks. It had cost Androv another fifty to learn the name of the woman who had arrived just after Balinska. The doorman told him she was the wife of a prominent financier.

His phone rang. It was Morse. "Where are you?" he asked.

"In my car keeping an eye on the lobby of the Marriott on Bay. Waiting for him and his bimbo to leave."

"How long has he been there and who is the bimbo?"

Androv gave him the details.

"Phone me as soon as he leaves. What about the hacker?"

"I don't know; he's not with Balinska."

That meant that Messi was still in his apartment. Androv had bribed the super and found out he was staying in the guest suite on the ground floor. Two birds with one stone would simplify everything. Especially with his tight schedule. He picked up his phone, looked for the number and dialed. There were several clicks as the call was transferred from country to country until it reached its destination. "Hola," a voice answered in Spanish.

"Hi, Jose, it's Morse. I expect to have everything ready to go this afternoon. Do you have your people in place?"

"Just as soon as I give them the word."

"I'll call you as soon as I have the signed confession."

He drove across the city to Balinska's apartment building, the Edwardian, on Lawrence. It was late morning, so he parked a few blocks away, and out of sight of Lawrence Avenue. From the trunk of his car, he removed his briefcase. It contained the document, an airline folder, his gun and silencer, and two sets of handcuffs. In a compartment were his 'open-sesame' tool collection, several lockpicks and a small microprocessor for reading the bit codes on digital locks. He walked to the tradesman's entrance at the rear of the building and found the door was open. No doubt the superintendent was too lazy to open and close it every time a contractor or service technician needed to get in.

Morse took the stairs up to the fifth floor and walked along to suite 504. The door had a pin tumbler lock, which made things easier. It yielded quickly to his lock-pick. He went inside and found himself in a small lobby with a flight of three steps that led up to a foyer, containing a wing chair and a small table. A door opened off it leading into the living room, with a large picture window. There was a good view of Edwards Gardens.

He checked the apartment from one end to the other, examining each room carefully. Once he had determined there were no unexpected surprises he went back to the foyer, opened his attaché case, replaced his tools and removed the document and a pen and placed them on the table. Then he sat down in the wing chair, going over the plan in his mind wondering how long he would have to wait. It was two hours later when his phone rang. It was Androv to say that Balinska was just leaving. Morse took out his gun, attached the silencer and placed it on his lap.

It was another thirty minutes before he heard the front door open, and Balinska came up the steps. He stopped in his tracks when he saw Morse sitting there holding the gun which was now trained on him. "Who the fuck are you?" he said, "and why are you in my apartment?"

"Such a lot of questions, have you forgotten Sutton Place already." He looked carefully and noticed the telltale bulge under his jacket.

"Just a minute you must be the Russian bastard who tried to eliminate me. Talk of screwing up. I don't know who you are working for, but I imagine the shit hit the fan."

"It was a setback, but we found you again. And this is payback time." There was a muffled report, a small puff of smoke, and Balinska crashed to the floor grabbing his left knee.

"You douchebag, you've shattered my fucking kneecap."

"It won't kill you. I needed to get your attention and let you know who's in charge. Take the gun that's under your jacket and slide it across to me. Do it very slowly and don't try anything foolish, my gun is trained on your head."

Balinska did as he was told, and Morse picked it up and placed it on the table. "I haven't phoned Inspector Mason yet, and if you don't know who he is, your stoolie Woodman worked for him. Before you put a bullet in him, that is. And there is the little matter of the two priests and the professor from Copenhagen. I know you're behind it, and after I've taken care of you and Messi, I plan on paying the Archdeacon a visit at the Castillo."

He noticed a flicker of surprise Balinska's face, as he wondered how much this guy knew. He didn't say anything, just sat there clutching his knee. He was in considerable pain, but he refused to show it.

Morse continued, "It's all here in this document." He picked it up from the table and held it so Balinska could see it. And there's the matter of the outstanding warrants in Russia."

"Why the fuck would you care about that? If you decided to pop me, I could understand but you were tossed out of the police force in Russia. They're hardly your friends."

"We'll get to that in a minute. First you need to sign this." He tossed the document to Balinska."

Balinska read it through, then said, "How do you know all this?"

"That doesn't matter. All I'm looking for is your signature as the paid assassin." Morse answered.

Morse hoped that the facts that he and Rodriguez had put together were accurate enough for Balinska to believe. It worked.

"So what if I am. Why would I sign it? Why would I shop myself and all the others at the Castillo? I'm probably going away for a long time anyway. I don't see any upside for me."

"Let me tell you about the downside; what's going to happen if you don't sign it in the next five minutes," he said looking at his watch, "I have some friends in Hong Kong. I shouldn't really call them friends, more like acquaintances; they're a pretty nasty bunch actually. One of them, in particular, loves little girls, especially the ones who are just nearing puberty, nice and fresh and juicy. He can't keep his hands off them if you know what I mean."

Balinska was now staring at him, his eyes getting even darker, and anger spreading across his face. He knew where this was going! Even with his shattered knee he made a grab for Morse but he was expecting it. There was a puff of smoke, and a bullet hit Balinska on the shin of his other leg. He fell back in agony now with both legs useless.

"Looks like you won't be walking for a while. But you interrupted my story. I was telling you about this pervert who likes little girls. I won't describe what he does to them. It turns my stomach. However, you might be interested that I could tell him where he can find one. You might know her. She's really cute. Her name is Lilette, and her mother's name is Lily. But you know that, don't you? You send them money all the time."

"You fucking bastard, you wouldn't do that? You would have to be a pervert yourself to even suggest it."

"All you need to know about me is that I'll do what it takes to get what I need. Either sign it or I make the call." He looked at his watch, "there are only two minutes remaining." He took out his mobile phone.

Balinska didn't know if he would really do it, but he knew he couldn't take the risk. And he had nothing else left to bargain with. He signed the document and tossed it back to Morse, who looked it over and made sure of the signature and date then placed it inside a folder. Then he opened his briefcase and placed it inside.

"Now let me tell you where you went wrong. You were doing alright running Metachev's drug business. You should have left it at that. When you signed on with those screwballs in Sanlucar, you became a marked man. We needed to know who they were and where they were located. We used you to lead us to them. I followed you from Toronto to the Castillo. I'm sure the security cameras picked me up."

"Fuck, I remember now, the kid at the Avis desk and the car reservation. But the name on the car rental wasn't Russak it was Moors or something like that, and the address was in London. I should have eliminated you then when I had a chance."

"That's right. I used a different identity—Leonard Morse—it's necessary in my business. I knew you didn't know what I looked like. At the Sutton Place, there was too much smoke in the room for you to get a good look. But I knew you would recognize the name, Russak."

"We've been watching you carefully; even followed you back to the Edwardian and the Marriott. How is Ida Goodwin by the way?"

Balinska wondered just how long they had him under surveillance, but he kept his face blank. "So what! And who the fuck is we?" he said with a grimace; the pain beginning to show, "don't tell me you're KGB or whatever they call themselves these days."

"Not bad. Right now I'm working with Interpol. Before that, as Waltmir Russak, I was working with Russian intelligence, investigating the drug networks in Russia. My dismissal in Primorsky Krai was faked so I could go undercover and infiltrate them. They were turning Russia into a haven for drug dealers."

"So you're the patriot who shopped them. I saw it on the news. But why come after me? I'm now a Canadian, nothing to do with Russia. I've already signed the document. What else do you want from me?"

"There's a second reason, and this one is personal."

"What do you mean?" he said, the pain beginning to show on his face.

"Before you were Boris Radovic, you were Borislav Radovic Sokalovsky—"

"So you know my background, so what?" Balinska interrupted.

"Shut the fuck up or I'll put another slug into you," Morse said then continued, "My real name is Waltmir Antonovic Russak." He watched Balinska and saw the realization on his face change, as he made the connection."

"The sailor on Okeansky Prospekt," he said, with the realization that his chances of coming out of this alive had just taken a nose dive.

"That's right, he was my younger brother and if I'd been home you would have died then and there. But I wasn't, I was fighting a bloody war in Afghanistan, and they don't give you time off, not even to avenge the death of your brother. But I vowed that one day I would hunt you down and kill you."

"He came at me with a knife."

"Not the way I heard it. He was so drunk he didn't have a chance."

Radovic didn't say anything; he still didn't know what had happened for certain, back then. His memory of it was still a blank; nothing between the drunk coming at him with a knife and then seeing him lying in the road, covered in blood, clutching his throat. Finally he said, "Who told you that?"

"Some old whore who would do anything for a few dollars to buy her next fix. She had the same eyes as you. Someone said she was *your mother*." Morse emphasized the last two words and watched Radovic, as the anger and shame tore through him. "That's right. She's the bitch that gave you birth, then abandoned you. You weren't worth keeping even by a hooker. You can't get much lower than that. And she's still working the streets. How does that make you feel?"

Despite the pain, Balinska somehow launched himself towards Morse and managed to grab his left leg, then began to pull him towards him. Morse couldn't believe the strength of the man. He was only able to use his arms; his legs were useless, but despite that he was gradually pulling Morse towards him.

"Let go," he warned, "or I'll shoot.

He ignored him and continued to drag him closer until Morse had no choice. There was a click as he pulled the trigger back.

Balinska heard it and knew it was the end. And in that final moment, on the edge of oblivion, he thought about his mother. He hated her for what she had done, but Morse was right.

'I wasn't worth keeping; even by a hooker. It wasn't my mother I hated; it was myself.'

Morse looked at him. This man was evil; he had killed a lot of innocent people, including his brother. But he had to respect his courage. There was no pleading, no sign of fear, almost the opposite. Something expected, even welcomed.

Morse released the trigger. The bullet went in through the right eye socket. The body jerked backward and collapsed in a pool of blood; what was left of the face no longer identifiable.

This was the moment he had visualized so many times since his brother had died. Revenge! He thought it would give him a sense of closure; a release. It didn't!

Chapter 64

Boulevard Lasalle
Montreal, Canada

It was phoned in by a jogger. Every night she ran the same route; along the St. Lawrence, then back through the park. She had seen the car parked there, on her run, almost out of sight behind a row of trees. It was a black Lincoln Continental. At first she thought it was just a couple enjoying a little recreation.

On the second evening, she called the police who said they would look into it. But they didn't and on the third day it was still there. She went over to it then quickly pulled back, holding her hand to her mouth. She crouched behind the car and threw up. There was a body in it and blood everywhere. This time, the police answered her call immediately.

The driver was slumped over the steering wheel with a bullet hole in the back of his head. He was missing the index finger on his right hand.

Forensics confirmed what the police and the jogger knew from the smell, that he had been dead for three days and had been killed elsewhere, then driven here.

Chapter 65

The Edwardian,
755 Lawrence East
Toronto, Canada

Morse was furious with himself. He was supposed to have found out more from Balinska about the Castillo. What security forces they had? Who else they had kidnapped beside the two priests? Why they were in Toronto? But he'd let his personal feelings come into it; lost his objectivity. Exactly why agents didn't work on operations that involved people they knew. He would have to get it from Messi, although he didn't know how much he knew.

Before he left Balinska's apartment, he phoned Jose Rodriguez and told him he had the signed confession. He picked up his briefcase, walked down the stairs to the ground floor and rapped on the door of the guest suite. Messi didn't open it. He just asked, "Who is it?" as he looked through the Judas hole.

"A friend of Balinska's. The police have a warrant out for his arrest, and there is no way he will be able to leave the country." Morse opened his briefcase and took out the airline folder. "He wanted me to give you this and tell you to get out now. It's a ticket to Seville, and the flight leaves Toronto in two hours. Once the police realize that you're associated with him, they'll arrest you. It's up to you. If you want the ticket, you have to open the door and sign for it."

Morse expected more questions, but Messi opened the door a crack, keeping it on the chain. Just enough space for him to squeeze the barrel of his gun through the gap. "Now listen and listen carefully, Messi. You are going to close the door and remove the chain and then let me in. I'm going to count to three and if I don't hear you opening it by then I'll fire a clip of bullets through the door. You'll be dead before you can move."

To emphasize the point, he withdrew the gun and fired a shot just to the left of where Messi was standing.

"Time starts now Messi," and he began to count. He could hear him frantically removing the chain. He had just reached three when the door opened. He stepped inside.

"Just give me the ticket and leave."

"Before I do, there are a couple of things I need to know," he said pressing the gun hard against Messi's head. The first is why you and Balinska came back to Toronto. And don't lie, we've been following you from Sanlucar."

Messi didn't know how much to disclose. This guy was dangerous, but if he gave him the information, Balinska would kill him. "I don't know. And even if I did and told you, Balinska would kill me."

"You don't have to worry about that anymore; he's dead."

Messi hesitated, wondering if he could believe him. He had to be sure; then he would gladly shop all of them. He just wanted to get out of the whole fucking mess. "Okay I'll tell you but first you'll have to convince me that you're telling the truth, that he really is dead."

Morse went behind Messi and pushed his gun into his back. "Okay, let's go. And if you try any funny stuff, you're a dead man."

He marched him up the stairs to apartment 504, with the gun in his back. When Messi saw what was left of Balinska's head, he threw up. "Satisfied?" Morse asked.

This guy is worse than Balinska. He tried to get a grip on himself, but he had to face the fact that he was probably going to die! But he didn't go to pieces. It had the opposite effect. It cleared his mind of everything, except how to survive. And his best bet was to tell him everything.

"I wish I'd never got involved. I thought I was just going to hack into a few computers. Once I found what they were really doing, I wanted out. But I knew that maniac would kill me. Can we go back to my apartment and I'll give you everything I've got. Then you can turn me over to the cops."

Messi told Morse everything and gave him a sheet that listed the names of the *Dialogue* members.

Michael Kinghaven:	Coordinator
John Hampton	Physics Professor
Marius Sorensen	Anthropology Professor
Maurice Svensen	IT professor
Emile Calderon	Priest
Michael Rodriguez	Priest

Messi continued; he didn't know much about who was in the Sotano. He'd only been down there once when Balinska was torturing the first priest. After that, he never went down there again. "And the reason we came back to Toronto was to kidnap the daughter of a professor at the University."

Morse remembered that Hampton was the name of one of the professors that Androv had found when he followed Balinska to the University.

So that is why Balinska was at the University, Morse realized. "Did you kidnap her? Where is she?"

"Yes, we grabbed her in a rental yesterday and took her to a house in Toronto. I stayed in the van. I didn't see much, but I remember passing a theater just before we got there."

"What was her name?" Morse demanded, standing behind Messi and pushing the gun against the back of his head.

This is it, Messi thought. He tried to prepare himself. As he heard the trigger being pulled back, a wet stain began to spread on the front of his trousers. He attempted to speak, but all he could do was stammer, making no sense.

Morse realized what was happening and lowered the gun. "Nothing is going to happen to you if you tell me her name and the name of the theater?"

"All I know is her first name, Kimberly; she is Hampton's daughter, and the theater had something to do with royalty."

"Like Queen or King?" Morse suggested. He wasn't an expert on Toronto."

"No, it wasn't that. I think it was Princess. The one who died in that car crash."

"Princess of Wales?"

"Yes, that's it. It was close to there."

"Where was the van rented?"

"I don't know the location, I didn't rent it, but it had a Budget sticker inside."

"What color and make?" he asked looking at his watch. He wouldn't have time to search for the girl.

"It was green, and I think it was . . . a Chevy," he managed to say, still not sure about this guy. He could be as crazy as Balinska. And once he had told him everything, he would just pop him!

Morse figured he had got all he could from Messi. It didn't tell him everything, but it would have to do. He looked around the apartment for something sturdy. There was a desk with a glass top and tubular metal legs. It had been fixed to the wall with brackets. He pushed Messi over to it and pulled hard on it. It didn't move. He took both pairs of handcuffs from his briefcase and used them to fasten his hands together and one of his feet to the desk. He checked the bathroom cabinet and found a roll of tape. He tore off a strip and placed it over Messi's mouth.

He looked at his watch; 4:30, he had to move fast. He left the building via the rear door, walked quickly back to his car, and headed for the airport. He entered Mason's number and hit call. When he answered he said, "This is Russak Inspector, you don't sound so good. Something wrong?"

"Yes, lots. You fucked me up last time with that fiasco at the hotel. I don't take kindly to being duped. You owe me. I want a meeting, just you and me so I can let you know that no one takes advantage of me like that, without facing the consequences."

"That isn't going to happen. I'm sorry about it, but I was acting under orders, and I don't have time anyway. Just be quiet and listen and you might come out of this with your reputation intact. I'm tying up the loose ends right now, and I can't stop. I have a signed confession from Radovic, also known as Balinska. He's lying on the floor of his apartment. I'm afraid he's dead but at least you won't have to worry about him anymore. And Messi is there as well. He's alive."

"Who the hell is Messi? And what makes you think that finding Radovic's corpse is going to help. They'll have to be another inquiry, and I'll be raked over the coals again."

"No, you won't. Get your spin doctors on it and you'll come up smelling like roses. Write down the details." He gave Mason the address and apartment numbers. "And according to Messi they kidnapped the daughter of a Professor Hampton."

Mason wrote down the information then said, "There was a rumor yesterday about it, from a police informer, but he didn't know any details. Are you behind this as well?"

"Not really, but I have some information about her. Her name is Kimberley Hampton. Her father is a professor at the University, and they've stashed her somewhere near the Princess of Wales Theater. Messi is handcuffed to a desk in the guest suite. He'll give you all the details."

"The van was rented from Budget. They often have a GPS in them, so you should be able to find her. Goodbye, Inspector. Hopefully, for my sake, our paths won't cross again."

Traffic was congested, the middle of rush hour, and it took him an hour and a half to reach the airport. The executive jet was ready with its engines already started. A few minutes later they were in the air.

He looked at his watch 6:00 p.m., right on schedule He used the plane's communication system to call Sanlucar. "Hello, this is *NightFlight*, on its way."

He got the required response, "We're holding *runway 6* for you."

"Balinska's confession has enough evidence for the search warrant. It names the Archdeacon and has details of who they kidnapped and tortured. The pilot says that the weather is good, and we should be on the ground in Sanlucar at 6 a.m. local time. Have someone meet me there and have everything ready to go."

Jose wanted to ask him about Papa Michael but before he could, the line went dead. Either Morse had hung up, or the communication frequency had been lost.

It was almost over. Morse had one final email to send. It used an old protocol, one that they had used when they had worked together previously. Charpentier would know the cipher.

John Leightell

>*To: c:*

>*Subject: Alice*

>*11:1:1 → 11:1:4*
>*11:6:1 → 11:6:5*
>*11:2:1 → 11:2:5*

>*m.*

There was something so illogical about it that it actually made sense. Reverse logic. Like looking at life backward, through a mirror.

Chapter 66

Interpol, Quai Charles de Gaulle
Lyon, France

Willi Charpentier was looking at the email he had just received from Morse. He checked his watch, just after midnight, six in the evening in Toronto.

He had stayed late, waiting for it, to confirm Morse was on his way to Sanlucar. And now he had to decrypt it. He knew the code and the cipher, they had used it in the past, but that was several years ago. He would now have to find it, and he was tired. He didn't need the aggravation.

He would have a word with Morse when this operation was over. It didn't take him as long as he thought. He still had the cipher on his system. He looked at the email again.

Subject: Alice

11:1:1 → 11:1:4
11:6:1 → 11:6:5
11:2:1 → 11:2:5

m

The format was: *verse:line:word*

Code	Cypher	Meaning
11:1:1 → 11:1:4	*The time has come*	*Happening Now*
11:6:1 → 11:6:5	*And whether pigs have wings*	*Flying*
11:2:1 → 11:2:5	*To talk of many things*	*He had the confession*

He was now flying [Toronto to Sanlucar] and he had the confession.

Chapter 67

Office of the Archdeacon
Castillo de Chipiona
Sanlucar, Spain

The Archdeacon was sitting at his desk in the Castillo wondering what had happened. He hadn't slept. He was too aware that the success or failure of their mission would be determined in the next few hours. They had agreed that Balinska would phone each day, at 10 p.m. Toronto time, to give him an update. He had called on Tuesday and told him that they had the girl. But he hadn't heard from him since. He looked at his watch; almost 5 a.m, 11 p.m. in Toronto, an hour past the time they had agreed. Why hadn't he called?

Something had gone wrong. They had agreed that he wouldn't call Balinska, but he couldn't wait any longer. He picked up his phone and dialed. It clicked through; then it rang for a few seconds before going to voicemail. No point in leaving a message.

He got a phone call from one of his security guards who was in Sanlucar, checking what was happening there. The police were still trying to get a search warrant, and there was a line of police vehicles being assembled, including a 'Hummer' with a hydraulic ram.

Now almost positive that the ransom had failed, and the police were getting ready to storm the Castillo, he phoned his security chief and told him to initiate the emergency plan. "Set the timer to start at six and set the delay for two hours, to activate at eight. Put everyone on standby, ready to leave as soon as they hear the siren. If you don't hear from me again, start the siren at seven o' clock."

"What about the people in the Sotano? Do I need to bring them out?"

"No. Leave them there. What they know can die with them. Get going. You've got a lot to do."

The security chief called him back ten minutes later to say that he had set all the timers, and everything was primed to go.

In a final attempt to stop the police from getting a search warrant, the Archdeacon had called Cardinal Karmazin, twice in the last twenty-four hours, but he had been forced to speak to his secretary. She told him the Cardinal was extremely busy but would return his call when he could. Yesterday he had phoned back. The Archdeacon explained what was happening then asked, "Couldn't you use your influence to bring some pressure to bear to prevent them."

"I am sorry Bernado but I cannot and will not. Remember that we agreed that the Vatican would completely deny any complicity if things went wrong. This now seems to be the situation. You are on your own. Do not try and contact us again." Karmazin didn't tell him that he felt the same way.

This was the final straw. The Archdeacon knew they had agreed that the Vatican could never be seen to be involved, but the Castillo was still a Church property, and they could prevent a warrant being issued on religious grounds. They were abandoning him. He was their scapegoat. But if he went down so would the Cardinal.

He took his pen and began writing. *Everything.* How he had been instructed by Karmazin to destroy the *Dialogues*; the capturing and interrogation of the Priests and the Professor. The death of Father Emile; how they had 'hacked' into the computer and found the names of the members of the *Dialogues*. The kidnapping of the girl in Toronto in a final attempt to destroy their data. He avoided mentioning Balinska or Messi by name, he would shoulder that responsibility alone. He ended it with a blistering denunciation of Karmazin.

When he had finished, he put it in an envelope and wrote on it, 'To be opened in the event of my death.' He sealed the envelope and placed it in on his desk.

At six-thirty, the Archdeacon called his security chief but there was no reply. He tried again but still no response. He tried the Control room, and a security guard answered. "Where's the Chief?" he asked.

"I don't know. I haven't seen him," the guard replied, "but someone said they saw him leave fifteen minutes ago for Seville."

"The coward, deserting a sinking ship. Who am I speaking to?"

"Avilar, sir, and we are wondering what we should do. We haven't received any instructions."

"Very well Avilar I'm putting you in charge. The Chief told me he had set the timer and alarm. Please check and if they aren't activated, set the timer to go off at eight and the evacuation siren at seven. Do you understand?"

"Yes, Archdeacon."

"Good. Thank you."

He took his Luger out of the safe. The moment had come. He wouldn't fail this time. He placed the barrel of the gun in his mouth.

Chapter 68

Everything was ready. The executive jet was on the ground at 5:30 a.m, thirty minutes ahead of schedule. As soon as it taxied to a stop, a police officer took the signed confession and a second envelope that Morse handed him. He jumped into the waiting police car and raced towards the courthouse where a judge was waiting to sign the search warrant. The police assault team were hidden behind an abandoned warehouse on the old road to Sanlucar. The convoy of vehicles had Jose's car in front, followed by a cube van with the words 'High Voltage' painted on the side, driven by Sparky. Behind that was an armored police 'Hummer' with a hydraulic ram mounted on the front. These were followed by an unmarked car, carrying the police chief, and four police cars, each with four uniformed officers carrying automatic rifles.

A police launch and a coast guard vessel were standing by in the harbor at Sanlucar. They had instructions to proceed directly to a point one hundred and fifty yards offshore, directly behind the Castillo, once they received the order.

Jose's phone rang, and he quickly opened it and checked the caller. This was it. "Rodriguez."

"Hello Jose, we have it, and we should be with you in five minutes. There's also an envelope addressed to you."

Jose called the police launch and coast guard and told them to go, then walked down the line of vehicles telling everyone to get ready, they would be on their way in a few minutes. It was 6:15 a.m.

They heard the sound of a car traveling at high speed. It screeched to a halt beside the convoy and the driver handed the search warrant to the Police Chief, and the other envelope to Jose. The Chief scanned it then passed it Jose, who had torn open the other envelope. It contained a single sheet of paper with the message:

jr:

The code you want is 2189. Good luck.

m.

He stuffed it into his pocket and gave the order to proceed. He led the way until they were almost opposite the clearing. He got out of his car and signaled the others to stay where they were. The road had been closed off two hours earlier, so there was no traffic to contend with. Jose led the way on foot, followed by Sparky, who drove his van up to the fence while the Hummer waited at the rear of the clearing.

Once he was at the gate, Sparky got out, took an electrical meter from the van, pulled on a pair of thick rubber gloves and clipped the wires to the fence. "Not enough to stop an elephant but sufficient to give it a nasty shock," he said as he looked at the meter. He went back and collected two thick cables that he connected between the fence and two terminals on the van. He opened a panel on the side, revealing a large switch. He looked back to the clearing and located Jose. He held up his thumb to indicate he was ready. Jose walked back to the road and signaled the other vehicles to follow. Sparky counted down, "Three, two, one," and threw the switch. The circuitry in the van shorted the electricity in the fence. There was a large spark. Sparky checked the meter which now showed no voltage at all. "If they didn't realize it before they sure as hell know we're here now."

Sparky moved the van out of the way, and the Hummer rammed the gate. It had dragged it and a large section of fence halfway down the road before they fell away. The Hummer continued and stopped just short of the main gates of the Castillo. Jose and the police cars followed. The officers jumped out and formed a semicircle with their automatic rifles at the ready.

The Dobermans came out of the trees snarling and tried to attack the police as they got out of the cars. No-one had brought a stun gun, so they had no choice but to shoot them.

A small door, to the side of the main gate opened and a uniformed security guard, came out. "What the hell is going on? What are you doing here?" he asked. "This is a private residence, and you are trespassing. Please turn around and leave." His voice had an edgy sound to it, as he looked at the sixteen police officers.

Jose walked forward and handed him the warrant. "This search warrant authorizes us to enter the Castillo and take into custody any property or persons that we deem suspicious. Now open these gates."

"I need to take this search warrant inside to my superiors to have them decide what to do."

"No, you don't. You are obstructing a police investigation, and unless you cooperate right now, I will place you under arrest and have you taken into custody. Then I will have the 'Hummer' ram the gates. Do I make myself clear?" He turned round and nodded to the armed police officers, who aimed their rifles directly at the Guard. There was an audible click as they released the safety catches.

It had the desired effect. He went back to the small door, with Jose right behind him. As they entered the compound, Jose thought he heard a gun being fired; a single shot. A few seconds later the gates opened. The Guard started to walk back towards the buildings when Jose halted him by saying, "where do you think you're going?"

"Back to the security building. Why?"

"You're not going anywhere; you stay with me. You're our eyes in here; you are going to take me where I want to go."

There were five main buildings with the largest an imposing mansion that he guessed was the original Castillo. The others looked newer, and he guessed they had been added fairly recently. He saw several cars in a parking area, including a blue Opel Corsa with the license plate 3762DCS. So I was right, he thought, let's hope he hasn't escaped. He assigned one of the police to keep an eye on the cars and to make sure no-one used them to try and escape.

He turned his attention back to the guard, "Which building houses the Sotano? And where is the Archdeacon's office?"

The guard pointed to the original Castillo and added, "His office is in there, and the Sotano is in the basement."

Morse, who had followed the police into the compound, overheard what the guard said and saw where he was pointing.

Jose turned round and directed six of the police to follow him with their rifles ready in case they ran into any opposition. He pushed the guard ahead of him, "You lead the way. If there's any gunfire, you'll take the first bullet. Let's go." They moved quickly towards the main building.

Suddenly there was an announcement over a loudspeaker system for everyone to evacuate, followed by the wail of a siren. People began emerging from different buildings, heading for the main gate. Jose told the remaining police to move them over to the wall to the side and to keep them there. He had seriously misjudged how many people lived in the compound. He radioed central dispatch and ordered them to send three more buses immediately.

A group tried to leave by the seaward door and were confronted by the police launch and the Coast Guard. They were given instructions over the bull horn to remain where they were on the dock.

Under cover of the people milling in every direction, and the sound of the siren, Morse slipped into the Castillo unnoticed and headed down the hallway towards the large door at the end. He guessed it was the Archdeacon's office and has he got closer his assumption was confirmed by the sign that read, '*Office of the Archdeacon.*' He removed his gun from the holster under his arm. As he neared the door of the office, he called out, "I'm coming in, put your hands in the air so I can see them."

There was no answer. He repeated his warning again, still with no response. He flattened himself against the wall, held his pistol in front of him in his right hand and turned the handle with his left. He pushed the door open with his foot. He quickly looked in and then relaxed the grip on his gun. What had once been the Archdeacon was now an almost headless corpse, in a purple and white cassock, flecked with blood and parts of his brain.

Switching his thoughts and eyes away from the body, he saw an envelope on the desk. He pulled on a pair of latex gloves and walked over. It had splashes of blood on it. It was closed with the Archdeacon's wax seal. Morse picked it up and placed it in his inside jacket pocket. He left quickly, closing the door behind him.

Once Jose had restored order, and the people had been organized into groups awaiting the arrival of the buses he turned his attention back to the Archdeacon and the Sotano. With the guard in front of him, he went into the building and down the hallway. When he reached the closed door, he stopped and called out, "Please open up, Archdeacon. I don't want to have to shoot my way in."

There was no reply. Jose slowly started to open the door, just far enough for him to take a quick look into the room and immediately pull his head back. There was no need for caution. The body of the Archdeacon was lying across the desk, and there was blood everywhere. It explained the shot he thought he had heard as he came through the gates. The guard who had guided them looked at the dead body of the Archdeacon and felt he was going to be sick. He assumed the police had killed him and thought he might be next. He leaned against the wall at the side of the doorway. His hands were shaking.

Jose grabbed him and pushed him forward down the hallway, away from the office. "Take us to the Sotano. And fast, if you want to stay alive." The guard took the threat literally and almost ran. They went past several rooms until they reached a large paneled dining room. The guard went to the far side and pushed a switch hidden by a protruding sconce. There was the hum of an electric motor and part of the paneling slid away, revealing a large door. It had the same security system, which Jose had seen on the ocean side. He turned to the guard, "Okay, where's your key?"

The guard gave it to him.

"Now I need the code that goes with it."

"I don't have one for this door."

"Why not, I thought each key had a matching code?"

"This door requires the master code, and only three people have it, the Archdeacon, Balinska, and the head of security."

Jose knew that Balinska and the Archdeacon were dead. "Where's the head of security," he asked.

"I think he left about an hour ago, to Seville, that's where he lives."

"Shit," he exclaimed, "do you know his address in Seville?"

"No," the guard replied, "but I think I could find it. I've been there a couple of times."

Jose thought about it for a few seconds; it might take forever to find him, and he suspected this guy was lying anyway, just buying time. Which is what he didn't have. If the timer had been activated, the explosives could blow at any moment.

He would have to do it himself and hope the code that Father William, Morse, and Sparky had given him was correct. There was some reassurance that they had all come up with the same number. First he had to empty the building. If it went up, he didn't want anyone else going up with it, just himself and whoever was in the Sotano.

He turned to the police officer to his right and said, "Take the guard outside, and put him against the wall with the others."

The guard turned white. "No, please I'm just a security guard. I had nothing to do with those monsters. I have a wife and two small children."

Jose didn't know what the guard was talking about and ignored him.

He told the other officers to make sure there was no one else left in the building and then to get out themselves.

Five minutes later a policewoman came back and told him the building was empty. Jose thanked her then opened his notebook to the page where he had written the code, *2189*.

Here goes. If Father William, Morse, and Sparky were correct, he would personally thank them. If they weren't, it wouldn't matter. He wouldn't be around to tell them they were wrong.

He checked his watch. It was 7:40 a.m.

He slowly inserted the key and turned it. The plastic cover on the keypad slid out of the way, and a small red light in the top corner began to blink. He took a deep breath then slowly and very carefully he entered the code. All he had to do now was press the 'Enter' key at the bottom of the number pad.

Chapter 69

DCI Mason was reviewing the information Morse had given him. He had sent two detectives to the Lawrence Avenue apartment, and they confirmed that there was an almost headless body in one and a scared, handcuffed, pasty-faced kid in the other. Mason told them to stay there and make sure no one entered either of the two apartments.

After he had got the confirmation, he had informed the Police Chief. "Fuck," the captain said, "I thought this was behind us. Now we've got to deal with it again. You say that that Russian detective called it in. Who the hell is he?"

"According to the information we have, he's a detective with the Russian drug squad. If we blame the deaths on rival drug gangs, and we can find the girl quickly, we might come out of it smelling good."

The Chief glared at him. "Cut out the bullshit, Mason. All I'm getting is the stink. Alright, I want your team in the conference room in thirty minutes. I don't care where they are or whether they're on or off duty. I want them there."

The detectives were all assembled wondering what was going on. The police chief and Mason came into the room, and they all stood up and stopped talking. "Thank you, said the chief. Sit down and we'll tell you why you're here. Chief Inspector Mason will give you the facts and then I'll tell you how we're going to deal with it."

Mason gave them the details about Balinska and Messi and that they had received a tip-off that it was gang warfare. He avoided any mention of Russak. Then he gave them the information on the kidnapped girl.

There was a buzz of conversation as the detectives reacted to the news, which quickly died down as the chief stood up and looked around the room. "Listen carefully because I don't want any mistakes. I want this handled with kid gloves and the only people you talk to are the DCI and the colleague you are assigned. If even a whisper makes it into the press," he paused and looked at each one individually, "I will personally haul your ass into my office and bust you back to uniform. Then I'll find you a posting somewhere north of the Arctic Circle. Do I make myself clear?" Murmurs of 'Yes Sir.' went around the room before he said. "Good. Mason will now give you your instructions. And let's get this wrapped up quickly so we can all move forward."

As the chief left the room, Mason stood up and issued instructions. He detailed four of his detectives to the Edwardian, to meet with the two already there. They were to request a police van, unmarked, to accompany them, with a body bag. Then get the corpse into the bag and into the vehicle without attracting attention. The kid was to be brought back to headquarters so that they could find out exactly what he knew.

When the four had left, he gave them the details of the search for the kidnapped girl. He had requested forty uniforms to go door to door in a radius of one mile around the Princess of Wales Theatre, to see if anyone had seen anything.

Two officers from Motor Vehicle Thefts were assigned to find out which Budget location had rented the van. He told the other detectives to coordinate the uniforms in the search area and to work with the MVT. He set up a lead for each group and told them he wanted a verbal report every hour.

Messi was brought back, and Mason questioned him. He was pretty sure he wasn't hiding anything, but all he seemed to know about was the Princess of Wales Theatre. "Did you see the house where they took her?" Mason asked.

"Yes, but I've no idea how we got there or what street it was on. I've never been to Toronto before."

"How long was it between the theater and reaching the house?"

"Just a few minutes," Messi told him.

Mason left the room and got the information to the police checking the area.

The first reports coming back from the house to house came up blank. But in the third report a woman on John Street said she was just leaving her apartment when she had noticed a green van going down the street. It was about the size of a minivan but without windows. What had caught her attention was that it was going very slowly as if the driver wasn't certain where he was going. She wasn't sure, but she thought it turned left onto Nelson Street. She didn't know the make, and she didn't remember any part of the license plate.

Then he got a call from MVT. They had found the Budget rental office on College, and it did have a GPS tracker in it. The van was a green Chevy, plate number AVBG 378. The GPS confirmed that it had traveled from the rental office to a stop on Devonshire Place and from there it had driven to Nelson Street. It would take them a little longer to get the exact number of the house. He ordered a SWAT team to Nelson Street to stand by for further instructions.

While he was waiting for MVT to get back to him, he got an incident report from an officer at 29 Nelson Street. He had seen movement in the building but when he knocked on the door several times, no one answered. He was sure there was someone inside.

Mason was sure that had to be it, but he needed confirmation. He didn't want anything to go wrong. He had the detective in charge take a photo of the house and send it to him. As soon as he got it, he showed it to Messi. "Does that look like the house?" he asked hopefully.

Messi looked at the image; it wasn't entirely clear, and then he recognized it. "Yes, I remember those symbols on the glass doors, they looked like dollar signs."

Mason looked over his shoulder and saw the two glass panels in the doors and symbols at the top of each. Mason called the SWAT team leader and gave him the go ahead, but told him to leave the line open so he could hear what was happening.

Mason put the phone on his desk and pressed the speakerphone button. He heard the sound of breaking glass and a door being broken down; then boots echoing down a hallway. Then nothing for several seconds, then a scream and a gunshot. Someone yelled, "Fuck, what's happening?" then nothing. He picked up the phone. He had been cut off. He was beginning to curse when it rang. "Yes, who is this and what the fuck is happening. I said to keep this line open."

"Calm down sir, we've found her. She was in the basement, and she's alive, but not in great shape. They roped her to a chair and used hockey tape to tie her legs and wrists together and wrapped it around her mouth so she couldn't yell for help."

"Thank God. Get her to a hospital as soon as possible."

"I'm already on it there's an ambulance on its way from Mount Sinai. It should be here any minute."

"Good work. I'll meet you there. I heard a gunshot; what was that?"

"Just a warning shot. They were trying to get out the back way. But we had a team stationed back there. We'll need to get forensics and the drug squad down here. It looks to me like a crack house. The uniforms are rounding up the residents, and we'll take them back to fifty-two division, that's the closest."

At Mount Sinai Hospital, Kimberley Hampton was checked carefully and thoroughly. She was dehydrated and had a few cuts and bruises, but they would disappear in a few days. The lasting injuries would be emotional ones.

Once he was sure she was okay, Mason dispatched a car to pick up her parents and then phoned them to tell them that they had found their daughter. He reassured them that she had not been assaulted in any way.

The Police Chief called a press conference for 4 p.m. that afternoon. With Mason by his side, he explained that as a result of police investigations and excellent undercover work they had found and rescued the kidnapped girl who was now back home with her parents. He especially thanked Detective Chief Inspector Mason, who had headed up the recovery that involved the coordination of several specialized units from different branches of the police force.

Mason was surprised by the praise, thinking to himself, 'maybe Slippy Mickey is learning to share the successes as well as the failures.'

The Chief also added that as a result of a tip-off they had found the dead body of Andre Balinska, previously called Boris Radovic, a leading figure in the Toronto underworld. "We believe his death was gang-related."

They had also taken into custody, Antonio Messi, a resident of Seville, Spain traveling on a Romanian passport. He was an associate of Radovic but not in any way involved in the kidnapping.

He closed the conference, "At this time we are not taking any questions. A fact sheet detailing what I have just said will be available from our media office within the hour. There will be another conference once all the information has been processed. Thank you."

The Police Chief and DCI Mason were commended for their quick thinking and actions in finding and recovering Kimberly Hampton. The death of Balinska was the subject of a police investigation, and the conclusion was, as expected, that it was gang related, and no further action was needed. The media didn't believe it and tracked it for three months, trying to uncover some dirt, before giving up.

Messi was quietly deported to Rumania to stand trial on an outstanding warrant for credit card theft.

Chapter 70

Castillo de Chipiona
Sanlucar, Spain

Jose's index finger was poised over the *Enter* key. He closed his eyes—he would have said a prayer if he had been religious—then counted down; three two, one, and pressed the button.

His eyes were still closed, but he neither heard nor felt anything. He opened them slowly. The blinking red light had turned to a solid green, and the door was slightly ajar. He pushed it with his hand, but it was too heavy, so he leaned against it and had to push hard to get it open. As he did so, he yelled at the top of lungs, "Papa Michael, Papa Michael."

The time was seven forty.

At the bottom of the stairs was a hallway leading off to the left with several doors. The first one and one near the end needed a key, but all the others were fastened with two bolts, top, and bottom. He listened carefully; there was a muffled sound, faint, somebody calling for help. *Thank God. He was still alive!*

Jose narrowed the source to one of the doors. He held his breath as he drew back the bolts, but it wasn't Papa. It was a man in his fifties with a blank look on his face. He looked at Jose but didn't say anything.

The detective helped him to his feet, and the man yelled in pain as soon as he put weight on his left leg. Jose placed an arm around his shoulder to help reduce the pressure and then led him towards the stairs. As he did, he asked him, "Is anyone else down here? A priest called Father Michael and another called Father Emile?"

The man looked at Jose and said slowly, "I don't know. . . . I can't remember . . . it." He paused trying to recall what it was he meant to say.

Jose realized that there wasn't much time. Did he have time to check every room? He looked at his watch; seven forty-five.

The man placed his hand on Jose's arm and said, "I know now. It's about . . . the other rooms. That's it. Someone else."

Jose looked at him. "Which room? Do you know?" There was panic in his voice.

The man shook his head. Jose didn't know whether that was because he didn't know which room or that he didn't understand what Jose was asking.

Jose moved quickly along the corridor stopping at each door and calling, 'Papa Michael.'

At the fifth door he thought he heard a low moan followed by a voice, barely audible, "In here. Help me. Please!"

Jose undid the bolts and pulled the door open with such force that one of the hinges tore away. There, on a bed in the corner, was Father Michael, shivering and hardly able to lift his head. All he had on was an undershirt and a pair of dirty trousers. Jose carefully lifted him and carried him to where he had left the other man. As he did so, he said, "Thank God, Papa. I was afraid they might have killed you. Is there anyone else down here?"

Papa looked at Jose and said slowly, "I think there was someone else, Jose, but I'm not sure."

Jose was thankful he had remembered his name, but they didn't have time to wait until he was sure. He turned towards the stairs still with Papa in his arms, and as he did so, Father Michael saw the other man. "That's him, Jose . . . we were the . . . only ones."

Jose wasn't sure if he could trust his uncle's memory; his thinking was confused. But he decided it was probably faster to get these two out then come back down and check to see if Father Emile was in one of the other rooms. Somehow he managed to get them both up the stairs and out of the building.

He looked around. The compound was empty of people. Everyone had been loaded onto buses and taken to the police station in Sanlucar. There were still several empty cars; one with its engine running, waiting for him. It drove over, and Jose recognized the driver, by the fact that he was too tall for the car and by the feather protruding through the window. "Franz, thank God you are here. Get these two into the car. I have to go back and see if there are any others."

"No you don't," Franz answered.

"What?"

"I asked the security guard who led you into the building. He's married to the cook, and she told him that she only prepared two meals for the people in the Sotano."

Jose wondered what had happened to Father Emile, but there was no time to ask them questions. He could do that later. Once they had the two of them in the back seat, Jose jumped into the front seat and told Franz to put his foot down." He looked at his watch, seven fifty-eight.

Franz didn't need any other encouragement. He was used to the autobahns and was well out of the compound and on the road to Sanlucar when they heard the explosion. Franz slowed the car, but Jose said, "Keep going, Franz. We can't stop, we need to get to the hospital as fast as possible."

Jose looked out of the window, back towards the Castillo. There were flames shooting into the air and debris flying everywhere. Large plumes of black smoke rose upwards, and a black residue was falling from the flames, covering everything with a thick coating of ash.

What Morse had told him about the basement being wired had been true. They had got out just in time.

When they got to the hospital, the doctors rushed the two men to Emergency. Jose stayed behind to fill out the paperwork and realized that he didn't know who the second man was. "Stay there," the attendant said, "I'll go and find out."

She returned a few minutes later and told Jose that the man didn't remember, but Father Michael told her that he thought he was a professor, but that's all. She added that he was still very confused and could well be wrong.

Franz, who was standing behind Jose, said, "You finish the forms. I can't use my phone in here. I'll go outside and see if I can find out anything."

Outside Franz contacted his assistant in Munich. He gave her a description and told him to check all missing persons' reports for the last month, looking especially for any academics on the list.

Less than twenty minutes later he got a return call. It was his assistant. "Did you get it?"

"I did. There were two professors listed as missing. One of them was on vacation and had disappeared in Australia, so that ruled her out.

The other one was a Professor at Andersen University, in Copenhagen. The girl on the switchboard knew who he was; apparently the whole University does. She put me through to his department, and I got a full description. It matched the description you gave me. His name is Marius Sorensen, and he's a professor of anthropology. Several weeks ago he left on a trip to Canada, Montreal, and Toronto, and never returned. According to the airlines, he was on the flights from Toronto to Copenhagen but after that, nothing. He vanished into thin air." Franz went back inside and gave the information to Jose and the attendant.

They both sat in the waiting room and half an hour later the doctor came out and told him that they were going to admit both Father Michael and the Professor. Their initial examination revealed some bruises and torn muscles, and Sorensen had a slight fracture in his left leg, but other than that they were physically alright. What concerned the doctor was their dazed condition and inability to answer basic cognitive questions. They suspected they had been administered some kind of psychedelic drugs. Both men had burn marks on their temples, consistent with electro-shock therapy given by someone who didn't know how to do it or didn't care. They were going to keep them at the hospital for further tests.

As they were leaving the hospital, Jose turned to Franz, "I never asked you what you were doing here? Not that I didn't appreciate the help."

Franz smiled as he replied, "You didn't think I was going to miss the finale did you. I put too much into the opening acts."

It took several days for the detectives in Sanlucar to process all the people taken into custody. Most of them were innocent, they just worked there and had no idea what was going on. They were released immediately, but the remainder were interrogated. Those charged with being accessories to kidnapping and murder were denied bail.

The press was desperate to find out what had happened. They questioned all those who had been released, as well as local residents, but they didn't know anything or weren't talking. The police released a terse statement that they were investigating charges of murder and kidnapping and would release a full statement once their inquiries were complete.

Chapter 71

Hotel Monterrey
Sanlucar, Spain

Morse booked into the hotel he had used when he was here before. Once in his room, he put on a pair of latex gloves took out the letter and used a knife to open it. He wanted to avoid contaminating it in any way, in case they needed to check it for fingerprints and forensics.

It consisted of five handwritten pages; he assumed it was in the Archdeacon's hand. He looked at the final page and it was signed:

> *Father Bernado*
> Archdeacon
> Castillo de Chipiona

It was a detailed account of what had transpired over a period of approximately eighteen months. It began with his appointment as Archdeacon and his call to Rome to meet with Cardinal Karmazin and the extraordinary assignment to remove the *Dialogues* by whatever means were necessary.

The organization of the Regents was described, and there was a reference to the hiring of a computer expert and a Chief Interrogator. No names were given, but Morse knew he was referring to Messi and Balinska.

Bernado spared no detail; the letter detailed the kidnapping of the Priests and the anthropology Professor, as well as the torture carried out in the Sotano. It even described the waterboarding and electric shock that was used.

It was obvious he did not know what had happened in Toronto, just the fact that he had lost contact with them. And feared the worst.

The final page was a vitriolic attack on Cardinal Karmazin and the indication that the Vatican must have known what was happening. He had pleaded with the Cardinal to use his influence to prevent the police from obtaining a search warrant. He had turned a deaf ear.

Morse sat back in his chair and exhaled. This letter was political dynamite. He called Charpentier and gave him an account of the contents of the letter. He was told to get back to Lyon on the next plane.

* * *

Interpol, 3-I, Lyon

Morse had arrived back the previous evening, and when he got back to his office, there was a lengthy voice message from Rodriguez giving him the facts about what had happened. He also thanked him for his part in getting the Balinska confession. Without it they never would have got the search warrant. The message ended with a personal thanks; the code he had given him had been correct!

After listening to the message, he took the Archdeacon's letter to Charpentier and waited for him to finish reading it. He could see the look of disbelief spreading across his face. "I've dealt with some damaging evidence in my career but nothing like this. If it's released to the press, it will almost certainly destroy this Cardinal Karmazin, the Pope and possibly the Vatican itself. That would only be the beginning, the Church itself may not survive. But we can't just sit on it. What do we do?" he said, directing his questions at Morse.

Morse thought back to the list of names that Messi had given him; in particular the coordinator Michael Kinghaven. Perhaps he should have the letter. The *Dialogues* were the ones that the Cardinal and the Archdeacon had tried to destroy. They would know better than anyone, what should be done.

Morse and Charpentier discussed the idea. It wasn't an ideal solution. Passing the buck in a way, but they couldn't come up with a better solution, so they decided to get in touch with him. Morse would personally deliver the letter. It was too sensitive to trust to anyone else. There was a caveat. If nothing had happened in two months, they would assume that Kinghaven had failed, and they would be forced to release it to the public .

* * *

University of Stockholm

Morse had flown to Stockholm that morning and was briefing Kinghaven on what had happened. A Castillo near Sanlucar had been raided by the police, and they had found a priest and a professor in the basement. Their names were Father Michael Rodriguez and Marius Sorensen.

Kinghaven let out a sigh of relief. "Thank God!" he said, then quickly added, "What about Father Emile? Wasn't he there?"

Morse looked puzzled for a moment; then he remembered the name from the voice message. "No. Inspector Rodriguez left me a message; Father Emile wasn't there. I'm sorry."

"What about John Hampton's daughter. Are they the ones who kidnapped her? Is she safe?"

The detective raised an eyebrow in surprise. "How did you know about the kidnapping?" he asked.

"John Hampton phoned and told me. I told him to forget about the *Dialogues* and just give them what they demanded. You still haven't told me what happened to her."

"She's okay and reunited with her parents. He explained the role played by Messi. The police found her, due in part, to his cooperation. Once he knew that Balinska was dead, he was willing to tell them everything."

Morse then explained about the letter then gave it to him. He watched Kinghaven's face seeing the expression change from shock to anger to disgust. "This suggests the Vatican planned the whole thing."

"I'm not sure they organized it, but they were definitively involved. The problem is what do we do with it?"

Kinghaven looked it over again before saying," Perhaps we should give the Vatican a chance to resolve it internally. I have a contact there."

The next day Kinghaven placed an ad in the Atfonbladet newspaper and left the letter with the bank.

Chapter 72

Papal Apartment
Vatican City, Italy

Cardinal Damien was shown into the Papal apartment. The Pope had suggested they meet there because it was less official and more private than any of the formal meeting rooms.

The Pope spoke first. "Good morning, Cardinal. I trust you are well. I am told you wish to see me on an urgent matter. How can *We* be of service?"

Damien noted the use of the word *'We'* and knew that the Pontiff was elevating this to avoid personal responsibility. Damien was equally determined to lay the blame directly on his shoulders.

Accordingly he began in a direct manner. "Thank you Your Holiness, but I'm sure you know why I am here."

"No Cardinal, I don't. Please explain." He made it sound like an order rather than a request.

Damien replied in a similar tone. "Very well. I'll *instruct* you. You must have heard about the death of the Archdeacon at the Castillo de Chipiona in Spain."

Damien had noticed a momentary flicker of concern in the Pope's eyes before he replied, "Yes, I heard. Terrible. Such a sad end."

"Who told you? Karmazin!"

This time, there was a definite look of unease. "Yes, I think it was, and I will thank you to address him correctly as Cardinal."

"If the letter is made public he will never be called Cardinal again."

The Pope tried hard to remain calm, but his expression betrayed his apprehension. "What letter?"

Damien removed the letter from his pocket and placed it in front of the Pope. "This is a copy of the letter the Archdeacon wrote just before he killed himself. Read it. Take your time. I can wait."

The Pope hesitated, afraid of what it might contain. He picked it up, took it out of the envelope and began to read. As the realization of what it meant sank in, his face turned white. When he had finished, he said, "This is the first time I have seen this letter. I had no knowledge of this. You should talk to Cardinal Karmazin. He apparently was behind it."

"That really doesn't matter. Karmazin is named in the letter as the person who instructed Bernado to destroy the *Dialogues*. But the letter makes it very clear that those instructions came from the very top."

"I never authorized this. I am not a murderer. This was Karmazin's doing. He told me they were questioning those Priests. That was all. I deny any involvement."

"Your denial is meaningless. Whether you admit it or not, you are implicated by association. You appointed Karmazin to your Council of Advisors. It was after he abandoned the Archdeacon, that he committed suicide. Can you imagine what the paparazzi will do with this? They'll tear you and your conservative supporters to shreds. And the fallout may well destroy the rest of us."

The Pope's complexion had gone from white to pink to red. "And what do you propose?"

"Let me repeat the words once addressed to the rump parliament in England, not long after the King had lost his head. They seem appropriate. *You have sat too long. Depart, I say, and let us have done with you. In the name of God, go!*"

"How dare you. Remember I am your Pontiff. Do not dare to insult this holy office."

"I do not insult the office. I insult what you have made of it."

"I think you have said enough. Now it is time for you to depart. *In the name of God, go!*"

"Not quite yet. You haven't heard my terms."

"How dare you. You cannot dictate terms to me."

Damien paused for a moment. He had asked himself the same question many times over the past few days; since he had received the letter. He had been raised in the Catholic faith to revere the Pope. He was God's representative here on earth. As such he was infallible.

He had wrestled with his conscience. 'Do I have the right to do this?' But he knew he had to. He had to remove this man, and his advisors, who had brought shame and disgrace to the Papacy and the whole Catholic Church.

He looked directly at the Pope, now certain of what he was doing and answered him. "I can, and I will dictate the terms. In a few days, you will tender your resignation. Freely and without influence as is required by Canon Law. Hopefully, that will give the press a scapegoat, in this case, the correct one, on which to pin the blame. Maybe, just maybe, the letter can be kept secret. And maybe, just maybe, the Church will survive."

Chapter 73

The resignation of the Pope had shocked everyone. The reason given—
that the Church must respect its history and reject attempts to change
it—had been misunderstood by some of his closest advisors. They had
mistaken his intentions and misapplied them. He refused to give any
more details and denied all requests for interviews.

Then he disappeared.

The paparazzi were frantic. They knew there was a bigger story
behind the resignation. They went in search of Cardinal Karmazin,
who was widely known to be the 'power behind the throne.' He too had
disappeared.

None of the press made any connection with the suicide of an
Archdeacon in Sanlucar or the gang-related death of a drug dealer
in Toronto. They certainly saw no connection to the deportation of a
computer specialist from Toronto to Bucharest, to face outstanding
charges in a credit card scam.

Chapter 74

St. Gregory's Church
Bethlehem, Pennsylvania

The town of Bethlehem was founded in 1741 by a group of Moravian settlers. They were given 500 acres of land at the confluence of Monocacy Creek and the Lehigh River, in Eastern Pennsylvania. The land was fertile, and there were abundant iron and coal deposits. The town prospered and in 1857, the Saucona Iron Company was incorporated.

Patrick William Damien emigrated from Ireland in 1858 and settled in Bethlehem. Observing that a war between the southern and northern states was inevitable, he knew there would be a need for armaments of all kinds. He invested all the money he had in the newly incorporated Saucona Iron Company. His observation proved correct and during the civil war that followed, there was enormous demand for railway equipment, especially iron rails.

Saucona prospered, and so did Patrick Damien. He made a small fortune during the war, and when it was over, he founded the Bethlehem Investment Company, which grew into the largest securities broker in the state. This was the foundation of the Damien Empire which through shrewd stock deals and investments eventually controlled over forty large public corporations. He was a devout Catholic and believed that his good luck was tied to the name *Bethlehem*; the birthplace of Jesus and the birthplace of the Damien family fortune.

He had two sons. The first born was christened, Patrick Bethlehem Damien and the second Fitzpatrick Bethlehem Damien; starting a tradition that all male descendants of the Damien family would have Bethlehem as one of their names.

It was mid-morning. The city of Bethlehem had grown from 2,500 when Patrick Damien emigrated from Ireland to its present population of 75,000. Normally the streets would be full of people at this time, but they were almost deserted. They were indoors, either at work, church, or at home. Sitting in front of a television or watching over the internet, they were caught up, like no other, in the Conclave taking place in the Vatican.

The church of St. Gregory, in the center of the city, was filled to overflowing. A large screen had been erected in front of the altar rail, and it was carrying the live transmission from Rome. They had a very particular interest in the events taking place there. One of their own was considered to be amongst the list of possible successors as the next Pope. William Bethlehem Damien was their native son. This Church was where he had been baptized, and where he had taken his vows as a priest. It was where he had committed his life to God and dedicated it to Saint Francis Xavier, whose life and example he followed into the mission fields of North West Africa.

All eyes were fixed on the chimney, waiting for the smoke to appear. The conclave had been in session for two days and four times it had been black.

In Rome, it was late afternoon and another ballot should have taken place by now. The result would soon be known.

The tension rippled through the congregation. They had trouble keeping still. They stood up, sat down, fidgeted with their hands, wiped the perspiration from their faces. Then as one they *came to their feet*. Smoke was coming out of the chimney. There was complete silence in the Church. It was impossible to tell the color from the first few wisps but as the volume increased they saw it was white. They had a new Pope! Now the very hard part began. They had to wait, to find out who it was.

* * *

The Vatican Rome

In the Sistine Chapel, the Cardinal Dean asked the pope-elect "Do you accept your canonical election as Supreme Pontiff?"

"I cannot accept this as a man. It is too great a burden to carry. But as the servant of Christ and with God's help I accept."

"By what name do you wish to be called?" the Dean asked him.

He told him the regnal name he would use, and then the other Cardinals approached him, in an act of homage and a pledge of obedience.

The new Pope was taken to the "Room of Tears", a small room next to the Sistine Chapel. He put on the Pontifical robes, choosing from the three sets—small, medium, and large—that had been laid out. With the white Papal zucchetto on his head, he was led towards the balcony of St. Peter's Basilica.

The Cardinal Deacon appeared first and waited for the crowd of 300,000 in the square below to be quiet.

"Habemus Papam." The dean announced. He continued in Latin:

"I announce to you a great joy. We have a new Pope! He has taken the name, Francis Xavier."

The Dean stepped aside and the new Pope, Father William B. Damien, who henceforth would be known as Pope Francis Xavier, stepped forward. The crowd in the square cheered and applauded; some said a silent prayer.

* * *

St. Gregory's Church, Bethlehem, Pa.

They hugged each other. They high fived. There were tears of happiness, joy and gratitude. Then a quietness descended as they realized the enormity of what had happened; to their church, their community, and their country. Their native son, their beloved Father Damien was now Pontiff, the Bishop of Rome, Pope of a billion Catholics around the world.

Epilogue

It took six months to bring the accused to trial, in what had been dubbed the Vatican Conspiracy. It was an anticlimax given what had already transpired. Five of the accused were acquitted for lack of evidence. Each of the Regents received three years, except Father Diego Paz, who was given six years for his involvement in the kidnapping of Father Michael. The rest received sentences ranging from one to three years.

Father Michael received treatment at a neurological institute just outside Madrid, and Marius Sorensen received similar treatment at a sanatorium near Copenhagen. They both improved but not completely. They would have ongoing memory and cognitive problems.

Once Papa Michael's convalescence was complete, and he had been discharged, Jose drove him to see Father William at the monastery at Espiritu Santo. When they arrived, all the monks were waiting outside and broke into spontaneous applause as Father Michael got out of the car.

Morse flew to Oslo and then drove to his cabin on Lake Mjosa just outside Lillehammer. He spent two weeks there fishing and sleeping, mainly the latter. Then he flew to London and his flat in Hampstead and resumed the identity of Walter Russak. While he waited for his next assignment, he visited his local, took in a few football matches at Stamford Bridge, and enjoyed a few of his favorite girls and restaurants.

Jose and Isobel had known each other for less than a year. But that was long enough for him to know that he wanted to spend more than just a few sleepovers with her, but he wasn't yet ready for marriage and all that that entailed. Maybe one day. He was on his way to see her. On the passenger seat was a gift-wrapped package containing a small bronze statue of a spaniel, and a card that read, 'maybe WE could get one together'.

Pope Francis Xavier ordered a copy of the *Dialogue's* reports to be sent to every Cardinal. It was accompanied by a requirement that they study them and submit their comments and recommendations to the Vatican Congregation charged with rendering an opinion on them.

Notes and Explanations

Cast

Walter Russak	was	Leonard Morse.
Boris Radovic	was	Andre Balinska
William B. Damien	was	*Bethlehem*

The rest of the characters played themselves.

The DIALOGUEMEMBERSS matrix was used as an example of data encryption. It is a very simple pattern for two reasons; it illustrates in a simple way how encryption is done, and it fit the story—*any hacker still in his diapers could have cracked it.*

Real world encryption is far more complicated, certainly beyond my expertise. Similarly, protection against hackers is far more complex than suggested in the novel but, as anyone who watches the news knows, hacking still goes on—often government sponsored.

The golden ratio can be illustrated by a golden rectangle:

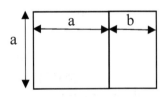

If $\dfrac{a + b}{a} = \dfrac{a}{b} = 1.618$

It is a golden rectangle

In the novel, the Castillo was built by Andreo Bonacci, and there is a reference to a Bonacci, who was a mathematician. This was Leonardo Bonacci (1170-1250), better known as Leonardo Fibonacci of *Pisa*. He is best remembered for the mathematical series named after him, in which each term, after the first two, is the sum of the previous two:

0, 1, 1, 2, 3, 5, 8, 13, 21, 34, 55, 89, 144, 233, 377 . . .

If you divide each term by the previous term, the ratio tends to the golden ratio. e.g. 13/8 = 1.625; 144/89 = 1.6179; 377/233 = 1.6180

There are many current applications of the Fibonacci sequence. One of them is the 'Fibonacci Retracement' method used for predicting future stock prices. So if you want to impress your bank manager, you might ask her if they use the 'Fibonacci Retracement' when deciding how to invest your money.

In the novel the symbols on the 'missing key card' are $f9$ and $f12$. *They* referred to the ninth and twelfth terms in the Fibonacci series; $f9$ is 21 and $f12$ is 89, giving the code 2189.

The names of the agents, Charpentier, and Morse, are French words that translate into English as Carpenter and Walrus respectively. The 'Walrus and the Carpenter' is from the poem, *Jabberwocky*, which appears in *'Through the Looking Glass'* by Lewis Carroll (1832 – 1898)—real name Charles Dodgson—a mathematics professor at Oxford University. *Jabberwocky* is a nonsense poem - *so illogical about it that it actually made sense. Reverse logic. Like looking at life backward, through a mirror.*

In the message sent by Morse to Charpentier, the cipher refers to *Jabberwocky,* using the code *verse:line:word*
11:1:1 → 11:1:4 refers to the text in the 11th verse, line 1, words 1 to 4.

Code	Cypher	Meaning
11:1:1 → 11:1:4	*The time has come*	*Happening Now*
11:6:1 → 11:6:5	*And whether pigs have wings*	*Flying*
11:2:1 → 11:2:5	*To talk of many things*	*He had the confession*

And as you may have observed, the lawyers— *in Boris' experience lawyers were all bloodsuckers*—were aptly named, Sweeney and Todd.

John Leightell
September 2015